"You're a complete innocent," he choked out. Gods, three kisses was nothing. She was contemplating a life well beyond the pale and had no idea of what changes would come in her life as a mistress.

"Yes." She lifted her chin proudly. "But I'd like not to be ignorant, too."

He rubbed his jaw, thinking hard of a way to turn her inexperience to his advantage. If he could distract her from her plan of finding a protector she might yet find a man to marry. A few poorly executed kisses wouldn't bring her too much harm as long as no one learned of them. "Very well."

Her mouth fell open.

He grinned at her shock. "I will be the one to answer your questions about intimacy on the condition you tell no one that you wish to be a mistress, for the time being. I must have your promise that this will be our secret. I won't be a party to your ruin."

"And you'll teach me what I need to know, too?"

He paused. An innocent bride was expected to know very little on her wedding night. He would be careful of what he taught her. "Yes."

HEATHER BOYD

BESTSELLING AUTHOR

AN IMPROPER PROPOSAL

Distinguished Rogues

The characters and events portrayed in this book are fictitious. Any similarity to real persons, living or dead, is purely coincidental and not intended by the author.

AN IMPROPER PROPOSAL
Copyright © 2015 by Heather Boyd
Edited by Kelli Collins

Dedication

———◆———

To those who must remember the good times for someone they love.
You are not alone.

Chapter One

———◆———

Iris Hedley was not afraid of the world, although a series of unfortunate events had taken away everything that had once been comforting in it. At one and twenty years of age, she should have been settled into marriage like so many of her former friends, rather than left on the shelf and a secret visitor to the Marshalsea Prison for indebted gentlemen.

"Come and eat, Father," she urged gently as she polished Alexander Hedley's spoon so it gleamed as brightly as the poor dented thing could manage then placed it beside the smuggled repast she'd served up to him. Oh, how there were times when the memory of her former happy home life caused a lump to form in her throat, and made her miss what had been lost in recent years.

Unfortunately, as had become his habit, her father did not budge from his slump on the edge of his cot in the room he shared with two other men in the musty barracks. He'd once been a fine man, wealthy, possessed of great wit and intelligence, courted by those in society who valued such things highly. Now he stared off into space quite often, absorbed in his own thoughts and lost in his memories of the past.

The change had begun prior to his incarceration and she feared for him. Her father had not taken his confinement well, but she supposed few independent gentlemen did. He was not in his right mind. He hadn't been himself in a long time.

"Father?"

He grumbled, "Goose again?"

Cold goose breast and turnip soup was a luxury in this place, but Iris didn't dare remind him of his situation. She was grateful Lady Heathcote's cook set aside this meal every day, but she was always aware she spent someone else's coin to care for her father. Pointing out that fact only added to his distress. "Yes, Papa. Come and sit down now so I might share it with you."

As hoped, her father brightened at the news she would share the meal with him and perched on the stool beside the makeshift table. She handed him the spoon so he could start on his soup. "I cannot stay long today. Lady Heathcote has given me a list of errands to run on her behalf before tonight's entertainment."

Her father stared at the spoon a moment then snatched up the bowl of cooled soup and drank from it directly. He shuddered, wiped his mouth with the napkin and then glanced sidelong at her plate, where a single slice of goose rested. "Lady Heathcote has servants to do errands," he grumbled. "And you should be resting so you are prepared for the evening."

"I don't mind helping her. Running errands to the dressmaker gives me something to do with my days, and in a small way makes up for the burden of providing me with food and lodgings. I am indebted to her." Esme, a popular widow of independent fortune, had taken her in before her father had fled the country and his debts. She didn't like to imagine what would have happened to her without Esme.

At first, her father had remained on the continent to assess his true situation, leaving Iris in Esme's temporary care with a promise to return soon. While away, the scale of his losses must have preyed on his mind and he'd returned much sooner than expected, only to surrender himself to his debtors. He'd entered the Marshalsea willingly, although few knew that small detail, and she planned to keep it that way. The tally of losses had steadily risen against him until Iris had feared he might never be free. Esme insisted they conceal his location for the sake of her reputation, but it was difficult to allow others to believe her father had abandoned her for a life abroad.

"A woman should have a home of her own, a child to bounce

on her knee and a respectable situation." Her father sighed and looked about them mournfully. "This is not the life I wanted for you."

What he'd wanted was for Iris to marry a viscount, have a home in the heart of Mayfair, and a dozen grandchildren perched on his lap as he sipped whiskey in a library. Unfortunately, a life of that nature would be forever denied them both. Her father was ruined good and proper and Iris, despite all Esme had done to protect her, had fallen victim to greedy, unscrupulous men.

She hugged him close. "We will win through Papa, never doubt it."

Despite her words, Iris did find it hard to remain optimistic, especially here in this dreary place. Perhaps it was better that her father often could not remember he was entirely at fault for the decisions he'd made that had brought him to this damp and undesirable place.

As her father finished his meal, she began to repack her basket and then prepare herself to face the turnkey. "The turnkey asked for the name of your governess this morning. I think he wishes his daughter had half your grace."

"He's only being polite, papa." The turnkey's real interest was blackmail. He might have a daughter, almost of an age to marry, but Iris was due to hand over funds to him to ensure her father was taken care of in her absence. More of Esme's funds. Iris bit her lip as worry filled her. Esme did too much already and an alternative source of funds to pay for her father's upkeep had to be found. One day soon, she must attempt to repay Esme for her many kindnesses.

Unfortunately, there were few honorable choices for a woman who needed to improve her life. Marriage, of course, was the preferred option for a young woman to elevate herself in society. Snaring well-to-do and titled gentlemen had been the ultimate goal for her friends. With her once substantial dowry, Iris had her pick of anyone and had chosen a young man with a modest title of viscount because she'd liked him best of all her suitors. Lord Grindlewood had not been a wealthy man and her dowry would have assured them a comfortable life.

However, before they could be wed, her father had lost his

fortune, including her dowry. Iris had felt honor bound to release Lord Grindlewood from their engagement.

Her chances of a second match had perished with her dowry and that left her with only unpalatable choices.

"I intend to speak to Fitzhugh on the way out to ask after his wife and daughters," she lied. "They've not been in the best of health of late."

"If you must single him out for conversation be sure to have a care for your reputation and stand in the open at a respectable distance," her father warned unnecessarily. "I don't want anyone to misconstrue your interest in his family as an attempt to curry pecuniary dispensation on my behalf."

Through her daily visits to the Marshalsea, a hoard of scandalous options for lining ones pockets had presented themselves. Thievery was rife around the Marshalsea and she'd learned to carry little of value or look directly at anyone for too long.

Prostitutes parading their wares in the yard in the hope of customers were almost impossible to sidestep but gave her a glimpse into one possible future for her. While he'd deflected any untoward advances from men, and women too, since her father's fall and retained her innocence, such a final profession might be the only means of securing a large regular income with which to take care of her papa. Gentlemen were said to pay their mistresses handsomely well if they were satisfied in bed. Fitzhugh had expressed an interest in bedding her that she'd rebuffed already.

She shuddered and pressed her gloves to her cold cheeks. "I will keep our conversation as brief as possible," she assured him. She would never give herself to Fitzhugh but she might have no choice but to become a mistress to someone else. "I must be going."

Her father stared out the tiny window of the barracks room with no idea of her inner turmoil; no idea Iris was contemplating a life beyond good society in the demimonde. His already battered pride would never bear the disappointment of her fall, so she would tell him nothing until she had settled her mind on the subject.

He caught her arm as she stood. "You will be careful out

there."

"Of course, Father." Truth to tell, it was more dangerous in the Marshalsea for a woman in her situation. The turnkey liked to remind her not to give herself airs above anyone else. Thieves, even thieves' accomplices, had to adhere to the pecking order. She was at the very bottom of the hierarchy and utterly expendable in the scheme of things. The turnkey took his cut of what she helped others steal, but the real wealth went elsewhere. Fitzhugh's solicitous behavior and kind inquiries masked his real intent, as he never failed to remind her who was really in charge of her life.

She kissed the top of her father's gray head. "I am always careful."

He stood too and placed her hand on his arm. He led her down the rickety wooden staircase to the courtyard as if they were arriving at a ball. On the way to the main gate, he nodded to fellow captives but kept a distance from them. Mr. Fitzhugh, surrounded by other prisoners, lounged against the gate following their progress with hooded eyes. He swung his keys, a tactic to remind everyone he was in charge. She hated him but didn't dare show how much. As she drew closer, she buried her loathing. If not for her father's need, she would tell him exactly what she thought of him and his so-called friends.

However, the men worth befriending in the Marshalsea, the most influential, were the turnkey, and those on the prisoner committee. Iris didn't dare slight them, no matter how dark or dangerous her thoughts became toward them. She smiled instead at them all, never singling out one over the other for attention. "Good morning, gentlemen."

Thankfully, the men gathered around Fitzhugh murmured a greeting in response but continued their own conversation and did not impede their progress.

At the gate, her father stopped. "I'll be thinking of you," he whispered, casting an anxious eye at the gate and back at the prison yard.

Mr. Fitzhugh strolled toward her father and placed a restraining hand on his shoulder. Her father was not allowed to leave the Marshalsea until his debts were paid in full. Iris, as a visitor, was free to come and go between the hours of eight in the morning and ten in the evening as often as she liked.

She hugged her father quickly. "I will be back before you know it."

Fitzhugh smiled, as a cat would when it hungered for a bowl of cream. "You're looking remarkably pretty today, Miss Hedley."

Go away! "Thank you. How is your wife faring of late?"

"Much improved." He strolled to the gate and held the latch, his ring of keys clanking against his thigh. "Does it look like rain today, Miss Hedley?"

A chill swept her at the question. "It won't rain."

"And the rest of the weather report?"

She glanced at her father anxiously, who stood a short distance back from the gate with his hands clasped together. "Lord Hazelton's library on Conduit Street tonight. Behind the portrait of his children," she whispered. "The safe is there."

She swallowed the lump clogging her throat. Being an accessory to robbery didn't make her a lady or honorable. One more reason to hate her life. Lord Hazelton had recently purchased a seed-pearl necklace and matching amethyst brooch for his beautiful young wife, and the flattered woman hadn't been able to stop talking about it to everyone she met. She had set herself up to be robbed by revealing where it was kept to a room full of gossipy women and gentlemen several times. There was no way Iris could be a sole suspect, so she felt safe enough to pass this intelligence along.

The turnkey smiled. "Mr. Talbot will see you at eleven. Do not forget what's at stake."

My father's life. She shuddered. "How could I?"

He shrugged and when a knock sounded on the gate, he managed to stand between her and freedom to open it. Although she tried her best, she could not get through without rudely shoving the new visitors aside. Many considered visiting the Marshalsea as a lark, unless you had family trapped here.

Fitzhugh tipped his hat to them. "Talbot said to tell you he will dance with you tonight."

"I will not agree to that." She looked for the comfort of her father but he'd already turned away for the company of other men, leaving her alone with this scoundrel.

"Were you about to tell your sweet old pa about your arrangements? I wouldn't do it if I were you. He'll froth at the mouth and start biting the balustrade. Should by rights send him where he belongs." He mimicked a shooting star and then slapped his thigh. "Straight to the madhouse for him if I had my way. You should be grateful a man like Talbot thinks to spare him."

She'd be grateful when they both dropped dead. "Leave my father alone."

"Then do your job." The turnkey opened the gate, so slowly she wanted to scream in frustration. When she could squeeze through, she marched away from the prison, furious but afraid. Iris lived in fear that her father would be sent to Bedlam if she did not do what Talbot demanded.

No one ever left a madhouse.

She squared her shoulders and set off for Lady Heathcote's home, Fitzhugh's threats following her into the better part of London despite her best efforts to forget. She had to find a way out of this mess, and soon.

Chapter Two

——◆——

The world crashed down on Martin Andrew, Lord Louth's, head at precisely eleven o'clock in the morning in the private residence he owned on Pollen Street, London. "What do you mean Vivian is dead?"

Mrs. Hughes, his former mistress' housekeeper, looked on him with sorrowful eyes. "She died, my lord."

"I don't believe you."

"I am sorry to be the bearer of such sad news." Mrs. Hughes winced. "I know you have no reason to mourn Mrs. Rose after all the trouble she put you through, but I thought you would want to know."

Martin turned away to hide his reaction. Shock. Dismay. Grief. He might not have been Vivian's protector anymore but he had cared enough about her welfare to allow her to lease the house long after their arrangement had ended. He had not laid eyes on Vivian in six months or more, at her request, nor had he shared a bed with her in closer to eight, also by her request.

Another protector had snatched Vivian up a few days after their parting, ensuring no reconciliation was ever possible between them. The bitter sting of discovering she'd fallen in love with another had tainted their last words to each other, and now he could never make peace with her.

He glanced around, at last noticing the house was draped in mourning colors. "Is she here?"

"No, my lord." The housekeeper clasped her hands together at her waist. "Lord Fallow took her body and made arrangements for a private burial. He was beside himself and would not permit us to see her or attend services."

Martin nodded slowly, an uncomfortable ache building in his chest. He might not have been Vivian's choice as a protector, but she had been in his life for a long time and he wished he'd known about her passing sooner. "Did she suffer?"

There was nothing Vivian had hated more than discomfort or being inconvenienced. He hoped her death had been swift and painless.

"No more than any woman," Mrs. Hughes informed him. "I thought everything was well but her death took me by surprise."

Martin turned slowly, unable to believe his ears. "What do you mean by 'no more than any woman'? She is dead, for heaven's sake."

Mrs. Hughes regarded him with widened eyes. "She delivered her daughter easily, looked up into my face smiling, and when I returned to her after taking the girl away for wrapping, she was gone. So suddenly. Without a whimper of protest or warning."

"Daughter?" Martin staggered back a step. "She was with child?"

Mrs. Hughes winced. "I urged her to write to you and explain. It would have been kinder."

The sadness that had begun with the news of Vivian's death surged into dismay at Mrs. Hughes' words. "I received no letter about any pregnancy."

"I wish I did not need to distress you more but the birth was very hard on her. More so than I realized." Mrs. Hughes glanced down at her hands.

Martin sank onto a chair, horrified that Vivian had died giving birth to another's offspring.

The housekeeper cleared her throat. "The child thrives. Lord Fallon has done all he can for my mistress but once he saw the babe, he washed his hands. The girl has none of his features. Now that I see you again, I am more certain than ever that she is your daughter."

It took a moment for Martin to gather his struggling wits to realize the woman believed him to be the child's father. He put his hands on his head and dug his fingers into his skull as shock swept over him. He'd always feared any child of his would be too large for a woman to bear easily, so in bed he played other sorts of games to avoid pregnancy. He'd always been careful with Vivian. Or so he'd thought until now.

Given the way she waited silently, Mrs. Hughes wanted an admission from him too. But that was impossible. He'd seen no hint of Vivian's condition during their last discussion. He could not believe that in her anger, in the volley of spiteful words that had been flung at him during their last meeting, that she could have held that back. Had she believed, hoped, the child belonged to Fallon? "I want to see the babe."

"Of course, my lord. Let me fetch her."

While Mrs. Hughes was gone, Martin paced the darkened sitting room. Was it a trick, a scheme to foist a motherless child onto him to raise as his own? He'd certainly heard of it happening before and it always caused a scandal for the men involved, and their families.

He tugged the drawn drapes open, determined not to be tricked into anything. Crying alerted him that the child was drawing close. He faced the doorway as Mrs. Hughes stepped into view, attempting to soothe the babe with soft, ineffectual words.

Wrapped snugly in a black shawl, the child's red face was the only piece of her visible.

Mrs. Hughes stopped before him. "The child has no name."

The woman held the bundle out to him and he immediately placed his hands behind his back. He stared at the child with no name and no mother, struggling to see a resemblance to his former mistress. In her distress and agitation, the child wriggled and a lock of dark hair peeked below the shawl. Fallon had been fair, if memory served.

Mrs. Hughes pressed the child against his chest and he had no choice but to capture her. A trickle of sweat ran from his temple. However much he tried not to show it, he was utterly terrified that he would crush her. "She's heavier than I expected a newborn to be."

"She was born large. The largest babe I've ever beheld." Mrs.

Hughes urged him backward when the child continued to cry. "Perhaps you should sit, my lord."

Martin sank into the chair gratefully, babe held carefully to his chest. It was a little better to be sitting. Safer for the girl. If she squirmed out of his arms, she would not have far to fall into his lap. He adjusted his grip a little tighter, determined that would not happen.

"Perhaps this way might be easier." Mrs. Hughes took the crying child back momentarily then placed her lengthways over his knees.

Martin squeezed his thighs tightly together, forming a solid platform for the wailing child to rest upon. He placed one hand on her midsection and, to his relief, she quieted a little. He exhaled. "Is that better?"

Her crying spluttered to hiccups.

He had no experience with children but thought that reaction boded well. "You are wise not to trust me. Not with my track record. A little thing like you would be so easily damaged." She could almost fit inside his two hands too. He glanced at Mrs. Hughes briefly. "What will be done with her?"

"That is for you to say." Mrs. Hughes perched on a chair opposite him. "My mistress had no family, as you must know. This little angel is all alone in the world."

"A bleak picture you paint. We are all alone. Even in a crowded room it is possible to feel lonely."

"It is not the same circumstances." Mrs. Hughes sat forward a little. "She will likely go to an orphanage unless I can find a home for her. She's a pretty child, isn't she?"

He glanced at the child's face. Now she was quiet and calm, her skin had changed from a mottled red to soft pink. Rounded cheeks spoke of a healthy child; squat nose; and a pair of murky dark-gray eyes that shifted to his own face when he spoke. He leaned closer, inhaling the scent of a newborn child and looking for traces of Vivian's features in her appearance.

He nudged the dark shawl away from her face a little bit.

"You might safely unwrap her, my lord. The room is warm enough for the child not to become chilled."

He did so carefully, noting the child was long rather than wide. Still big for a newborn babe. The housekeeper had dressed her in a fine white muslin smock, embroidered with flowers at the hem, and her tiny legs were curled upward beneath the gown. Her fists clenched and unclenched haphazardly, revealing the tiniest pale fingernails he'd ever seen. He studied them carefully in fascination.

When she squirmed, curling into a tighter ball and yawning, he was spellbound and used two hands to hold her still. There were no certain hints of Vivian in this creature, but was there any of himself? He inspected what he could see of the girl.

Her ears were tiny shells beside her head, perhaps similar to his own in shape but he could not honestly recall the shape of Vivian's. Her eyes were not the color of his but they were framed by a pair of straight dark brows, rather than the curve of Vivian's elegant ones. Of course the color of her hair lacked the vibrancy of Vivian's. Where this child was dark, Vivian had been the color of a bright sunset. And the dramatic widow's peak Vivian had always accentuated was also absent from the babe's appearance.

The only reason to suspect the child was Vivian's was Mrs. Hughes word. "She doesn't look a bit like the late Mrs. Rose."

"Not yet. Children change as they age, my lord. Do you not have portraits of yourself at a young age that seem strange when compared to your current face?"

He shifted in his chair as unwelcome remembrances of his childhood flooded him. She was correct. He'd hidden his childhood portraits the minute he'd come into his title. He'd been made to wear decidedly girlish curls as a boy, which was why he kept his dark hair cropped short now.

He carefully turned the child's head to the side. There at the back, previously hidden by the shawl, the babe's short hair was crimped with the hint of a wave. He set the child back to rights, disturbed by that observation.

Vivian's hair had been straight and stubborn. She'd complained of it often enough upon waking in the morning that he remembered her ire all too well.

Which meant the child *could* be his. He'd been Vivian's protector nine months ago but it depended on who else had shared her bed. He had believed her to be faithful until she'd revealed her preference for another man. The housekeeper surely would know what Vivian had done behind his back. "What has Lord Fallon to say?"

Mrs. Hughes glanced at the child. "Lord Fallon, of course, knew of the pregnancy early in their arrangement but the child does not resemble him in the slightest."

He rested his hand again on the child's middle and earned a half-hearted grumble as his reward. "Did Mrs. Rose have any other gentlemen callers?"

"There was only Lord Fallon, and he doted on her." Mrs. Hughes swallowed hard. "I'm so sorry to be the bearer of such difficult news. Especially so long since parting ways."

Even after nine months, he experienced pain at the mention of Lord Fallon replacing him. He'd thought he'd doted on Vivian too and he'd done his best to make her happy.

"I believe I can return the child to bed now." Mrs. Hughes smiled softly. "You have the touch. She's fallen asleep." She took the babe from him before he could deny her, spoke softly to the girl when she whimpered, and slipped from the room.

Martin followed to see where the child was being taken. He might not be entirely sure of his fatherhood but he did feel the beginnings of obligation. The child was alone in the world, denied her mother's love.

The door to the chamber beside Vivian's old room stood open and when he stepped inside, more white lace and frills surrounded him than he'd ever seen here.

"My mistress was looking forward to the birth and I couldn't bear to change anything to proper mourning, but I will if you insist." Mrs. Hughes hummed softly as she tucked her charge into the wicker basket, clearly smitten over the lass, and began to rub her softly.

Martin glanced over the housekeeper carefully, considering his options and Mrs. Hughes. He judged her at least fifty, with her white hair and well-rounded figure any child would like to cuddle up to. Although Vivian's employee, she had a value beyond price. She was here. She would do for the child.

"Leave everything as it is." He gestured at the tiny shape the woman leaned over. "An orphanage isn't necessary."

Mrs. Hughes met his gaze, eyes boring into his. "Will you take responsibility for her upbringing?"

"Yes." He sighed deeply. His life was about to get a great deal more complicated and that couldn't be helped. An illegitimate child could be embarrassing for his family so he would have to make plans to remove her from London soon. He truly wished he had known of it before so he might have made better arrangements. "The child is to remain here, under your care for the time being."

"Mine? Oh no." Mrs. Hughes shook her head. "I am the housekeeper, not a nursemaid."

"Appearances to the contrary. You have the touch too." The babe had fallen fast asleep under Mrs. Hughes' gentle hands. "And you seem more than capable to care for the child."

She straightened and met his gaze squarely. "It is not as simple as that. As much as I wish to help you, it is out of the question. I had but a week of service left to my mistress at the time of her death and I have already delayed long enough. You don't need me. She has a wet-nurse to appease her hunger, but the woman is owed wages already in order to keep her coming back."

Martin dug into his pocket and considered what coin he had. A wet-nurse often had other responsibilities, didn't they? A family of her own to feed. He'd pay well to keep the wet-nurse coming back to look after the child. He handed over a generous payment. "I will pay you double your previous wages."

"Double? Sir, you misunderstand. It is not a question of money but of affection." Mrs. Hughes skimmed her fingers over the little girl's cheeks. "She's a darling girl and I will miss her so much."

Martin scowled. "Then don't go."

"I had forgotten how formidable you could be, but it changes nothing." Mrs. Hughes straightened her shoulders. "I am sorry to let you down, my lord. I'm letting you both down, but a woman my age doesn't get too many second chances. You see, I am to be married. My Reginald is a dear man and willing to wait until you've found my replacement. But you must be quick about it. I am leaving this place as soon as arrangements can be made."

He scraped his fingers over his skull. This couldn't be happening to him. First the mother of his child and now her housekeeper. He glanced down at the cloth-wrapped bundle sleeping in blissful ignorance while he discussed upending her world, and the beginnings of panic crept over him. He could not care for her himself. She had to remain a secret and safe from mishap. Perhaps forever. "If I were not as I am, I would not need you to stay."

Mrs. Hughes sighed. "There are many good women who could easily take my place as housekeeper. Nothing has to change in the arrangements already made. The house is more than adequate; the staff is loyal and discreet. You must think of your reputation. Your cousin's reputation is at stake as well."

He glanced at her sharply. "What do you know of my cousin?"

Mrs. Hughes appeared abashed and glanced down swiftly. "Only that you have one living with you. My mistress took an interest and spoke of her often in respect to her prospects of making a match."

He'd clearly unburdened himself once too often if Vivian's servants were aware of his cousin's dubious chances of making a good marriage. "My cousin's prospects are the reason no one must ever learn of the child, do you understand?"

"I understand completely. Your secret is safe with me." Mrs. Hughes stepped back. "I will speak to my Reginald and maybe he could be willing to wait a bit longer."

Surely the additional funds of her doubled wages would sway him. "I would appreciate that. This situation has caught me unawares."

"Of course. A man in your position must do the right thing, and carefully, to protect the innocent from harm. I always thought you a kind man. I know you will take good care of the little one."

Martin tucked the blankets a little more snugly around the child's tiny shoulders. He would never hurt the babe. Not intentionally. When he compared his hands to the child's size, he had even more incentive to keep a distance. When he glanced up, Mrs. Hughes beamed at him. He jerked his hands back. He should not get too attached to the girl. Once his head ceased to spin from the shock, he'd send her away from London for his own piece of mind.

He groaned under his breath. Juggling one more demand

could prove difficult. He didn't want to think of how his friends would look at him should they learn he'd a bastard child living near his home. He'd be a laughingstock among the *ton* and he had no excuse for his carelessness. And as Mrs. Hughes had pointed out, there was Whitney. His cousin had to be kept in ignorance, if that was even possible. "I'll visit the Godwin Employment Agency today and see about a replacement housekeeper."

"That would be for the best." She fussed with straightening the room then paused at the door. "Should you like me to interview the women they send?"

By rights, he should do that himself. After all, the woman he hired would be responsible for the child, but perhaps Mrs. Hughes would understand what her needs might be where he did not. If he was not present, no one might connect him with the child for some time as well. "I will make arrangements for all interviews to be conducted here."

"Very good, my lord." She slipped from the room.

Martin stayed to watch the child sleep for some minutes. A daughter? He couldn't help but reach out to touch the soft hair on her tiny head even as his hand trembled. It was hard to believe the child could be his but Mrs. Hughes seemed sure, and he could admit to some similarities in features to his own.

Why hadn't Vivian revealed the pregnancy to him? He would have married her and made sure the child had the protection of his name. For the well-being of his own child, he'd have done anything, suffered celibacy for the rest of his days if necessary, so they might have his name.

He touched the curve of her ear gently and she squirmed, her face scrunching up in a delightful picture of sleepy protest. What should he do with her later? He could always send her to the country for strangers to raise.

He had some understanding of the difficulty finding homes for orphans could bring, through his association with Lord Carrington and his wife. It wasn't easy to find kind families, good people willing to overlook the circumstances of an irregular birth, but it could be done.

But could he do that to his own flesh and blood and never think of her again?

He lingered one more moment without finding an answer before turning away, heading for the front hall and stepped out onto the street. He didn't know the first thing about children but if he was to be responsible for one then he'd better learn, and quickly. The first step was finding a competent woman to replace Mrs. Hughes.

And then he'd decide on a name for the child.

Chapter Three

The walk from the Marshalsea to Lady Heathcote's modest home on Conduit Street was a good three miles, and had given Iris ample time to think about her situation. She was in trouble, with few options before her. She didn't know how to save herself or her father. If anyone connected her to the recent robberies among the *ton*, she'd be ruined, imprisoned or transported, and might never see her father again. She sniffed but then lifted her chin, determined not to show her overwhelming emotions on the very street where she'd once lived as a rich man's daughter, oblivious to the harsh realities of life.

Unfortunately, she sighted Mr. Charles Talbot ahead and a new chill swept over her. Would he never give her a moment's peace? Would he ever allow her to end their arrangement? He was making himself rich off the misery of others and she feared there'd be no end to his greed. In the beginning, he'd suggested her help would be settlement for her father's debts. In the months that had past, he'd refused to discuss how much longer she had to aid him.

Iris ducked behind a slow-moving carriage to avoid his notice, as she'd been doing every day for the past week on her way home from the Marshalsea, and followed behind it a short distance. She was starting to suspect Talbot followed her and that was extremely unsettling.

Since she knew the area well, as soon as the carriage drew

near a particular corner, Iris made a break for it and sprinted the short lane to reach an adjacent street then pretended nothing was amiss. As she'd been doing for the last year, and especially so since Talbot had threatened her father.

But she couldn't lie to herself anymore. She was lost. Her future taken away, leaving her to the mercy of others. She would rather choose her life than have it thrust upon her. To live the life her father had raised her for.

She let herself into Esme's home by the servant's entrance and hurried up to her room, her chest aching with panic. Tonight was yet another ball. Another opportunity to commit a crime. She checked her appearance in the mirror and saw a windswept woman with blazing cheeks and none of the accomplice. Exactly as Talbot wanted. "How can I do this again and not hate myself for the rest of my life?"

"You are beautiful," Lady Heathcote murmured as she slipped into the room with her maid trailing after. "But very late indeed."

Iris turned away from the mirror quickly, embarrassed to be caught staring at her own reflection, and rushed for her wardrobe to begin dressing for the evening in the first gown her hand encountered. "I am sorry. My father was talkative today and made me late to reach Madame du Clair. I promise I will not be long."

Esme's maid replaced Iris' selection with a different gown of burgundy silk and finished the task of her dressing so she'd be worthy of attending the night's ball. She murmured her thanks and sat down to have her hair styled, grateful that her own shaking hands were put to better use fitting her gloves in place.

Esme drew closer. "What troubles you, my dear?"

The widow arched one elegant brow and a teasing smile graced her lips. Closer to forty than thirty years, Esme had retained the skin and figure of a much younger girl, which men openly appreciated. Iris had heard many other women complain of it. What they never mentioned often enough was how kind Esme could be.

Iris darted a glance at her reflection as she secured the last button. "Am I that obvious?"

Esme pulled a string of amber beads from her reticule and

toyed with them, allowing the colors to flash and distract her. "I have become well acquainted with your frowns and sighs over the years of our acquaintance, my dear. You have something on your mind and don't want to tell me."

Esme slipped the necklace around Iris' throat when the maid stepped back. The coldness of the gems sent a shiver down her spine and she removed them immediately. "You're too kind but I cannot wear your gems." Talbot would see and might try to take them away under the guise of another payment toward her father's safety. She could not bear to have anything stolen from Esme, so she declined all jewels in favor of flowers and never shared the location of Esme's safe, or suggested there might be one.

"I have been thinking that it is time I moved on with my life. Away from society."

Esme shook her head firmly and motioned her maid out of the room. "I won't allow you to consider such a thing. I want you here where I can look after you until your father's release."

"You always have looked after me," Iris said then bit her lip. Esme couldn't protect her from Talbot. Not really. "But I think its time to find someone else to do that."

Esme's gaze narrowed. "Are you in love?"

The question surprised her. Once she'd been engaged to marry a viscount but since she'd released him from their engagement on account of her lost dowry, she'd not missed him enough to consider herself to have been even a little in love with him. "Goodness, no."

"Then what?"

Iris rubbed her hands on her arms. The friction settled her nerves a little. She couldn't tell Esme the whole truth. Esme would never forgive such duplicity. She had to lie. A hot blush heated her cheeks. "I miss having a home of my own."

Esme smiled and sank into a chair. "Of course you do, and one day you will have one again."

"I want that now. I want somewhere to call my own. A man to call my own, at least temporarily."

Esme straightened. "You're not speaking of marriage are you?"

"No, I am not." She winced as Esme glanced away, a frown

marring her beauty. Wasn't it better to be thought a wanton than a thief? She needed a good excuse to remove herself from Esme's life, and from society at the same time. Once she could legitimately avoid entering the homes of the wealthy, her part in Talbot's schemes would cease. "I am sorry if I disappoint you."

"I am not disappointed but I am sad you feel unhappy here."

Iris bit her lip. She might be happy living with Esme if not for Talbot and worry over her father. "I have no dowry, few connections to recommend me. I have thought about this long and hard. If I were to become a wealthy man's mistress, , I would have a home and at least some money of my own to spend instead of taking yours."

"More money than you can imagine now, I suspect." Esme stood and brought her to her feet. Her gaze raked her from head to toe with the cool detachment with which she usually regarded strangers. She stretched out Iris' arms wide and then circled her. "Do not ever underestimate your appeal."

Iris blushed and glanced down. Esme quickly captured her chin and lifted it high.

Her stare was firm. "A woman who chooses to be a mistress must be confident at all times in order to capture the right man's notice. She must work even harder to keep his interest afterward, too, because men are sensitive creatures and easily disappointed. This missish behavior of yours will never do."

The clocks chimed and Esme sighed. She gathered Iris' wrap and placed it about her shoulders. "Tomorrow you and I will talk this matter over in greater detail. However, tonight I want you to consider what you would give up. Mistresses are shunned, as you well know. I want you to think carefully every time you greet someone tonight. Will they speak to you once you become a mistress?"

She was shunned now to a fair degree, and at first that had been painful, but what she hoped for was an end to her association with society altogether. There were some ladies who were still kind despite her status. Thief or whore, losing their regard was inevitable no matter what she did. "Will *you*?"

Esme hugged her tight. "I would never abandon you. I'd never hold a lady's considered choice over her head but many other ladies are not at all forgiving."

Iris stared at her in dismay. She needed Esme to turn her away too. She had to be put to the gutter for Esme's own good, like week-old refuse. Without utter abandonment, Talbot might still punish her father for her failure.

When Esme drew back, the widowed sniffed. "Now we should be going, or Lord Hazelton will think we mean to snub him by our tardy arrival."

Her heart squeezed. Hazelton was a kind man but tonight he would lose something precious to him. The set Lady Hazelton had worn to the masquerade ball last week was exactly what Talbot wanted most. Not too distinctive but valuable all the same. It could be remade and sold as smaller pieces and turn a substantial profit without anyone the wiser.

Lady Heathcote and Lord and Lady Hazelton's houses were not far apart, so they walked the short distance escorted by three footmen. On the Hazelton front steps, after Esme's servants had been dismissed, Esme faced her. "Did you have someone in mind for a protector?"

She blinked at Esme's question. She'd thought merely announcing her intentions would be enough to make Esme disapprove but clearly she'd underestimated the woman. "No, I hadn't thought that far ahead."

Esme nodded firmly. "Good, because if you think I have strong opinions on what makes a good husband, you should know that I have even greater ones about the sort of man you should be making love to the first time."

Iris blushed at the idea of giving her innocence to a stranger in this scenario. She hadn't truly thought that far along. Her main concern was getting out from under Talbot's thumb.

Apparently, Esme's love knew no bounds.

She straightened her shoulders and glided after her friend into the heart of the Hazelton ball with a heavy heart. The *ton* was where Esme belonged. Iris didn't, but in a place like this she could find Talbot's next mark.

She paused when Esme did, murmured polite greetings but engaged in few actual conversations while she studied the gems sprinkled liberally amongst London's wealthiest residents. All the while she was aware she was tolerated merely because she was part of Esme's circle.

When Lady Ames, Esme's closest friend, arrived it was a considerable relief to see an honest smile and a woman not dripping with jewels. The woman liked to talk and could be counted on to say something pithy about those who gave themselves airs about their income. She was kind and Iris had never felt beneath her.

"I have the most astonishing news," Lady Ames gushed immediately on seeing them, but instead of sharing her confidence openly, she drew Esme aside and whispered in her ear. It was always a serious matter when Iris was excluded from a conversation but she didn't feel slighted. If it were truly important and might involve her, Esme would likely tell her later over a cup of tea.

Left to her own devices, Iris glanced around at the gentlemen as she considered them dispassionately. As future protectors, they all had potential she supposed but choosing one seemed impossible, given the variety. Lord Avery Hill, Lady Ames' frequent lover, was in attendance tonight and dazzled every lady around him. He winked at her but kept his distance. She's spoken with him many times in Lady Ames' company but it was clear he avoided women such as Iris—an apparently virtuous woman—like the plague.

Her gaze flittered about the room and rested immediately on a tall naval officer, laughing with friends. He was handsome, and cut a fine figure in his perfectly pressed captain's uniform. A man like that would certainly protect his home well. He turned, but his gaze passed right over her head as if she was not there and then he smiled at a woman who'd just arrived. The woman didn't see him but she wore a fascinating ruby pendant around her neck. Talbot would want that gem one day, if he'd already caught sight of the woman. If Iris remained in society, she'd have to find out who the woman was and where she resided.

Her arm was touched and then Esme's soft laughter filled her ears. "What tasty tidbit has captured your interest tonight, my dear? I spoke to you three times and you did not answer."

Iris leaned closer to her friend, ready with a new lie to match their earlier conversation about becoming a mistress. "Am I invisible?"

Yet that invisibility allowed her to move around the

wealthiest members of the *ton* undetected to learn where they kept their valuables.

Esme's brow furrowed. "I assure you that could not be the case, and I'll prove it."

She linked their arms and led her about the room. It was true many men turned their attention in their direction, even the naval officer bowed to them, but she wasn't the least bit surprised that the bulk of interest rested on Esme's trim figure rather than hers.

She shook her head and tried her best to affect a bitter tone. "I am merely a touchstone for someone hoping to see you. I simply don't hold the same appeal to that sort of man and I should probably begin my search away from the *ton* for a protector. You're likely wasting your time trying to help me, you know."

Esme's brow creased but she nodded to friends and continued their path through the throng to reach a quieter spot. "What sort of man are you hoping to catch the notice of?"

Astonished that Esme still imagined there was anything more to discuss about the scheme to become a mistress, she floundered but fell back on her old fears about finding a husband as inspiration. "Someone..." She gathered her courage. "Someone who doesn't care a wit for my connections, of which I have few, or my experience, which precisely is none. Someone kind."

"Someone wicked," Esme countered.

A wicked man would never consider an innocent but there might be something to this new direction she'd not considered. Iris had always been a good woman, if you didn't count her duplicitous nature, and since she'd begun living with Esme, her eyes had been opened to the possibilities around her. Esme and her friends enjoyed the attentions of men and lived by their own rules. Iris wanted to do that too but because of her father and Talbot, that had been denied her. She needed to be well and truly ruined.

To reach that point, she would require assistance.

Iris glanced across the room eagerly. "How can you tell a man is wicked just by looking at him?"

"There are many ways, my dear, and we can discuss them

tomorrow." Esme smiled. "Let me ask you this: What would you do if a wealthy man, who cares naught for connections and experience, fell madly in love with you?"

"I would suggest to his friends that he should be committed to Bedlam posthaste," she answered immediately. Love would only lead to trouble.

"What am I to do with you, Miss Hedley? You say you wish to be bold and strike out on your own yet you constantly sell yourself short. You want an open-minded gentleman, not one of these fellows who constantly fret about how they are viewed by society. A gentleman with a healthy disregard for societies rules is just the place to begin, I should think."

Iris had known Esme long enough to believe her sincere, and that was a problem. "You might be right."

"Of course I am right." Esme squeezed her arm affectionately. "What you need is a man who would move heaven and earth to give you what you require, and that, my dear, is a wedding."

Esme suggested a fairy tale and Iris has long left such fantasies behind. "How about a protector first, and then I can chase the dream."

"If I had my way, you should have both and more." Esme stopped as Lord Avery approached. "Mr. Hill. Good evening to you."

"I was just thinking of you," he murmured in a deep, seductive voice meant usually for Lady Ames. The fact that Iris understood the intent behind his warm tone and no one thought twice about her presence just went to show that she really was invisible. She backed away, leaving them to spar with each other. Esme didn't really approve of Lord Avery Hill's private life. Wicked seemed an insufficient description of him.

To ensure Talbot's men entry to the Hazelton townhouse later that night, she slipped into the hall. She took a calming breath when she found herself alone and smoothed her gown. Since the safe and gems were located in the library, she had to unlock a window in that room and return to the ballroom without being detected.

She had visited Lord and Lady Hazelton's lovely home often with Esme in the past year so she knew her way around. She could be done in a few moments. She'd even been given leave to borrow the occasional book from Lord Hazelton's library, which would later account for her lingering in the library if someone questioned her being there.

As soon as she turned into the hall, she spied Lord Hazelton and his wife arguing just inside the library doors. They often argued, usually about his tardiness, but Iris winced as his wife berated him with more heat than usual.

Not wishing to reveal herself, she fled down a dark hall to hide before they noticed her presence. If she remembered correctly, there was a small alcove beyond the music room doorway where she might wait for their argument to end without being seen, and then she could slip back and complete her task unnoticed.

The dark music room and secluded alcove were mere steps away when she collided with a large shape crossing the darkened hall and toppled onto her backside on the carpet runner.

"Botheration," she muttered unhappily.

A gentleman, judging by the soft grunt, rushed to her side and fumbled about, trying to find her fingers. His hands slipped over her thighs and upward until she almost couldn't breathe from the shocking sensations he stirred in her. "Forgive me," he murmured.

He caught her hands eventually and with a little tug, had her on her feet once more.

"Thank you, sir," she said as she brushed off her skirts and shuffled into the little moonlit alcove she been headed for to assess if her gown was damaged and bring her racing heart under control. She'd never reacted to a man in such a way before and was quite unnerved by how she'd not stopped him from touching her sooner.

She put her hand to the nearest window latch and, out of habit, flipped it unlocked.

"Completely my fault," the man assured her as he squeezed into the small space with her. "I should have been far more careful. I am so sorry."

She spun around, praying he'd not seen her action to unlock the window. Her gaze slowly rose up his body, and given her lack of height and the excess of his, she had to crane her neck to look at his face. "For myself, I cannot imagine how I missed seeing you soon enough to get out of your way. Good evening, Lord Louth."

He winced. "Miss Hedley? I am so sorry. Have you suffered any lasting hurt?"

Her smile widened at his earnest concern. "Only to my dignity and that is easily recovered," she promised him. He was always so considerate and he always asked her to dance when they met at balls. It was a pity his kindness was wasted. She wasn't worthy of his smiles.

However, her breath caught on two interesting facts.

Louth wasn't married and, despite his kindness, was considered a rogue by many.

If he wasn't married, and might never hold a ball, she did not have to worry about learning the location of his safe. She might even safely entertain the notion of securing his help toward her ruin.

He reached for her elbow, his grip firm, and the warmth from his gloved hands seeped into her bare skin. "Are you certain you are all right? A fall can be dangerous to your health."

She even liked him enough that the idea of becoming his mistress wasn't the least bit daunting. He would be the perfect man to snare as protector too, since his estate was far away in Lincolnshire. Could he be persuaded to set a mistress up in the country?

She let her gaze drop to his wide chest and imagined him pressed against her. She had never imagined him or anyone this way and it seemed a good time to start. She set her hand against his chest to steady herself as her legs turned to butter at the idea of being his.

Esme had said she should look for a wicked man. She'd never mentioned she might think wicked thoughts about him too. "Yes, of course I am. I am perfectly well. In fact I am so pleased to see you tonight."

He smiled warmly. "And why is that?"

She couldn't baldly state her intent to ruin herself, so she chose something less shocking until she found her courage to press for more. "I wonder if I might trouble you for a dance."

Ladies did not ever ask gentlemen for such a thing unless

they were fast, and she was aware he might already be engaged to dance with another woman in the next set. She also needed to get him back to the more populated part of the townhouse so she could inform Talbot that a different window had been opened.

However, he smiled. "I would be pleased to, Miss Hedley."

He held out his arm and she wrapped hers around it. He was quite tall and the muscles flexing under her fingers were thick and strong. Was he like that all over?

A blush filled her cheeks as they reentered the ballroom and joined the set newly forming. Unfortunately, the dance was a quadrille, which meant they would be too far apart to continue an improper conversation. But she could look at him all she liked and imagine being with him. For a large man, he was an accomplished dancer. His touch was light, his steps precise. His eyes never left hers and shivers raced over her skin when he smiled. She would have to find a way to keep him at her side after the dance and be brave enough to pursue him for what she wanted.

When the set finished, Louth caught her fingers lightly and placed her hand on his arm. "Thank you for the lovely dance, Miss Hedley."

"Thank you, my lord. I enjoyed it too."

"I will take you back to Lady Heathcote now."

Well, that will not do. She needed to spend a few more moments with Louth to ask her questions. "Oh please, might I have punch first?"

"Yes, of course. Dancing is thirsty work." He smoothly led her through the throng, his larger size immediately clearing a path, and for that she was grateful. She usually had to ask guests to move out of her way several times or scoot around them. A few steps along, however, Talbot materialized before her, stammering a false apology for stepping on her toes.

Lord Louth released her and moved back a few steps.

"East hall, alcove window. The library was occupied," she whispered and then hurried after Louth.

Once punch was secured, Iris moved to a quiet corner of the room that was still in full view of everyone present and tried to control her racing heart. She felt badly for the Hazeltons.

Tomorrow the family would be in an uproar over the robbery. There was nothing she could do to stop these awful events. She was as guilty as the thieves who took the jewels.

She sipped her punch then glanced up at Louth. "Are you enjoying the evening?"

He grunted. "My cousin is here, so no."

Iris spotted Miss Crewe on the far side of the room in the company of the mysterious Lady Taverham and other acquaintances. Miss Crewe was wearing the most beautiful pink silk gown and Iris sighed wistfully for days gone past, when she might have worn something similar. The strand of seed pearls around her neck took her by surprise. She'd never noticed that lady wear any truly valuable jewels before tonight. She was also surrounded by a gaggle of young gentlemen who clearly were entirely besotted by whatever she was talking about. "She looks to be popular."

"If only it could last," Louth murmured. "My cousin never fails to prove she's an original, as you probably have already heard. They'll be scared off like the rest by tomorrow afternoon at the latest."

She grinned and fluttered her fan before her face. "You suggest she does it on purpose but I've never seen any proof."

"She once suggested painting a suitor then listed all the ways she could soften the impact of his jowls." He laughed softly. "Ten minutes in my home listening to that sort of talk and you would not doubt my belief that she'd determined never to wed."

"I'd love to visit you at home, my lord." Her heart stopped. Was that too bold?

He seemed to choke a little but then smiled broadly. "Will your party go on to another entertainment tonight?"

She frowned, sensing the change in topic had robbed her of a chance to feel him out about the depth of his interest in her. "I believe Lady Heathcote has other plans for later that involve Mr. Meriwether, so I will be left to my own devices for several hours."

"Ah," Louth murmured and said no more on the subject.

"They are intimate friends and spend much of the evenings alone together." She handed her empty punch glass to a passing waiter. She couldn't let this opportunity slip away without trying harder to make an impression. "It must be nice, having someone to hold at night."

Louth froze with his glass almost to his lips. "It can be," he murmured before draining the glass entirely in one swallow and grimacing at the sickly sweet taste.

"Might I ask you a question?" When he nodded she took a deep breath. "What is it like to keep a mistress?"

He blinked slowly and tilted his head to the side. "Is your question part of a dare my cousin tricked you into tonight, Miss Hedley?"

"Absolutely not," she assured him. "I want to know for my own interest. I'd never speak to your cousin about so personal a matter."

"Then forgive me for being blunt but what interest could you have in such a discussion?" His frown grew. "Perhaps I should have returned you to Lady Heathcote, after all. I fear your fall has overset your good sense."

She gripped her fan tightly until the blades bent under the pressure. "If you'd rather not explain then I'll simply have to ask someone else."

Her irritated tone seemed to startle him because he eased closer. "You cannot run about a ball asking that sort of question."

Louth towered over her and those sensations he'd stirred in her when they'd touched earlier returned full force. Her pulse raced at the idea of being trapped in his strong arms, of being held by him. Kissed into senselessness.

She glanced across the room to where Mr. Talbot stood. He watched them with a curious expression on his face. Her heart raced a little faster. "Would you answer me in private then? I'd very much like to discuss the topic in greater detail."

Louth stared at her with widened brown eyes. He shifted to stand immediately before her. "I will return you to Lady Heathcote now."

He was so tall and wide; his shoulders blocked out Talbot entirely and for that she was grateful. A trickle of satisfaction filled her, even as he caught her elbow in a light grip. She took a risk to ask one more question, the most important one. "What sort of talents do *you* look for in a mistress?"

He squeezed her elbow firmly, and then dragged her back in the direction of Lady Heathcote and friends. Although she dug her heels in discreetly in a vain hope of slowing him down, she was no match for his power or determination to return her to her chaperone. Seeing it was futile to resist, she gave up the fight and plastered a smile on her face. She would have to ask someone less prudish next time indeed, if she wanted an honest answer.

Chapter Four

<hr>

Martin handed his card to the butler of Lady Heathcote's home and paced the short hall while he waited to be announced. He regretted his errand, he truly did, but he was doing this for Iris Hedley's own good. He had barely slept a wink last night, fretting over the questions the innocent woman had uttered in the crowded Hazelton ballroom. She could not ask men what they wanted in their mistresses without risking her reputation and being labeled shockingly fast.

Any scoundrel could have heard her unguarded remarks and taken advantage of her mistake. She was lucky he wasn't the sort to take advantage or spread harmful gossip, as so many in society were prone to do these days. Unfortunately, he suspected she might not be so lucky the next time she dared to ask a man such an impertinent question if he didn't put a stop to it himself.

When the butler led him into the drawing room, he discovered Lady Heathcote and Iris alone beside the crackling fireplace and the vision was so lovely and warm, he faltered. Tiny Iris wore her dark hair softly gathered at the back of her head in a loose chignon, and the deep-blue day gown fitted snuggly around her ample curves accented the paleness of her skin. She would be a temptation to any man who thought he might have her in his bed. Given her questions, even a sane man might think he had the right to have her anywhere and anytime he damn well liked.

Lady Heathcote smiled widely. "Ah, Lord Louth. So nice of you to call."

"Lady Heathcote, Miss Hedley, the pleasure is all mine, I assure you," he said as he took a place on a delicate seat opposite them and made small talk as expected of any normal caller. When the pleasantries were over, however, his throat seized. He had planned out what he would say but now, faced with the moment to deliver the warning, he grew uncertain whether to proceed. He would harm Iris' standing in Lady Heathcote's eyes if he were to reveal her scandalous inquiries to him last night.

Lady Heathcote smiled and glanced between them. "Iris mentioned this morning that she asked after your requirements in a mistress, and I must say I appreciate your early visit more than you can possibly know. Are you come to offer her your protection?"

"You knew what she was up to?" His temper flared and he bit out, "Of course I would not."

Iris shook her head. "I tried to tell you that you were mistaken over Lord Louth's reason for calling, Lady Heathcote. He is just being as polite as he has ever been."

"Absolutely," Martin insisted. "I came to stop this nonsense."

"A pity." Lady Heathcote's frank gaze raked him from head to toe and she squeezed Iris' hand. "I should have listened but you cannot scold me for hoping that such a fine specimen of man admired you. There are certainly others who would want someone as lovely as you in their bed."

Martin stared at Lady Heathcote in disbelief. The woman knew about Iris' impertinent questions and wasn't even offended by the idea of Iris Hedley joining the ranks of the demimonde. "Are you not going to stop her from pursing this ridiculous topic?"

Iris flinched and he chastised himself that he'd raised his voice enough to frighten her. He didn't mean to bellow like a bull but he was horrified. He'd thought Iris to be Lady Heathcote's friend, but clearly their friendship only went so far and did not cover preventing decisions that could destroy her reputation.

Lady Heathcote regarded him curiously. "Iris is a beautiful and intelligent woman. She knows her own mind, my lord. It is not a direction she has chosen lightly, but since she feels she has no choice, I've had to accept her decision and so must all her real friends. I certainly entertain the hope that she will marry well instead one day. Perhaps even fall in love. However, we've spent the whole morning discussing the subject and she is determined to strike out on her own and soon, with or without my help. She will find a protector and leave my home for the delights of his bed. I had hoped that man might be you."

"Make her stay with you." Martin jumped to his feet and began to pace. The idea of offering his protection was a joke. He'd only harm her.

"I cannot make her do what I want. She is my guest and not a child. She can stay for as long as she wishes to stay and take as much time as she needs to find the perfect man as her first protector." Lady Heathcote stood. "All I can do is guide her toward a gentle man who will take proper care of her, especially given her past experience."

"What past experience?" A hot flush swept over his skin at the idea of Iris Hedley having given her body to another without the benefit of marriage. "If your former betrothed or some other bounder has taken advantage, you should tell me."

Lady Heathcote shook her head. "And then what? Do you plan to call them out? That would cause an even greater scandal."

He glanced at Iris and found her staring at him, narrowed eyes, arms folded beneath her full breasts. "If you two are finished discussing my future and past as if I am not even in the room, I should like you both to calm down."

"Forgive me," Esme murmured and indeed she did look chastened. "I simply wanted Lord Louth to realize what was at stake and to have no doubts of your determination."

"I think you've managed to convey that. My decision is made and will not be changed, my lord."

He closed his eyes. "A shortsighted decision that will only bring you regret."

Lady Heathcote murmured, "Excuse me a moment."

Martin opened his eyes in time to see her leave the room and shut the drawing room door firmly behind her.

Iris waved her hand toward a chair, her skin glowing pink

from embarrassment. "Forgive my friend, she is determined that I must approach my choice with honesty and utter conviction or not at all. I had not expected her to importune you on my behalf. Please do sit down, my lord, or if you are too disappointed in me, I can understand if you'd rather leave."

He returned to his chair. "Why this mistress nonsense? Why not just marry?"

She looked on him in consternation. "I am not exactly marriage material, my lord, without a dowry."

True. And yet... "That would put off many men but certainly not all. You never lacked for admirers in the past."

"They admired my father's money and connections far more than me."

He winced. "Have you heard when your father might return to society?"

Her attention dropped to her hands and he recalled his prior questions had always produced the same shy response. "I don't expect my father will ever return."

Her words were filled with such sorrow that her father had abandoned her along with his financial responsibilities that he leaned forward to take her hand in his. "Surely there is still room for hope that he will come back and put things right again."

She bit her bottom lip and then shook her head. "There is none and it is high time I started earning my way in this world. I cannot live on Esme's charity for the rest of my life. I want something of my own again and to be away from London." She stood and paced away, abandoning his offered comfort. "Esme has been all that is kind and welcoming but I am always aware that my presence in her home is an imposition. My only hope for a secure future is to become a mistress. At least I would be out from under Esme's feet. I wish you had not come today. It is easy to see that you doubt my appeal."

Martin was glad he had come and he did not for a moment doubt her appeal as a woman. While she was distracted by the view outside, Martin let his gaze rove over her discreetly. He'd always had a soft spot for Iris Hedley, especially so since her father had fled to the Continent to avoid his debtors. That she lived with Lady Heathcote in London ensured she was well cared for and he always made sure to dance with her whenever their paths crossed. Many in society had snubbed her for her poverty and that made him furious. How was she to blame for anything that had happened?

However, no matter how appealing she might be, tiny, delicate creatures such as this were strictly off limits for a man of his proportions. Since his parting with Vivian, looking at a woman was often the only pleasure he allowed himself. He could not offer for her even if he didn't think it the most appalling idea. "Of course I would come, if only to warn you not to ask gentlemen such questions ever again. Other men would have assumed you were bent on seduction and pounced on you immediately."

Her gaze flittered to his shyly. "I will be more circumspect next time and ask someone who might like what he sees."

Martin did like what he saw very much but she could never be more to him than this. He could be her friend and offer some guidance. Maybe if he answered her questions, she'd change her mind about the whole thing and consider the alternative: marriage to the right man. "I won't allow you to ask anyone else. The risk of censure is too great. What do you want to know?"

Her eyes widened and then she smiled warmly and drew closer. "How often would I be expected to be intimate with my protector?"

He gave the matter careful consideration, stalling for time in the hope Lady Heathcote would return. Iris was beautiful in a way he suspected she didn't understand. An ordinary-sized man would likely want her daily. He could tell her the truth but to be so honest might frighten her away from marriage entirely and that wasn't his goal. He didn't want to turn her off all men so he chose a lesser answer. "At least a handful of nights each week."

She held out her hand and flexed her fingers. "So when you saw your mistress, you were intimate at least five times?"

He winced. In truth, he'd been intimate with Vivian less than that. He'd always ensured her pleasure first and often. "We are not talking about my desires but those of an ordinary man."

She frowned. "What is the difference?"

He raked a hand through his short hair. He could not be that honest with Iris Hedley. "What is your next question?"

Her gaze fell to his lips and a bright blush filled her cheeks.

"What is it like to kiss someone so deeply that you lose yourself in their embrace?"

He peered at her closely, noticed the rapid rise and fall of her breasts and felt the unwise stirrings of arousal in himself. Just how experienced was Iris with men? If she did not know a good kiss could devastate the senses then the "past experience" Lady Heathcote eluded too might not be as ruinous as he had first feared. "It is wonderful."

"Could you show me?"

He rocked backward in surprise. "I beg your pardon?"

She clenched her hands together at her waist and wrung them together. "As Lady Heathcote mentioned, I have limited experience in these matters."

He sagged in relief. Lady Heathcote's choice of words had led him to imagine the worst and that was not the case. "That is good news."

"How could you believe that?" She sighed. "I have no choice but to press forward if I want any sort of life of my own. I want to know what I'd be expected to do with men and I'd like help in gathering some skills to prepare myself for that day."

She wanted lessons? His mind reeled that she might have asked someone else for that improper education. She'd be expelled from all good society if she were ever found out. "How much experience do you have exactly?"

"Three kisses," she answered immediately. "I know there are any number of degrees to a lady's experience but Esme assures me a woman should be able to tell that the man she is with has the necessary skills to deserve her affections by the expertise of his kiss."

"You're a complete innocent," he choked out. Gods, three kisses was nothing. She was contemplating a life well beyond the pale and had no idea of what changes would come in her life as a mistress.

"Yes." She lifted her chin proudly. "But I'd like not to be ignorant, too."

He rubbed his jaw, thinking hard of a way to turn her inexperience to his advantage. If he could distract her from her plan of finding a protector she might yet find a man to marry. A few poorly executed kisses wouldn't bring her too much harm as long as no one learned of them. "Very well."

Her mouth fell open.

He grinned at her shock. "I will be the one to answer your questions about intimacy on the condition you tell no one that you wish to be a mistress, for the time being. I must have your promise that this will be our secret. I won't be a party to your ruin."

"And you'll teach me what I need to know, too?"

He paused. An innocent bride was expected to know very little on her wedding night. He would be careful of what he taught her. "Yes."

"I do promise." She drew closer. "Show me."

"You want me to kiss you now? Here?" He glanced around wildly, hoping Lady Heathcote might be on the verge of rejoining them. However he heard not one sound beyond Iris' rushed breath. When he'd imagined her education, he'd not envisaged undertaking it in Lady Heathcote's drawing room where anyone might walk in.

Iris, however, stared up at him seriously. "Well, where else might be as private as this? If we were to sneak away at a ball, someone might see us. If we were to meet at a private residence you own, that too would be fraught with the risk of detection. Esme would not have left us alone had she not wanted me to continue my inquiries with you under her roof."

"I see your point." Now was indeed the perfect moment. He could kiss Iris and no one would know, and then tomorrow night she'd hopefully forget all about these ridiculous lessons and return to a search for a suitable husband.

Decision made, he gripped her shoulders and pressed his lips to hers in a smacking kiss that ended before it truly began.

When he released her and stood back, she stared at him in disapproval. "I thought you'd be better at kissing than that."

So much for his good intentions. He ground his teeth. "Why do women always want something more from me than I offer?"

"I don't know." Her head tilted a little to the side as she studied him. "I've never asked you to show me more than what a proper kiss entails, but if it's too much of an inconvenience…"

Despite the situation, he was impressed by her pluck. The challenge she presented intrigued him. Tiny Iris Hedley was remarkably stubborn and he'd never noticed that trait before. How much could he teach her without going too far, though? He'd have to tread carefully.

Since the disparity in their heights was too great to kiss comfortably standing, he caught her hand and towed Iris toward the window seat at the rear of the room. He sat and left her standing before him. "How about *you* kiss *me*, since you clearly have some idea of what constitutes a proper kiss?"

Her brow creased in consternation. "Do mistresses do that? Kiss their protectors first, and can they also do that without his encouragement?"

His certainly had before. Nothing aroused him more than an impatient woman. He nodded slowly. "A man likes a woman who knows what she wants when it comes to passion."

"I see. Then I was correct that I must learn everything I can." She set her hands to his shoulders and lowered her face to his. He stared into her pale-green eyes, waiting for her to change her mind until the very last minute when she brushed her lips softly against his.

It was a gentle kiss but Martin's heart began to clamor hard against his ribs immediately. Her hands drifted slowly up his neck and when she touched his jaw, her little fingers were warm and distracting. She lifted her face a moment then kissed him again as if she had all the time in the world to experiment on him. She learned fast. She was courageous and brave even if her eyes were shut tightly, and she grew enthusiastic about her chance to kiss him into senselessness.

It might be a mistake to encourage her but Martin caught her head and pulled her down onto his lap, her tiny weight balanced on one thigh, her skirts tangled between his legs. He wrapped his arm across her hip and with the other stroked her shoulder firmly. He closed his eyes too and discovered that an innocent's kiss was ten times more arousing than the most experienced courtesan he'd ever draped over his knee.

Her lips parted without prompting and her tongue danced across his lower lip. Martin tucked her firmly against his body and thrust into her mouth hungrily with his own tongue, lost in the moment of exploration he'd never once expected. When she stroked his tentatively in return, he pressed her hip harder against his growing erection and plundered the sweet taste of her mouth.

Iris whimpered softly and the sound checked his urgency. He eased back, glancing up into a face grown flushed and dazed from arousal. He groaned under his breath. Perhaps educating the innocent hadn't been the best way to convince her to marry, but he could not say he regretted that kiss or the feel of her tiny body in his arms.

He deposited her onto an adjacent cushion and waited while she caught her breath. That was probably more than he should have "taught" her but she had asked for it boldly and he'd answered in kind. Hopefully, his actions would prove to her that passion belonged with a husband and not with some near-stranger who would use her then walk away each morning, leaving money or jewels beside the bed and no certainty of when she'd see them again. The very idea offended him. "Do you see?"

"I believe I understand," she said at last after clearing her throat a few times. "So it is possible to receive such a kiss when the man doesn't even want the lady."

He shook his head. How wrong she was. He *did* want her, and for proof she had only to look at the growing bulge in his trousers, but being an innocent she had no idea of the condition her kisses had left him in. However, since Martin was all wrong for Iris Hedley, he said nothing to convince her that his interest was genuine. He sat a moment, waiting for his arousal to subside. "Promise me you will limit voicing your inquiries to this place and to me."

Her face turned to his and he could see her struggle for composure after such a heady kiss. The way she stared at him, glassy eyed and breathless, meant the first lesson was likely an unabashed success in her eyes. Her fingers rose to cover her flushed lips and eventually she nodded. "I would be most happy to receive further lessons from you, my lord. Anytime."

The doors burst open and Lady Heathcote rushed inside, holding a note aloft. "You'll never believe it but Lord Hazelton was robbed last night during the ball and struck down by the villains."

Iris shot to her feet, pale and trembling. "Is he dead?"

"He survives but everyone is a suspect, it seems," Lady

Heathcote reassured her. "Meriwether is on his way."

Iris nodded. "I'm sure he will be a comfort to you."

"Yes, it will be nice to see him, however, he is coming to interview us about last night. At last he's been promoted to lead the investigations into the spate of thefts prevalent among the *ton* these past months."

When Iris burst into tears, Martin waited a heartbeat then gathered her close, despite Lady Heathcote's understandably shocked expression. Clearly, her nerves were overset by the kiss and her brazen request. Iris didn't understand that such an interview was merely a formality. Meriwether would ask his questions and go because no one in their right mind would ever imagine a proper lady would stoop to theft.

Chapter Five

"**I** love you, Papa!" Iris clung to her father and buried her face in his collar. She needed the comfort of his arms after the distress of being interrogated by Mr. Meriwether about her movements at the Hazelton ball the previous night. She had been beyond relieved that Louth had not mentioned their pleasant interlude alone in the alcove. The alcove that the thieves had used for egress to the Hazelton library and which might have led the inquisitive Mr. Meriwether to consider her a prime suspect in his investigation had he but known.

She drew back to peer into her father's face, desperate for the comfort of his love. The lines around his eyes appeared deeper and darker today, his once-bright green eyes were dull and tired.

He pushed her away. "Mind your pretty clothes."

"I don't care about my clothes," she assured him, but settled for holding his hand. "Are you well?"

He nodded and drew her toward the only chair in the room, situated near the window. Overnight another bed had been crammed into the chamber but they were alone at the moment, the other men having excused themselves upon her arrival. "We had a to-do here during the evening just past, a few fellows fighting over nonsense, but everyone calmed down eventually with no harm done."

Iris glanced out at the yard. A handful of men lingered outside, resting against the walls and talking in small groups.

She'd not noticed anything amiss in their mood upon her arrival but tempers always flared quickly in this place. The last fight that had erupted within the Marshalsea had ended up with bloodshed. One of her father's chums had been stabbed. Luckily not fatally but it was a side of life in the prison that terrified her. Her father was not accustomed to the rough and tumble of the grim world.

Her father patted her hand. "I am glad you were not here for it. At least with you gone, I don't have to worry for your safety."

She wasn't safe anywhere and her heart ached anew. "I am safe with Esme," she promised

Her father nodded. "She's been a good friend. Very particular of observing the proprieties."

Well, not all the time. Esme had left her alone with Louth in the hopes she'd be seduced and Iris had failed to experience more than a kiss. Not a very auspicious beginning for her new career but she would persevere. She glanced at her father and sadness consumed her. "She speaks fondly of you still."

"If only she might find you a husband then I would not worry so."

"Father, please." She stretched for his hand again. "Do not concern yourself over that?"

"Well, it is the done thing for a woman to make a match. I'm just telling you what everyone knows." He raked his fingers through his hair. "You must consider how it looks to others. Lady Forsythe is particularly cutting of women who drag their feet on the way to the altar. We might never be invited to dinner again, and you know how your stepmother feels about making the right impression."

Iris squeezed his hand to halt the flow of his words. Her heart ached that he'd forgotten that what Lady Forsythe and her stepmother felt mattered little anymore. Her father's second wife had fled to Bath as soon as the money was gone, and good riddance; and Lady Forsythe had refused to acknowledge her existence for some time. "I am sorry I haven't married yet too, Papa," she promised him sincerely. A nice husband with a large fortune might have saved them both but the chances of that were far behind her. A protector, and a residence outside of London, was all she could hope for now. "Lord Louth asked after you yesterday."

Her father appeared startled. "Do I know him?"

"Yes, Papa. He came to dinner quite often and you thought he possessed a keen intellect."

He frowned at her hand then nodded. "Oh, yes. I did think him very smart. Why did you not think to set your cap for him?"

She had been engaged at that time but she would not mention Grindlewood today. If she did, it would undoubtedly set off a series of conversations that would leave him confused about why her dowry had been used to pay off his last landlord. As for Louth, he was not interested in her or matrimony. "Lord Louth is a friend, sir, and he only pays me attention out of respect for you."

Her father settled on the end of his bed with a groan. "Nonsense. He'd make a fine husband."

Iris pressed her lips together. He might make a fine lover too except for his unwillingness. "He has expressed no interest in matrimony."

"Sounds like a young woman I raised." Her father regarded her with narrowed eyes. "Charm him and you'll win his title in the end."

"Father." She laughed and cupped his face. When he got an idea in his head he was impossibly determined. "That is not what I will do. I will not throw myself at the only man who still asks me to dance."

Her father dismissed that with a wave of his hand. "Does his appearance offend you in some way?"

Her eyes widened in astonishment. "No, of course not. He is a very agreeable and gentle man." And attractive. Thinking of their kiss had lost her several hours of precious sleep last night. She'd tossed about so much, she'd needed to straighten her own bed this morning before the maids could come in.

He smoothed his waistcoat, one that had seen better days, with one hand. "Oh well. Forget I mentioned the man."

Now that was impossible to do, and especially so after thoroughly kissing him yesterday. She could still feel his large hands pressing her body close to his, his taste in her mouth. The slight rasp of stubble had been a wicked surprise that she'd enjoyed too. She'd almost forget the trouble in her life just to have a chance to kiss him again.

"What about Lord Ettington? I know his uncle."

And had offended the marquess' uncle, the Duke of Exeter, rather thoroughly, too. "Ettington is married, Papa. Don't you remember me telling you of his public displays of affection for his wife?" She patted his hand again. "Anyway, never mind your matchmaking attempts. Is there anything I can do for you?"

Her father reached into his trunk and removed a crumpled shirt from the low pile of clothing inside. "I lost a button."

Iris shook out the shirt and spread it over her lap. "This will take only a minute. Why don't you tell me your news while I work?"

She dug into her reticule for scissors, needle and thread, and a spare button she carried with her just in case of such a need, while her father related the details of recent events in the Marshalsea. His recounting, as always, included news from weeks ago too. Things she already knew. He spoke of them as if they had just happened and she didn't care to upset him by reminding him of the passage of time between then and now. She just wanted to hear his voice and she was done with the shirt before he finished. She folded the garment neatly away in his trunk. "Perfect again."

Her father cleared his throat. "Iris, there is something I want to talk to you about."

"Of course, Papa."

He took her hands and stared into her face. "When you leave here today, I don't want you to come back. It is too dangerous here for one so lovely as you."

Iris shook her head violently. "You cannot mean that."

"But I do." He gripped her hands even tighter. "My daughter, I love you more than anything in the world and I never wished to drag you so low. You have a good situation with Lady Heathcote. You live in comfort, and have the respect of those you meet. You should do everything you can to protect your reputation."

She nodded numbly, having heard it all before and knowing he made sense in a way. However, she couldn't do as he asked. She was buried so deep in muck she had no way out yet. "I will not leave you, and nothing you say will ever make me decide otherwise."

He turned away as if she'd not spoken. "While you can, you must use this opportunity to find a husband of means and save yourself."

"Father, I'm not going to abandon you. We discussed this. We can recover and find a little place to rent in the countryside. Won't that be a nice change from London?" She dug into her reticule and removed the coins that Esme had pressed on her this morning. She placed them into his hand and folded his fingers over them. "I will have more, and soon."

Her father did not refuse the money but his expression told her he was not happy to take from her again. "My dear child, your heart is so large, but you must realize that you will never have enough to cover the debts unless you marry exceedingly well."

"Not this again. Please, Papa. I would not argue with you today about this. We have so little time left before I must return to Esme."

He touched the sleeve of her gown and rubbed the fine material between his fingers. "Consider it well, my dear. Seeing you like this, in gowns so fine and grand, makes sense. You belong among the *ton*."

She met his gaze. "We belong where we choose. Isn't that what you've always told me?"

"Then work toward making a good match for yourself. You deserve to be happy."

"I will be happy when you are free," she assured him. Iris kissed his cheek as tears filled her eyes. Yes, a good marriage would solve many problems but no man would want to marry a thief's accomplice. Being a mistress was entirely different. At least the situation would be honest and only ever about a little passion. She was sure no harm would come to her future protector if she were charged with a crime committed before their arrangement had begun.

She kissed her father's cheek again, fussed about him until it was time to depart for the three-mile trip back to Esme's home, and when she took her leave, promising to return the next day, she thought her father might cry. He expected her to obey him and never return. She always would.

Partway down the rickety stairs, she came face-to-face with the turnkey. "How dare your men attack a lord?"

"Toff should have stepped out of the way," Fitzhugh grumbled but he looked distinctly uncomfortable.

Iris punched her hands to her hips and glared. "I refuse to be a party to murder."

"Complaining won't do you any good. He'll never let you go. You do your part and I'll do mine."

He glanced up at the barracks doorway where her father's sad face looked down upon them and waved. "We'll all pay in the end."

"You have to save my father," she whispered. "You have to get him out of here. Please."

"Can't even save myself. There ain't no salvation for the fallen. There ain't money enough to silence wagging tongues and hide him, not the way he carries on some days." He trudged up the stairs, eased past her father and disappeared into the room.

If Fitzhugh did ever escape Talbot's influence, what then would become of her father if he were left here alone?

Father might not last a day.

She hurried down the stairs, nodded politely to Fitzhugh's burly assistant as he fumbled with the lock and stepped out through the Marshalsea prison gate as fast as she could with tears streaming down her cheeks.

No one had died yet, but that didn't mean they'd be so lucky next time.

Once she reached the nearest corner, she hailed a hack and gave directions for Lord Louth's Golden Square townhouse. She was going to call on Miss Crewe as a pretext to seeing the earl and arranging when her next lesson would occur. She could be a mistress to him if she could encourage him the right way; experience pleasure such as Lord Louth had teased her with yesterday, and be protected from Talbot.

The trip in the carriage took significantly less time than the long trek on foot but even so her anxiety soared. She'd never deliberately paid a social call to a man before. There was always the possibility that Louth wouldn't be at home, wouldn't offer for her, wouldn't wish to see her.

When the carriage stopped before his home and she applied the knocker, the kindly faced butler greeted her with warm smiles and apologies that Miss Crewe had not yet arisen. "Should you care to leave a card?"

She bit her lip uncertainly. It was a pity to waste the entire trip when it was really the earl she'd come to see. It was a risk but she might not have another chance to see him for days. "Would Lord Louth perhaps be at home?"

"Yes, Miss Hedley." The butler gestured toward a nearby room. "If you'd care to wait a moment, I shall see if he has time to speak to you today."

Iris entered a drawing room so elegant, her breath caught. A fine chandelier hung above an exquisite Oriental rug. Deep-cushioned chairs surrounded a fireplace screen fashioned in the Oriental style. The setting took her breath away. She'd had no idea the earl possessed such remarkable taste.

Talbot would rub his hands in glee over the twin jade vases flanking the hearth too.

Lord Louth hurried into the room, straightening his elegant coat into place. "Miss Hedley? I am so sorry to keep you waiting."

"My lord. The wait was nothing." She dipped him a curtsy to hide the disconcerting blush sweeping over her skin like a lover's caress. "Thank you for seeing me at such short notice."

"Always." He turned toward the butler and dismissed him. Louth shut the door. "I trust all is well at home and that you've recovered from Mr. Meriwether's appallingly rude questions."

"Yes, I have." Her heart clattered against her chest as he drew closer. The man had been so offended by Meriwether's questioning she'd feared the pair might come to blows. "In truth, I came to see you to discuss my lessons. You rushed away yesterday without deciding when the next would be."

"I had hoped you'd put that behind you." He folded his arms over his chest, presenting an intimidating façade. "Were you not satisfied enough with the first lesson?"

She nodded quickly. Louth had not liked the idea she might approach another gentleman in her quest to become a mistress. She hoped to trigger his protective instincts even more today. "Oh yes. But now that I see you again I cannot help thinking perhaps you'd prefer I should ask someone else and be done with the chore."

His arms dropped to his sides and he took another pace closer. "Miss Hedley, I must make one thing perfectly clear. I know exactly what lesson you need next."

He swooped on her, dragging her up into his arms and kissed her soundly. With her feet dangling off the floor, she wrapped her arms about his neck purely for self-preservation. However, once she was in his arms again, her senses took over.

She'd been thinking of his kisses every other moment but had feared the desire he'd stirred in her could not be repeated. Clearly it could. He pressed her back to a wall as their tongues tangled in a frantic dance. If he could make her feel this way she'd enjoy her life as a mistress, but she still had to convince him to offer for her.

He drew back, panting hard. "Desire only takes a moment to flare beyond control, and no, I don't want to be replaced."

Her eyes widened as she slid down the wall and landed on her feet. Unfortunately, or perhaps fortunately, her legs had turned to butter so she had no choice but to hold onto his coat to remain upright. He towered over her in a navy wool coat and buff pantaloons, the epitome of good taste and breeding, and she wished to climb back into his arms again and continue kissing him. She licked her lips. "Is it normal to feel this way? So alive?"

"Yes." He frowned and kissed her again, his hands sliding down her sides and back up to her shoulders. He eased back a little to whisper. "What are you thinking in coming here to see me?"

Iris tangled her fingers in his short hair and met his gaze. "I did ask after your cousin first, so no one would suspect my real motives were to see you."

He stared at her steadily then he nodded. "At least in that you were sensible. I paid you a visit this morning, only to be told you had gone out on a private errand. Where did you go?"

Her heartbeat sped up. "To purchase lace," she said quickly, latching onto the most boring errand she could think of. It was the response of a brainless twit. She didn't want Louth to know she visited her father in the Marshalsea every chance she could. She withdrew her hand from his chest and glanced around.

"Whitney will be down soon," he murmured as he straightened. He caught her elbow and guided her across the room to a comfortable settee. "I sent three maids to peel her away from her art. If she's not here in precisely the next five minutes, I'll go in with pistols."

Iris couldn't help but giggle at the image. "You really do have a shockingly low opinion of your cousin."

He reached out and grazed her cheek softly with his thumb. "Do remember my remarks are based on years of experience in living with the brat."

Iris perched on the edge of the cushion, concerned for him. "She has you under siege."

"Something like that. I do have trouble understanding what she wants most of the time." He sat forward too, staring into her face with such direct focus that she shivered. "I am glad you have come."

She studied him openly, liking what she saw very much. Liking his honesty and to-the-point manner. "Why is that?"

He pressed his lips together a moment. "You asked for lessons but I want to assure you I will not make the mistake of going beyond what is needed."

She stilled, aware she had enjoyed his attentions very much and would prefer he continued them and make her his mistress. "I was not concerned about that."

"You should be." His smile slipped away. "I'm not one to take what should belong to another."

She smiled. She would be no trouble to him. If he did not want to be her protector she would accept his decision. "I believe, my Lord, that we understand each other. I assure you I will have no expectations beyond each lesson."

He nodded and was about to say more but Whitney flung the doors wide. "Not a moment too soon," Louth mumbled.

Whitney strode across the room wearing another pink gown, muslin this time, and a spencer with violet-spotted cuffs. "Miss Hedley, what a lovely surprise to see you here."

On closer inspection, however, Iris determined the spots were actually paint splotches. On anyone else, the gown would have caused laughter at her carelessness. Iris, however, thought Whitney Crewe very original. A trait she admired very much despite Lord Louth's occasional complaints. She dipped a curtsy. "Good morning, Miss Crewe. How lovely you look today."

Whitney held out her arm and displayed what might be finely drawn butterflies on the cuffs. "I was inspired by my morning view of the garden."

Iris smiled in awe at the patience required for the task, but her attention slipped to the gold cuff around her wrist. She dragged her gaze away. "Intriguing."

"Would you care to join me on an outing?" she asked as she pulled on her gloves, hiding the bracelet completely. "I was just on my way to the park in search of further inspiration."

"With us. You are not going out alone anywhere," Louth corrected his cousin.

Miss Crewe smiled. "What harm could there be in a short walk through the park? It is quite safe at this time of day. I don't think I will sleep a wink worrying over who might creep into our home. These robberies are quite terrifying."

"I would not allow that to happen. I personally make sure all the windows and doors of the lower floors are locked and secured each night."

Miss Crewe smiled sweetly at him. "That is a relief. It is a comfort to live in a home with such a large cousin to protect me. I am ready to go if Miss Hedley is ready to join me. We can begin without you if you'd prefer."

"You will wait for me." He stalked out grumbling, "I won't have you both galloping around the park unescorted."

Whitney sighed. "Ill tempered at odd moments but I assure you, Lord Louth is a perfectly rational gentleman in all other respects."

"Perfectly amiable," she agreed swiftly.

Miss Crewe began to laugh. "Oh, don't say such horridly bland things about my cousin. He deserves a better description, surely."

Iris glanced swiftly at Louth's cousin in confusion and found the woman grinning. "I beg your pardon?"

The girl fussed with her gown. "Come now, I would have waited outside longer so you and my cousin could continue your fascinating conversation about why he won't bed you, but Gibbs was looking at me strangely so I had no choice but to barge in and pretend I hadn't heard a word. I apologize if I interrupted precipitously, and promise I will endeavor to provide further opportunity for privacy at a later date. He must like you a great deal or he'd never have met with you without a chaperone present."

A blush swept up her face. "You heard it all?"

Miss Crewe winked. "But never would I breathe a word. I just want you to know you do not need to pretend indifference to my cousin around me. He is a generous man but like all men, can be ridiculously blinkered."

Iris did not know what to say to that but she was relieved Miss Crewe was not at all scandalized by what she'd overheard. But she wouldn't be so friendly if she knew what she'd done to others in society. "Thank you," she whispered.

When she heard Lord Louth returning she was vastly relieved. Miss Crewe noticed too much for her comfort.

"The carriage will be a moment or two more," he assured them.

"A slow carriage trip?" Miss Crewe threw a pained expression at him but then turned and winked at Iris again. "Martin, you are being unnecessarily proper but at least we will have Miss Hedley's presence to add some excitement to the day. We should have invited her to visit long before this so we do not grow bored with each other's company, as we often do."

The suggestion sounded so reasonable as it came out of Miss Crewe's mouth, but given the girl had overheard her conversation with Louth, there was no way she could dismiss the calculated potential for dalliance. Iris counted that a blessing.

Chapter Six

The empress, as Marin had once privately dubbed Iris years ago when her father had the funds, was in her element riding through Hyde Park in his carriage. It seemed impossible for her to belong anywhere other than in society, in his opinion. However, with Whitney at her side and grinning like a loon, he wasn't sure if his decision to accompany them was in his best interests. The two seemed to be becoming fast friends on this ride, but he was afraid, given the sly glances in his direction, that Whitney was also very likely up to something.

He hoped she was not leading Iris to believe there might be more between them. He couldn't bear to see Iris hurt. He could not court or wed her. He couldn't be her protector either. He wanted only to be her friend and divert her from the folly of her own making.

He settled more comfortably against the squabs of his barouche and let his gaze fall on Iris, as it had done constantly since leaving his home. Iris again fidgeted with her pale-gray gloves that matched her carriage dress. Pretty, and proper, and unbelievably desirable. The earlier kiss had affected him more than it should have and he cursed his foolishness for indulging in the unnecessary lesson. He felt on edge. Certain he was making a mistake in giving in to this attraction. She had felt very good in his arms.

Unfortunately, he could not walk away and let her education

be taken over by another man. The very idea sent his temper soaring.

"Are you enjoying yourself?" he asked her quietly, when Whitney's attention was drawn to a passing carriage containing artist friends of hers.

"Yes, my lord. A carriage ride in the park is always an enjoyable outing." Her genuine smile encouraged his. Their gaze held and the beginnings of unwise desire warmed her eyes, turning them round and luminous. Unfortunately, if Iris continued to look upon him with unabashed lust, he'd have to do something he'd really rather not. One kiss always led to another, and another. Indulging again was out of the question unless he wanted to ruin her life.

Her smile turned hesitant. "The Ettingtons have invited Esme and I to dinner on Thursday next week. Are you by chance attending?"

If any other unmarried woman had asked that question with such hope in her voice, he would have edged around an answer and not dared commit himself either way. However, he'd always looked forward to seeing Iris in society and making sure she was comfortable, so he nodded. "I am. They are great friends. You will find the marchioness a trifle unconventional but she is also a great deal of fun," he added.

"I like what I've heard of her very much. And I have been fortunate enough to have witnessed firsthand how happy she has made the marquess."

"That she has, although many suggested he'd chosen rashly at the time." He shrugged. Ettington had married for love. As had all of his friends. He did not begrudge them their happiness but being stuck in a room full of grinning spouses made a bachelor long for the nearest exit.

Whitney smacked the door of the carriage suddenly. "I just remembered. The duke is in Town and sure to be at the Ettington dinner party, isn't he?"

Iris frowned. "Which duke?"

"Why, the Duke of Exeter, of course. Lord Ettington's reclusive uncle." Whitney sighed dreamily. "Aside from determining if the resemblance is as strong as everyone claims, I'm so looking forward to making his acquaintance."

"Whitney," Martin warned. He doubted his cousin would set her cap for a man three times her age, which likely meant she wanted an introduction for other reasons. Exeter would be livid if Whitney even attempted to stir up trouble for him. He could see social disaster looming if he did not put a stop to her schemes. "The duke isn't a man to bait with careless conversation, as you do with everyone else."

Instead of being chastened, she smirked. "Well, everyone insists I must meet the man and at last that day has come."

"Meet him, not embarrass the family in the process. Get on his wrong side and you could find your eccentricities fodder for his amusement. You will not find the experience pleasant. There will be no one to appeal to for peace. Ettington will take his uncle's side, as always."

"Your cousin is correct," Iris agreed softly. "Exeter is not a man to cross."

He smiled his thanks for her support but Iris was wringing her hands instead and looking down. "Are you acquainted with His Grace?"

Her chin lifted. "A long time ago. I'm sure he won't remember me?"

Only a blind man wouldn't recall such sweet, gentle beauty. Instead he said, "He forgets nothing."

Iris winced and turned her attention to the park.

Whitney grabbed Iris' hand the next moment as her eyes widened. "Look there. I see Mr. Talbot has ventured to the park today."

Surprised by Whitney's mention of a man of little fashion or distinction, Martin turned to look too. Wealthy but not particularly well-shod. They'd had little to do with each other in society. The fellow normally moved in an entirely different social set, but due to recent inclusion by some hostesses who should know better, had begun climbing the social ladder and had been seen everywhere.

Iris kept her hands clenched together in her lap. "There are many others of interest in the park today."

Whitney's disappointment in Iris' disinterest was swift and curious. She glanced his way with a second haughty smirk. "Well, we must say hello anyway."

What was his cousin trying to do, engineer a deeper acquaintance between Talbot and Iris? She must know how wrong that was. Iris Hedley deserved the very best in a husband.

To his considerable shock, Whitney turned and waved wildly at Mr. Talbot, giving the man no choice but to acknowledge her. When his coachmen slowed to a stop, Talbot left his companions and strolled in their direction.

Martin held his breath as the man noticed Iris for the first time. The man's eyes glowed with happiness. Eagerness. He stopped beside the carriage and whispered her first name…*Iris.*

"Mr. Talbot." A slow blush crept over her cheeks. "It is a pleasure to see you, sir."

"And it is a pleasure to see you." The man glanced at him and Talbot's smile dimmed a little. "And with Lord Louth no less. What an unexpected surprise this is."

"Talbot," he acknowledged, but he was keen to see the back of the man. Iris, for all her warm greeting, appeared unimpressed with the man.

Iris sighed and gestured to Whitney. "Are you acquainted with my friend, Miss Whitney Crewe?"

Whitney held out her hand, bare of her glove and sparkling with gold at the wrist. Talbot took her fingers in a light grip and grinned. "Not as yet. Well met, dear lady."

"Sir. It is such a pleasure to make your acquaintance, too."

His attention returned to Iris immediately. "Any news of your father?"

Iris winced. "No."

Talbot nodded, and then squared his shoulders. "One does hope he remains in good health."

Martin's eyes narrowed when Iris paled. It pained him that she was so hesitant to speak of her father to acquaintances. She kept her gaze averted. "I hope so too."

Talbot smiled and was about to speak again when Martin tipped his head to the group the man had recently left. "I believe your party is moving on without you."

Annoyance, quickly masked, flickered over Talbot's face but he smiled and took his leave, with a promise to see Iris again soon.

Whitney frowned after his retreating form. "Well, I must say he has a distinct presence but rather abrupt in his manner of leaving."

Iris grimaced. "I'm sure he has many demands on his time."

The frown and the words combined did not give Martin the impression she'd meant to compliment the man. "Do you know him well?"

"Not really. He was an acquaintance of my father's some years ago and always speaks of him when our paths cross."

Whitney patted Iris' hand soothingly. "Then I shall overlook his haste just to make you happy."

What the devil was Whitney blathering about? By her own account, Talbot hardly knew Iris Hedley. What did it matter if he was not liked?

"I've no care for him either way but it would be rude to ignore him." Iris met his gaze and the corner of her mouth lifted into a tentative smile. Despite Whitney's odd behavior, a tremor of anticipation, of shared purpose, filled him. He shifted his position on the bench seat as her smile widened. She leaned close to Whitney. "You cannot say no one of interest comes to the park, Miss Crewe. Lord Acton is headed this way, and he is very handsome."

Astonishment and then a keen sense of loss filled Martin at the sound of Iris' earnest praise for another man. He turned. Seated atop a dappled gray gelding, Lord Acton presented a fine figure and quite likely inspired passion in many women. To hear Iris speak so well of another cut him to the quick.

Acton trotted up to the carriage and greeted them warmly. "Good afternoon, Louth, and ladies. 'Tis a fine day for it."

Whitney's mouth turned down in a frown. "Have you been prowling Rotten Row long, my lord, in search of a victim for your next amusement?"

"Not particularly." The earl patted his horse's neck as the beast pranced. "I was just leaving the park and thought to pay my respects when I saw you waiting here."

Whitney smirked. "Are you on your way to call on your sister then? She came to Town last week. How long has it been since you've spoken to her?"

Martin froze. The earl's recent estrangement from his sister wasn't a subject to discuss openly. Whitney didn't approve of

Acton. The harm his sister had done to the Marquess of Taverham's marriage had cost the couple a decade of lost time and trust. Whitney, who still insisted Acton must have played a part in the estrangement, made no bones that her loyalties were with the couple.

Acton ignored her remarks and turned his attention to Iris and nodded. "A pleasure to see you again, Miss Hedley. Louth. Good day to you."

He kicked his mount and left them without a backward glance or a word to Whitney.

"Drive on," Whitney called out to the coachman and they lurched forward.

"Stop," Martin countered and was immediately obeyed. He exchanged a worried glance with Iris then faced his cousin. "Were you trying to be inexcusably rude?"

"You *were* impolite," Iris agreed softly.

"Well, he had it coming." Whitney protested.

Before Martin could say another word on the subject, Iris twisted to face Whitney with a dark expression. "As I understand the matter from Lady Heathcote, the earl's only crime was ignorance. Lord Acton placed his faith in his sister and she betrayed him. That must be painful enough without other people pouring salt on the wound."

Whitney's eyes widened. "You dare take his side?"

Iris shook her head. "It is not fair of you to hold him accountable for his sister's actions. Believe me, I know how it hurts to have been that ignorant. My father made a lot of bad decisions I had no control over, and I continue to pay the price."

At last, Whitney appeared abashed. "I didn't think of it that way. You know he was beastly to her."

"And he has been trying to make amends by all accounts in any way he can ever since," Iris insisted.

A warm glow filled Martin's chest. When he got Iris alone, he would kiss her in thanks for making the attempt to straighten out his cousin. He'd tried many times to calm her ire but to no effect. "Miranda is at ease with Acton and that is all that matters," he added.

Whitney shrugged. "Then he should stop bothering us."

Martin frowned. "He doesn't bother me in the slightest. It

would have been rude not to have spoken to each other."

Whitney shrugged again and he studied her sullen expression.

"Apparently he bothers you a great deal though. Why?"

Whitney smiled and she turned away. "Don't be ridiculous. I could care less about what that scoundrel does."

As he opened his mouth to continue his line of questioning, he caught Iris' warning glance suggesting he should not. What had Acton done, what more than he already knew, to provoke such spite in his cousin? They'd actually had very little to do with each other, though any recent meeting between the pair had always held an edge of hostility. The bachelor had never asked Whitney to dance but perhaps she felt slighted for being overlooked as a partner. He would have to find out what was going on but Hyde Park wasn't the place for such a discussion.

"Perhaps we could step out and take a stroll," Iris suggested softly.

He glanced at her face and noted her pallor. "An excellent idea. Exercise is just the thing to turn the mind from unpleasantness."

Martin waved the grooms aside and assisted the ladies down from the carriage. As they strolled along the paths together, Martin took the rear but was constantly forced to direct his gaze away from the sway of Iris' hips. He loved the feel of her curves beneath his hands, tiny though she was. However, he wasn't the man to pursue her and so he turned his mind back to the real problem—how to convince Iris to find a husband instead of seeking a protector.

Despite a few promising and enthusiastic conversations with several bachelors along the path, he could detect no overt sign of her interest in other men.

There was her earlier glowing praise of Acton, though. He at least had been friendly toward her.

Martin glanced away as distaste filled him. He was no matchmaker and had no right to choose a husband for Iris Hedley. He didn't know the first thing about what Iris looked for in a man but he could guide her in the direction of every decent bachelor he knew, and would. Acton, for all his past mistakes, wasn't an utter scoundrel when it came to women and rich enough, he suspected, to marry a woman without a penny to her name.

He let his attention move ahead, where it landed on a lady pushing a wicker perambulator along the path toward them. A tall older man walked slowly at her side and they appeared quite cozy together. His breath caught as he recognized the woman.

That was his daughter's housekeeper coming toward him.

His glance fell to the wheeled contraption she pushed. Dear God, was his daughter in Hyde Park, or did she have a child? He'd never thought to ask.

He glanced around discreetly, hoping to avoid a meeting but the nearest dissecting path was too far away. He'd prefer to avoid a meeting without drawing undue attention but it seemed he could not avoid the encounter.

When Mrs. Hughes finally saw him, her step faltered as she took in his party. He nodded to her politely and stepped aside so she could pass him by, and hoped she would go on her way without stopping. The man at her side, a stranger to him, smiled fondly down at the perambulator as the child gurgled. He caught a brief glimpse of his daughter and his apprehension grew.

"Wait," Iris cried out and bent to pick up a white cloth that lay upon the path unnoticed. "Is this yours, by chance?"

She hurried toward Mrs. Hughes, casting a glance at his child where she lie wrapped up snuggly and protected from taking a chill. As Iris stared down at his daughter, a soft smile teased her lips. "What a beautiful child."

"She's a lamb, truly," Mrs. Hughes claimed as proudly as any mother, with a nervous glance in his direction.

Mrs. Hughes tucked the scrap of cloth more firmly at the end of the wicker basket as Iris leaned close to stroke the child's cheek. "She is so very young."

"She is," the gentleman agreed. "She lost her poor mother at birth, I'm afraid."

"Oh, I'm so very sorry," Iris murmured. "Is there anything I can do?"

Mrs. Hughes' eyes bulged. "No. Nothing is required for the child. She has everything she needs and is well cared for now."

"That is such a relief." Iris folded her hands at her waist, and he sensed she was restraining herself. "Might I ask her name?"

At the question, the housekeeper paled. "I just call her 'my lamb'."

Iris looked at her curiously but accepted the response. When she opened her mouth to speak again, Martin called to her. "Miss Hedley?"

Iris quickly said her goodbyes, touched the babe's cheek and hurried toward him.

"Forgive me." A blush filled Iris' cheeks as she glanced up at him. "I adore children of that age."

"Quite all right," he assured her, tipping his hat to Mrs. Hughes. He certainly didn't mind her admiring his offspring but if Iris knew he was the father, would she feel differently? Would she condemn him as a careless cad and scorn the child for the irregular nature of her birth, as many in society would?

Whitney spotted a female acquaintance and hurried forward, leaving Iris alone with him.

Iris gripped his arm. "Do you think it strange that the woman did not share the child's first name or her connections?"

"Not terribly," he said carefully, alarmed by her continued interest in the child's identity. He was at a loss to decide what to call her and that confused him too. It shouldn't be so hard to name a baby.

"I've never met anyone who would not share a babe's first name when asked. I wonder whose child it is? Perhaps I ought not to have spoken to her but I couldn't help myself."

"Why do you say that?"

Iris worried her lip a moment. "She is so very young and normally would be kept at home, protected from the elements and disease until she is much older."

His heart flipped at the mention of risk to the child. "I'm sure the woman knows what she's doing."

"I do hope so." Iris did not seem convinced, judging by the growing frown on her face.

He leaned toward her ear and pitched his voice low, eager to change the topic of conversation. "Have you thought what you would do if you became pregnant to a protector?"

"I would keep the child," she said immediately. Her brow furrowed and she glanced over her shoulder toward Mrs.

Hughes' retreating back. "I've no idea if it's the done thing or not but that is my answer."

"You would allow your child to suffer an irregular birth?"

She licked her lips. "I should not like to see them suffer of course, but that is likely what will happen, isn't it?"

"Very true, and yet there are some gentlemen who would do the right thing." Martin would have married Vivian if he'd been given the choice. "What if your protector were to propose marriage just to give the child his name? Could you marry the man if you did not love him?"

"Many women do marry for a title rather than affection." A tiny smile twisted her lips. "I would have to consider the matter at that time, of course."

He stopped. "You would hesitate to live a respectable life?"

"Well, I cannot say with any certainty what I would do at this moment. I've not even begun to be a mistress." She smiled cheekily. "Perhaps he picks his toes at the dinner table and drinks custard with his pork chops."

What nonsense. "These are serious matters, Iris. You cannot make light of them. Mistresses get with child every day and it is the children who suffer for their father's mistakes."

She seemed taken aback by his fervor. "Why are you so concerned?"

Why indeed? He steadied his temper. "I don't want to see you hurt."

She glanced behind her toward the retreating form of Mrs. Hughes and the baby once more but they'd already left the park, her expression wistful and sad. "If I had a child, I would likely marry the father if he cared to ask but then I would not have any other choice in my life. I could never earn my own money, as a mistress can do."

"If you were to marry, you would not need to be a mistress who earned a living. Your husband would provide for you."

"I still cannot say what I would do until I am in the situation." She peered at him. "However, as you are not interested in being my protector, and certainly you've never shown an interest in offering marriage, then I think this conversation must end. I will decide what to do if and when the time comes."

"But—"

"Enough now." She squeezed her eyes shut then opened them. "You are drawing attention. I should like to go home to Lady Heathcote."

She hurried after Whitney and whispered in her ear. Whitney scowled at him, said her goodbyes and, ignoring him, marched Iris back toward his carriage.

The carriage ride to Lady Heathcote's abode was the most uncomfortable journey he'd ever experienced because Iris never glanced his way even once. He'd grown used to her smiles and easy welcome. As a large man he'd never felt invisible before and he had to say he didn't enjoy the sensation one bit.

Chapter Seven

Iris loved everything about Esme's home. From the soft cushions on every chair, fresh flowers filling every room, to the raucous laughter drifting from the private parlor where Esme entertained her closest friends. It was a far cry from the shabby decor of the Marshalsea she'd just returned from, and this was exactly the home she would create once she became a mistress. A place where she could be herself and damn anyone who disagreed.

She tossed a plump cushion back onto her bed with a heavy sigh and began to strip off the practical dull-brown gown she wore to the Marshalsea so as not to draw attention. Despite how well her mistress education had progressed so far, she was angry, and that was rare for her. The earl's habit of pointing out her ignorance of certain aspects of a mistress' life had embarrassed her. She hadn't even enjoyed her visit with her father very much today, being too aware the decision she made would end her respectability in his eyes. She had one choice left to be rid of Talbot's demands.

It annoyed her too that the earl was correct in one particular respect. She hadn't the faintest notion of what she might do if she became pregnant with her protector's child. Her father might very well never look at her again if that circumstance happened, but then again, he wouldn't speak to her if she was revealed as a thief's accomplice either and sent to New South Wales for the crime. She certainly hadn't expected her feelings to matter so much to Lord Louth but he appeared hell bent on making her change her mind by pointing out all the flaws in her decisions.

"Horrible man to see my greatest wish and use it against me," she grumbled. She did indeed love little children with all her heart and had always wished for a family of her own. Louth had certainly witnessed her interest in them in Hyde Park yesterday and homed in on her greatest regret. When she'd been a debutant, she'd hoped to have a pair of children by her current age. She had even gone so far as to choose her favorite names from among the flowers. Violet would be her eldest daughter's name if she had any say in naming them, but that wish would remain unfulfilled forever at this rate.

She laid the gown she'd worn to the Marshalsea over the back of a damask chair and glanced about her fine room. Another beautiful room in someone else's home, and more often than not extremely soothing, except today it felt like a prison. Talbot had no idea of the riches surrounding her daily and she planned to keep it that way to protect Esme for as long as possible. She rubbed her face, tired to her core of pretending everything was all right.

Iris changed into the elegant dove-gray muslin Esme had ordered laid out in readiness for an afternoon of callers. Esme was a popular widow and entertained lavishly in her home at all hours, and she'd insisted early on that Iris look the part despite her poverty. She'd also placed a string of amber beads beside the gown. Iris could not wear them. As she returned the string of amber gems to a drawer and out of sight, she caught her reflection in the looking glass. Was she really pretty enough to be a mistress men wanted? Was it possible to kiss a man and feel absolutely nothing for the rest of her life?

She laughed softly, knowing the answer immediately. It took one good kiss and she was putty in a man's hands. When Louth had kissed her, she had become swept away by the experience. However, he was determined not to be her protector. She had to stop thinking of him and imagine someone else kissing.

It wasn't easy when he was the only comforting male

presence in her life.

Once properly attired, she made her way to Esme's private parlor and tapped on the sturdy oak door, determined to forget Louth and move forward. At Esme's entreaty, she slipped into the room and surveyed the occupants with a warm smile. There were two other ladies in the room and two men, all of them whispering furiously.

"She's the devil in human form," Lady Matilda James promised with a delighted smile that belied her harsh words. She glanced around at her companions and nodded sagely, setting her feathered headpiece to bobbing. The woman also glittered with fortune in rare gems and Iris averted her eyes from them. "That's one young lady headed for ruin, mark my words."

Despite her discomfort, Iris smiled. One of the more frivolous pastimes of Esme's friends was predicting which new face on the marriage mart would soon risk making a fool of themselves over some handsome scoundrel. No doubt they'd speculated on her character once too but she knew from experience their hearts would always be on the ladies side in any situation. "Lady Ames, Lady James. How lovely to see you both again."

"Darling," Lady James gushed, and patted the space nearby. "We were just beginning to fret when you might return."

Only Esme and Lady Ames knew where she'd gone and the time it took to visit Southwark and return. Lady Ames had made no bones about her disapproval that Iris visited her father in the Marshalsea and put her reputation at risk. Although engaged in a tumultuous affair herself with Lord Avery Hill, Iris feared that when the woman learned Iris intended to become a mistress, Lady Ames might fall entirely to pieces.

She turned to Esme. "Madam du Clair will have everything you ordered ready and delivered by Friday morning."

"Thank you, my dear." Esme smiled warmly and poured a cup of tea, added milk and passed it to her. "You are almost too late."

"For what?" Iris glanced at the gentlemen gathered on the chaise lounge. One of them was very familiar and she was certain she'd seen him recently. If memory served, this was the tall naval gentleman who'd looked right through her as if she hadn't been standing in the Hazelton ballroom. Today he was dressed for riding, a fine-looking gentleman with pale-blue eyes and a scar just visible above his brow. "If someone would care to introduce me."

Esme smiled. "Yes, of course. I forget you might not know Lord Somerset, who has recently returned to Town, and this of course is Captain Hastings. Gentlemen, might I present my very great friend Miss Iris Hedley?"

She curtsied to them. "A pleasure gentlemen."

Somerset was a widow with a somewhat scandalous past but Captain Hastings had distinguished himself in battle, though was very much an unknown face in London society.

Hasting's nodded but his eyes strayed back to Esme immediately. "I am afraid I must be going. I'm expected at the admiralty this evening."

Esme smiled widely. "Do give our love to Lord Admiral Ford. He is such a sweet and dear rogue."

"Sweet and dear are the last two descriptions I'd give to my superior," Hasting's said somewhat bitterly. "If the opportunity presents itself I shall certainly pass along the message."

He excused himself, leaving Lord Somerset the only man in the room.

"Well, how fortunate this is. Four lovely ladies all to myself." He rubbed his hands together. "What shall we drink to?"

Iris glanced about. No one was actually drinking the sort of thing one toasted with so she assumed his question was rhetorical.

"Let's drink to passion," Lady Ames declared.

"And all the delights to be found in renewed acquaintances," Lady James insisted with a flutter of her lashes at Lord Somerset.

"To happiness," Lady Heathcote countered. "Passion is all well and good but a contented life makes the every day worth living through."

"Happiness is an excellent idea. Might I see what your delightful butler can scare up for a repast, Lady Heathcote?" At Esme's nod, he stood and rushed for the door. "I will be back momentarily."

Iris glanced at Esme quickly and saw her hide a smile. Since

Esme usually did not allow even her lovers to give her servants orders, she quickly concluded Lord Somerset's spur-of-the-moment toast was prearranged.

Lady James smiled warmly after Somerset's retreating figure and when he was truly gone, she sighed and flopped back against the pillows. "I know you will think me foolish but I don't think I could bear to be parted from him again."

"I'm sure he feels the same way," Esme assured her. "He followed you here after all, although he was not specifically invited to my home today. He proved very insistent on seeing you, I'm told."

"My dear, you are the most ridiculous romantic in society," Lady Ames scolded Esme. "You've grown so in love with love that I barely recognize you as the carefree woman of years past."

Lady Heathcote glanced toward Iris. "Pay no attention to my dearest friend. She's in an irritable mood today and refuses to be jollied out of it."

Lady Ames jumped to her feet. "As you would be too."

"But the difference is I would never expect Avery Hill to change his ways," Esme sighed. "Please smile today."

Lady Ames' expression soured even more as she strode to a window. Lady James joined her there and put a comforting arm around her shoulders. Clearly something was amiss but Iris didn't dare ask for particulars. If she needed to know they would include her in their confidences.

"Did you place an order for that new gown I suggested?" Esme asked of Iris, drawing her attention away from Lady Ames.

"I did not."

Lady James returned to the chaise and regarded her seriously. "You will be noticed for all the wrong reasons if you wear last season's rags over and over."

"Some of my gowns are favorites," she murmured. Some of them were not, too, but she did not want to spend any more of Esme's funds on her wardrobe if she could help it. "What I have must be enough. People either like me as I am or pay to improve me themselves."

Iris relaxed as Lord Somerset returned, the butler hard on his heels carrying a heavy tray of refreshments and sweetmeats.

Judging by the quantity, this would become one of Esme's more rowdy gatherings.

Somerset glanced about. "Did I hear a suggestion that someone is in need of improvement?"

All eyes turned her way. Iris had a moment of indecision then met Lord Somerset's gaze. "They suggest I do."

Somerset handed round full glasses of champagne to the others. "Nonsense. You'll make some young buck a perfect wife." He admired his champagne a moment then drew near Lady James. He sat at her side. "As *this* lady shall surely do if I have my heart's desire."

He set his champagne aside and caught up Lady James' bejeweled hand in his. "My dearest love, I can contain myself no longer. Would you do me the honor of becoming my wife?"

Iris gasped but noticed neither Esme nor Lady Ames appeared surprised by his request.

Lady James froze and then threw herself into Somerset's waiting arms with an incoherent shriek. Esme quickly rescued Lady James' champagne glass while the couple kissed passionately. Somerset even pulled the woman into his lap so he could properly embrace her. They broke apart after a little while, laughing. "So that was a yes to marrying me?"

Lady James wrapped her arms around Somerset's shoulders and buried her face in his neckcloth. "I feared your mourning for Abigail would never end," she whispered.

Abigail had been Lord Somerset's first wife, and well-liked by everyone. "She was a good woman and we had many contented years together," Somerset told her. "The children were inconsolable."

"She was their mother."

Lady James' understanding was misplaced in Iris' opinion. The children Somerset spoke of were married women with families of their own. Grown women who should not have forced a two-year mourning onto their father.

The couple kissed again and after a while it was clear that the pair had forgotten they were not alone. Iris glanced longingly for the door and a reason to slip away.

Esme and Lady Ames cleared their throats loudly.

Somerset drew back and glanced around with an apologetic

smirk. "Forgive us. But I find it impossible to contain my happiness that this remarkable woman had the patience to wait for me."

"Quite understandable," Esme said warmly. "We are so happy for you both."

Iris grinned and lifted her glass. "A toast. To love and passion and happiness. Might you have all three with each other forevermore."

"Well said, Miss Hedley. Well said." Somerset wiped a tear from his future bride's cheek. "Lady James has indeed made me the happiest man in London."

"Where will you make your home?" Esme asked, and conversation soon turned to the practicalities of combining the substantial contents of two avid collectors under one roof. It seemed a certainty that the decisions would not be made swiftly, although Somerset was anxious to protect Lady James from the society thief as soon as possible.

Through it all, Lady Ames was silent. She met Iris' stare with a raised eyebrow.

Iris gained her feet and approached the lady. "Is everything all right?"

Lady Ames smiled wryly. "As you get older, hope can seem like a thing of the past."

She glanced at the happy couple, holding hands with eyes only for each other. "It is clear he loves her."

"Love is all well and good." She sipped her champagne and grimaced. "It is the rest of the relationship that matters so very much more."

"I don't understand."

Lady Ames cupped her cheek. "And I hope you never shall. Women like me, and Esme to some extent, go on with our lives never daring to believe that such happiness belongs to all. The lucky few like Lady James gain their heart's desire to marry for love and we are happy for them. But I don't believe I shall ever be as lucky to fall in love a second time."

Lady Ames' husband had died long ago, but Iris did not believe Lady Ames referred to him. By all accounts, the marriage had not been a happy one. "Of course you will!"

A fleeting smile crossed the countess' lips. "The first man I ever made love to broke my heart. Take my advice and never fall into love, Miss Hedley, if you can possibly avoid it."

The pleasant mask Lady Ames wore slipped away, revealing a woman ravaged by grief. The expression was fleeting, but so clear Iris caught her breath.

"Love is a painful and messy business with no end but heartbreak in sight," Lady Ames continued before she moved away, back to congratulate the soon-to-be-married couple and lend her opinion on the necessity of haste in the matter of moving.

Iris was left reeling. She had always admired Lady Ames and had never suspected her heartbroken. If a woman such as Lady Ames had failed to find love a second time, what hope did Iris have of achieving such a feat when the odds were stacked against her?

Chapter Eight

Martin eased the door open a crack and shook his head firmly. Inside the small parlor, Mrs. Hughes heaved a sigh and smiled at the woman sitting with her back to the door. The other woman, Mrs. Battle, continued to babble about her past experience without pause and never even noticed the tide had turned against her. He would not hire that woman to look after his daughter. No one should ever talk so much in one sitting.

Eventually, Mrs. Hughes got rid of Mrs. Battle and poured herself a cup of tea. "If you refuse every woman the employment agency sends, you'll be looking after the girl yourself soon," she warned him.

Martin emerged from the adjoining room. "I do not want to have my ears assaulted endlessly like that on my every visit. They are still ringing."

"Just remember you are not marrying the next housekeeper. She doesn't have to be exactly what you prefer in a woman." Mrs. Hughes smiled wryly. "But as for that woman in particular, I really can't blame you for saying no this time. If you had not refused her yourself, I certainly would not have pushed you to employ her."

From the next room, the babe began to cry and he rushed toward the sound eagerly. The little girl was about ready to explode judging by the look on her face, so he quickly scooped her up and rested her head against his shoulder.

He rocked her back and forward and patted her bottom as Mrs. Hughes had shown him and received a quiet belch as his reward. He smiled down at the girl's face. "Is that better?"

"It doesn't hurt her to cry, my lord. You will spoil her and ruin her temperament if you do not make her wait even a little bit for your attention," Mrs. Hughes chided him as she entered the room and took his daughter from him. She attended to the girl's needs and dressed her in fresh garments then handed her back into his waiting arms. "You should name her."

"I know." But he was still beset by indecision. He had three names in mind but couldn't choose between them. Regina, Penelope, or Audrey. "I will."

Mrs. Hughes gathered the soiled clothing and smiled up at him. "The wet nurse should be arriving very soon to appease her hunger."

Mrs. Hughes left to go about her duties while Martin carried his daughter back to the drawing room wedged in his arms, as had become his habit over the past week. He'd managed to spend a few hours here each day, mostly watching the child sleep or talking nonsense to her about what her future might entail. Even that he couldn't decide on.

He'd grown accustomed to seeing her every day and the thought of living even farther apart did not sit well with him anymore. He settled in his favorite chair and rested the girl on his knee. She was healthy and inquisitive, alert to new sounds and voices more so than he ever imagined a child could be. He'd grown profoundly protective of her too and carefully watched how the servants treated her when they didn't think he was looking or listening in. The wet nurse was a kind woman; breasts always full of milk for the child. But she had a coarse manner about her speech at times that he did not particularly care for. Once the feeding was done, he was quick to send her on her way, home to her own family and concerns with enough coin in her fist to ensure her return.

Mrs. Hughes treated the child best and that pained him. He had met her future husband earlier that morning and it was clear the man loved Mrs. Hughes dearly. They would be married soon and then the girl would have no one to love her but him. He feared he wasn't enough for the babe.

He would give anything for Vivian Rose to have lived to mother the girl instead.

He touched the girl's cheek softly, and then regretted it as she sought a breast to suckle. "Soon, my little one. Not long now I expect."

She grizzled a little and he rocked his legs too and fro. "When you've grown a bit, how about your papa buys you a fine pony to ride? A small white mare with a long tail and mane to swish about. How would that be?"

The child could ride all over Holly Park quite easily, but especially through the west field, which had been kept as a beginner's riding track since before his grandfather's time. He could tether the mare and follow them about, ensuring she was never afraid and could never stray too far to become lost in the nearby woods. It was a nice dream to imagine taking her home with him.

"I wouldn't mind a pony myself to carry me around," Mrs. Blake remarked suddenly. "But I'll settle for some ease."

He studied the wet nurses face and noted today's expression was as unhappy as yesterday's. "Is anything the matter?"

"No, my lord." She held out her hands. "Might I take her?"

Concerned that she didn't answer his question, he passed over the babe. When she crossed the hall and entered another room he followed her at a distance. He'd learned little about the woman's life before she'd come into his employ and he was intensely curious about her.

Mrs. Hughes joined him. "There will be no further interviews for the housekeeper's position today, my lord."

"Oh," he frowned. "I thought your note mentioned three candidates were coming?"

"Yes, but one found another position this morning so there is no one else expected in her place. Mrs. Godwin was very apologetic and promised to send another candidate tomorrow."

Martin sighed, uncertain what to do. He desperately needed someone to look after the child and he was running out of time and options. "Damn this waiting."

Mrs. Hughes smiled apologetically. "It is usually not such a chore to find good help."

Soft singing reached them. Mrs. Blake was humming softly to his daughter as she often did but the tone was sad. "Is there anything more I need to know about her, Mrs. Hughes?"

She nodded and drew Martin away. "It's her husband. He's sent their children away to his sister's without warning her of their going. She's fair upset with him over it."

"I see."

"Do you?" Mrs. Hughes grimaced. "Reading between the lines, I assume he's got a bit of fancy on the side and he's showering her with trinkets paid for by his wife. I'd be furious but she's resigned to it."

"For God's sake, why would any woman put up with that nonsense?"

"She's got nowhere else to go." Mrs. Hughes slipped into the room with his daughter and wet nurse, where the woman had begun to sing in earnest about lost love and broken hearts. Martin was torn over staying but he'd never dared watch the woman at work. Her situation sat ill with him but it wasn't his place to interfere. He had enough problems of his own to deal with—namely, preventing Iris Hedley's ruin.

After yesterday's disagreement on the subject of her future, he was even more certain she was making a colossal mistake. Every instinct he possessed told him she needed his protection, not as a lover but as a friend. If she would agree to see him again.

He was at her door in no time and requesting an audience with her.

Laughter drifted down from a room above his head—male laugher. His anxiety soared that she might be entertaining other men in the pursuit of her plan to become a mistress already.

A door opened and closed and the tap of footsteps drew near. Iris appeared at the landing and she slowly descended to the front hall with a scowl on her face.

Despite the cold welcome, his heart skipped a beat at how fresh and lovely she was to behold. He bowed to her. "Miss Hedley."

The woman kept her distance. "Lord Louth, what an unexpected surprise."

She shouldn't be surprised. She'd neatly wrapped him up in

her concerns until he couldn't bear to imagine her in someone else's arms. "Might we speak somewhere other than the hall?"

Her expression grew wary. "I cannot imagine you have anything left to say to me. I believe you've been most thorough in expressing your opinions."

Another burst of male laugher sounded from upstairs and she glanced up, a smile forming over her lips.

Were those her guests, too? Men come to make her their mistress? He would not let her throw her life away on some pretty face with deep pockets. He gritted his teeth and glanced into a nearby doorway, noticing a dining room beyond. "There is a great deal more to say to each other. Please."

She lifted a brow at his demanding tone but she slipped into the room ahead of him. "Just for a moment. Have you come to apologize?"

"No." He closed and locked the doors behind him and leaned against them. He kept the key hidden in his palm. "I've come to deliver your next lesson."

"That is not necessary, my lord." She shook her head. "I think I've learned everything I can from you."

"Is that so?" He moved from the door, passing Iris with a smile and testing the table for strength. Undoubtedly sufficient for today's lesson. He slipped the key into his waistcoat pocket. "You asked me once how often a protector might want to share your bed, and I should admit I gave you a halfway correct answer."

She folded her arms over her chest, pushing her breasts up. "A small detail."

He let his gaze linger there on her breasts long enough to see her fidget. "When a man considers taking a mistress, he is most times only interested in satisfying his own pleasure. And he will take it as often as he can, several times a day even, until he grows bored."

She appeared startled by the increase in number, as he'd hoped, but quickly squared her shoulders. "I shall ensure I have a sturdy bed."

He moved toward her, looked down into her stubborn face and smiled. "There's no need to wait for a bed when any situation will do."

Before she could react, he caught her under the arms and deposited her on top of the mahogany dining table. He crowded her so she was made uncomfortable by his proximity. "Are you prepared to be set upon and taken at a moment's notice because the blighter paid handsomely for your body?"

Her eyes widened, her breath came fast.

He stroked his fingers down her cheek, along her throat and down to her breast. He cupped it firmly and thumbed the nipple. "Because I tell you that being alone with you for as long as possible is most definitely at the foremost of my mind at this moment."

Her mouth opened. "But it is only eleven o'clock!"

She truly had no idea of what she was headed for, but he did. "Any time of day is the perfect time for a dalliance."

The idea of her laid out on the table was too much temptation to resist. But unlike the blighters he'd been trying to warn her away from, Martin was determined to show her what would be missing in those cold couplings. He kissed her hungrily and rejoiced when her arms twined about his neck. However, today's lesson wasn't about kisses. He'd planned something entirely more shocking. He broke the kiss and was pleased at her whimper of complaint.

He snagged a chair, sat upon it and widened her legs so he was seated between them. "It is never certain that a protector would consider your needs first before taking his own, but it's all I can think about."

A strange smile flickered over her lips. "So you *do* desire me?"

Did the woman not understand passion at all? Desire such as this could not be pretended. "Unbearably."

Her smile was radiant as she leaned down to kiss him again. She cupped his face and traced the seam of his lips with her tongue before drawing back. "Show me."

He set one hand behind her bottom and dragged her to the edge of the tabletop before reaching for her ankles. He drew both feet up to rest on his spread thighs. Iris gripped the table edge, her eyes wide, her lip caught provocatively between her teeth. He removed one shoe and then placed her foot close to his hip so her knee remained bent. "Leave it there."

He caught her other foot and repeated the procedure, but

then lifted it to his mouth and placed tender kisses on her ankle as he stripped away her stocking and revealed bare skin.

A soft moan left her lips. "Might I ask questions?"

"Of course."

"Why kiss me there?"

"Why not? I would like to kiss you all over." He kissed her shin, inching her gown and petticoat up as he went. When the fabric slid to her hips, revealing her bare sex, his cock ached. He kissed the inside of her knee and met her gaze. He placed his fingers lightly on her inner thighs and brushed them along her trembling leg. "Your neck, your back, your breasts, your bottom. I should like very much to push my tongue into your sex so I can taste you."

Her eyes widened and he brushed across her sex lightly with his thumbs. Iris said nothing to his declaration but her knuckles showed white on the edge of the table. He teased her curls again, and then pinched both lips lightly.

"Yes," she moaned as her eyes fluttered closed.

He smiled at her provocative reaction. She might be innocent but the woman certainly wasn't in the least prudish. He hoped what he offered would be enough. "Then lie back and I will give you the best lesson of all. I will show you how pleasurable making love should be."

Iris crumpled to the hardwood table, obedient and pliant and his.

He glanced down at her sex and stroked her lips again, hearing a soft whimper leave her throat. Very carefully he parted her folds, and blew softly over the sensitive area. Her hips lifted from the tabletop toward his mouth.

He rested one arm over her hips, holding her down with light pressure while he traced her entrance gently, breathing in the scent of her arousal as his fingers teased her passions higher. As he dipped near her entrance, he found greater moisture. Iris, for her part, couldn't seem to stop moving. He gripped her hips firmly and leaned in to kiss her sex.

Iris bucked and gasped as Martin flicked his tongue along her opening. Her hands landed on his arm where it draped across her stomach. Her fingers dug in as he found her clit and lightly sucked on the sensitive nubbin.

She twisted, arching on the table so provocatively he was dislodged. He stifled a laugh and kissed her thigh and returned to kiss her sex hungrily as soon as she settled. Iris gasped and bucked but he was prepared for her response now.

All of a sudden, her body convulsed beneath his mouth and she sobbed out loud.

Martin turned Iris onto her side, bringing her knees together while she calmed down. Her breath was rough and fast and he stroked her back soothingly. Her white bottom, however, faced him and he couldn't resist kissing her soft flesh just once.

He scooped her off the table and onto his lap and straightened her skirts. When he was satisfied he'd set her to rights, he ran his hand up her torso and cupped her breast. The soft orb filled his hand perfectly.

He kissed her brow and cuddled her against him. "That is how you should always feel after a lover's touch. Sated, boneless, exhausted from too much pleasure."

"I must be wicked, too, because I must insist you do that to me again." She sighed. "I had no idea."

He stiffened. "I should not."

"Why do you say that? You said it yourself that you want me."

"You don't understand. There are very good reasons we would not suit."

She was silent for a long time, but her fingers played with his cravat. "I cannot accept that decision until you explain yourself. Do you already have a mistress?"

He kissed her brow and relaxed his grip. "No, not for a long time."

She eased away from him but did not leave her perch on his knees. She glanced down at where her fingers toyed with his cravat. "Are you engaged to be married? Esme suggested I avoid taking a lover when they have formed an attachment elsewhere. I think that is a very sensible idea. No one's feelings should be hurt if you chose me."

He smiled at her persistence. Clearly she liked the way he made her feel and he couldn't deny making love even in a limited fashion satisfied his senses. He traced her bottom lip with his thumb. "I have no attachments."

She lifted her brow. "Then what? Am I not pretty enough for your taste?"

"You are beautiful, but…"

Her brow furrowed. Clearly she had no inkling of what the problem was.

"You are so tiny," he said in the end. He compared the size of their hands. His dwarfed hers. "Too small for a brute like me."

She linked their fingers together. "I'd hardly describe you in that fashion. In my first season I suffered bruised toes many a night. Never once were you responsible for my discomfort."

Martin teased the skin of her neck, unable to stop touching her even though he must. "And if I got a babe on you? What then?"

She blinked at that. "Then we would have a child."

"No. Any child of mine would likely kill you." He tossed her off his lap and stood, trembling with panic at the idea of her in peril. "I won't allow any harm to come to you if I can prevent it."

There was silence at his back for a long time. "So the only reason you *do* resist is out of concern for my health."

"Of course it is." He threw his arms wide and turned. "Look at me."

"I am. I have been." She strolled closer and laid her hands upon his abdomen. "I've come to realize I like large men. You, specifically."

Her appreciation sent a rush of blood to his cock and he caught her wrist. "Everything about me is large. Too large."

He laid her palm over his aching length.

Her eyes widened impossibly and then she looked down. "Oh my."

He waited for her stammered retreat and leave to go. Instead, her fingers curved around his length, still contained by his trousers, and she squeezed. "I see." Her voice came out unsteadily and then she stroked down his length with the edge of her thumb and back up.

A virgin should be quite rightly terrified of his condition. As a young man he'd been compared to a bull and it was true. Iris, however, continued to explore his proportion through the barrier of his clothes without revealing too much shock or concern. His cock grew heavier with every move of her hand until he was panting, hard, and desperate to ease the pain of his confinement. "Stop. Please."

Her gaze darted to his then she pressed her head to his chest. "Touching you makes me ache again."

Her admission of renewed arousal stunned him. There were not many women who expressed their desire so honestly. He stood immobile for a moment then swept her back up into his arms and carried her to the chair. This time he held her in his arms and worked to bring her pleasure. He kissed her and teased her and slid the tip of one finger inside her entrance. Heaven and hell. Iris was tight but wet from arousal. Her lips parted as her inner walls clenched his digit and she lifted her face to be kissed.

As had happened before, Martin lost himself in the kiss, his finger lightly teasing her until she climaxed, sobbing against his lips without any hint of embarrassment or feigned interest.

For himself, he was fit to explode at a moment's notice from the slightest provocation. He kissed her brow and tugged her skirts over her knees a few long minutes until he'd regained control and accepted he had but one choice.

He would not make her his mistress, he couldn't disrespect her that way, but he would give her more than anyone else wanted to. He would marry her. "I'll have the contracts drawn up immediately."

Chapter Nine

———◆———

When Iris entered Lord Windermere's home at Esme's side, she wondered if she really could avoid carrying out Talbot's wishes to aid him tonight. She was a mistress, or would be if Lord Louth's contract had been delivered as promised. She had not seen him for several days but he had sent flowers each morning and had promised to meet her here later tonight.

"You will break your neck looking for him," Esme teased. Although her friend was not happy about Louth's disappearance, she was not surprised by their arrangement. Esme had not even chided her for spending time alone with him in the dining room, though she hoped her friend had no idea of what they'd done there together on the mahogany table.

She fluttered her fan to stir the air as her cheeks heated. "He said he would attend but I don't see him anywhere."

Esme huffed. "Well, I'm sure he will come as soon as he can. Let us find Lady Ames and then secure a glass of punch for us both."

Iris glanced at Esme swiftly. "Punch?"

"Oh, do be quiet. I'm not feeling in the best spirits tonight. These robberies are hell on my nerves and I worry for Meriwether."

Concerned too, Iris linked their arms. She couldn't wait to be Louth's mistress and have an end to this dangerous game. She had so many questions to ask of him later. Where would she live, how soon could she leave London for a safer life far away from Talbot? "Lady Ames is standing to the left of the hearth with our host and Lady Bartlett."

A grimace passed over Esme's face at the mention of Lady Bartlett and she scanned the room. "Perhaps we should have champagne to soften the impact of that woman's gloating," Esme murmured, changing her mind about refreshments.

Iris glanced ahead. Lady Bartlett was standing at Lord Windermere's side. "Has he proposed?"

"I do hope not."

She glanced at them again but saw nothing unusual. "I thought you liked her."

"I did, but that was before I discovered my sense of fair play extends in unexpected directions." Esme snagged a glass of champagne from a waiter and sipped slowly. She glanced at the glass in her hand, her frown returning. "One can always expect the best from Windermere. 'Tis a shame such sentiments are not returned."

"Esme, I truly don't understand, and if you keep throwing out hints without answers I'll become cross with you." Iris stared hard at her friend. "Do you know something scandalous about our host?"

Esme passed her glass back to a servant and then cupped Iris' cheek. "I am concerned by some sensitive information that fell into my lap earlier today. However, this is not the place to discuss what should not be overheard. Do forgive me."

Curious about what Esme's information might be and what she would not say, Iris trailed along and closely observed Lady Bartlett as they met. It was not like Esme to become so stirred up by gossip that did not concern her. It must be truly awful. Lady Bartlett beamed at Esme and spoke warmly to everyone, though Esme and Lady Ames were both reserved in their responses. Windermere said little but his eyes lingered on Lady Bartlett often while she spoke, so perhaps Esme was worried for no reason.

Lady Ames turned to Esme. "I was just about to tell Lady Bartlett of a scandal in the making. A most dangerous and foolhardy scheme indeed. As you all know, the society thief is leaving a trail of terror in his wake but I heard of another scheme to replace the marble statue in the square with a replica of painted pine."

Iris frowned. "Why would anyone do that?"

"Why, for the money of course," Esme murmured. "There is a lot of money to be made in forgeries, as there is in gems."

Windermere cut in, "To those who choose to only look upon the surface, they might not have detected the scheme. However, it would take a lot to fool those with taste. One would only have to set their hand to the surface to know what was underneath."

"I do think you're wise," Esme agreed with a warm smile for Windermere. "A man should be sure to know what he's getting in any bargain."

Windermere appeared startled by Esme's agreement, but then his attention diverted to a spot beyond Lady Ames. "Do excuse me, I am needed elsewhere."

He kissed Lady Bartlett's hand and hurried off. The viscountess watched after him with a small smile tugging her lips. When Iris glanced at Lady Ames and Esme, however, they were not smiling. In fact, they both appeared furious.

Iris touched Lady Ames' arm, keen to find out more. "How did the scheme come to be exposed?"

"An excellent question, my dear," she said. "It seems when you do scratch beneath the surface, lift the barriers as it were, the lack of quality is clearly evident. All it took was only the barest investigation for the plan to come undone."

"What happened to the statue?"

Esme smiled sadly. "I've suggested it be sent to Windermere."

"What would he want with an imitation?" Lady Bartlett asked, frowning.

"My thoughts exactly." Esme scowled. "Perhaps he will find the situation pertinent, considering the scheme you're currently attempting on him. You do know he would expect you to deliver."

Lady Bartlett froze like a wounded doe in a hunter's sights. "Oh, do excuse me, I see Lady Hazelton has come and I must ask after her health."

The viscountess rushed off as Lady Ames beamed. "I think

that went quite well. She knows we are onto her."

"Onto what?"

"A false statue is as easy to uncover as a false pregnancy."

"Oh," Iris whispered, finally catching on. "Oh!"

"I wish he was as clever as you." Esme frowned. "I fear he must be told outright before he gets swept up in it all."

"Foolish man." Lady Ames sighed heavily and caught Iris' arm. "I've never met a Hill who knew what was good for him."

Iris allowed Lady Ames to move her away from Esme and withheld her questions for later. Lady Ames led her to a group of young women closer to her own age. "Ladies," she began. "Are you acquainted with my dear friend, Miss Hedley?"

Several nodded and introductions procured with the rest. A few looked upon her with a slight frown but she ignored their hesitant welcome. Very soon the chatter turned to the robberies. "I simply cannot believe I've attended every ball where a robbery has occurred," Miss Beasley said with widened eyes. She pressed her gloved hand over the necklace she wore. "It's almost certain I must have passed the thief."

"As has everyone else," Lady Ames reminded them all with a smile. "Try not to worry. The culprits are only after gems kept under lock and key, not gems openly worn."

"But how do they find out where the gems are kept, is what I want to know?" Miss Beasley exclaimed loudly. "They must walk among us."

"Or employ spies," Alice Quartermane, a shy young woman, added quietly. Her gaze landed on Iris. "What do you think, Miss Hedley?"

Although afraid of giving herself away, Iris nodded. "That is a possibility."

All eyes turned to stare at the other guests. "We shall have to watch everyone," Miss Beasley decided, her eyes narrowing on a passing gentleman. "Tomorrow, we shall gather at my home and compare notes. You will come too of course, Miss Hedley."

Iris couldn't attend no matter how much she wished to. She couldn't sit among these young women while they suspected others of her own misdeeds. Besides, mistresses were not good *ton*. No matter how kindly invited, she would do them all a disservice by socializing with them. But how to get out of it gracefully?

"Oh my, he's here," Miss Beasley stammered and hid herself behind Miss Quartermane.

Iris turned in time to see Lord Louth striding toward her party. Instant warmth flooded her face as he smiled and took her hand to squeeze it. "Forgive me for being late. Is this our dance?"

Her card was so bare she'd put it away long ago. A low murmur began at her back and she hated the sound of speculation. "Indeed, my lord."

"Do excuse us, ladies." Louth placed her hand on his arm and led her to the edge of the dance floor. "You look beautiful tonight. Good enough to eat, actually."

She glanced up at him as her body trembled. "Am I expected to say thank you to that or should I suggest we skip the dancing for a more private location?"

"Privacy can come later. I want to dance with you first."

His arms slipped around her as the strains of a slow waltz began. Iris bit her lip as she reacted strongly to his presence. He had been intimately acquainted with her body, his mouth and hands teasing her to ecstasy, and she craved his attention even worse than she'd ever imagined possible. However, she was being watched. Miss Beasley stared at her and Lord Louth, mouth agape. In the other direction, Mr. Talbot was regarding them with barely concealed hostility.

She forced her feet to follow Lord Louth's lead, but stumbled as her mind drifted to what would happen when her part in the robberies was discovered. Humiliation was too mild a word for what Lord Louth would say about her. She was very glad when the dance ended and they rejoined her friends and the safety of conversation.

———— ◆ ————

From his slightly higher vantage point in the Windermere ballroom, Martin reached the conclusion that Iris was not at ease with him anymore. It was several days since he'd last seen her and he'd hoped she might have missed him while they'd been apart. However, her right foot beat a constant cadence beneath her gown and she'd barely made eye contact with him since their dance. It was as if she couldn't wait for him to leave her side.

Lady Heathcote, too, stared across the room with a constant frown and that worried him. The countess had initially been very happy to arrange to meet at tonight's ball but her attention was clearly elsewhere. His intentions were honorable. As soon as he ran Alexander Hedley to ground, asked permission to marry his daughter, he was planning the largest celebration London had seen in many years.

He glanced at Iris, only to find her gaze darting away again.

Had he shocked her the other day when he'd pleasured her on the dining table of her chaperone's home, and again on his lap? Had she changed her mind about him? Martin had no idea what had possessed him to get so carried away by lust that he'd almost taken her on top of Lady Heathcote's dining table, but he hadn't regretted it until now. It was clear she found no joy in his attention or presence anymore.

Whitney joined him, having finished a set with young Mr. Easton. For the first time ever, she'd raised little fuss about attending Lord Windermere's ball. She waved a fan before her face. "Such a lively party, cousin."

Martin signaled a footman carrying a tray of punch and procured enough for her and everyone else. "I'm glad to see you're having fun at last," he told her.

"I enjoyed seeing you with a pretty woman on your arm and causing her to blush." Whitney sighed. "I do approve."

"Of what?"

"The imminent addition to the family." She tapped his arm sagely. "I know what you're up to."

He caught Whitney's gaze. She expected him to marry Iris and set up his nursery but there were other ways to avoid conception and he planned to use them all with Iris. "Don't set the cart before the horse."

"Of course not." She winked. "I like her too much to ruin your chances."

"Well that's a relief." And it was. Whitney frequently detested women so easily for a lack of intelligence and self-possession.

But he might have ruined his own chances. Acting on his baser instincts without proper thought to the likely awkwardness later had never occurred to him, but then again, he'd only ever dabbled with experienced women before. He should have waited until he had her father's permission and the banns had been read at least, before continuing with lessons. It had seemed in his best interests to prove his intent that day.

He glanced away from his cousin. Iris met his gaze at last as she sipped her punch, but her expression was troubled. He craved the sweet sound of her passion and her easy smiles. It was also very hard to forget that look in her eyes as her desire peaked, and had hoped to see her come apart again and again in his arms. He excused himself from Whitney and moved around the group to her side. "Are you not enjoying the evening?"

"A slight headache. Nothing to worry about."

"Would you care to sit? We could find somewhere quiet to rest awhile."

She looked up at him. "I would like that very much, but then tongues would really wag if we linger too long in each other's company."

"True, unfortunately." He'd like nothing better than to get her alone, but having her draped across his knee at a ball wasn't likely to preserve her reputation.

Iris sighed. "They will talk anyway about you singling me out, given my situation. You should ask Miss Quartermane or Miss Beasley to dance so the gossips have nothing to consider."

Martin shook his head as irritation gripped him. Propriety be damned. After making a few discreet inquiries, he'd learned a little more of Iris' life. Her so-called closest friends had dropped her acquaintance as fast as they possibly could after her father's indebtedness had been revealed. Once her engagement to Lord Grindlewood had ended too, she had been rudely snubbed. It was no wonder she'd believed herself a poor candidate for marriage. He wasn't leaving her side tonight to dance with someone who didn't interest him in the slightest. "I only dance with you from now on."

Desire to kiss her into a happier frame of mind grew and he eased closer to her side until her arm touched his. It was a comfort to stand beside a woman and know that tomorrow, or the next day, or the next, she might always be there.

Across the room, an older woman with silver hair waved her fingers in his direction. Martin didn't recognize her and looked to Iris for information.

"Lady Catherine Berry," Iris supplied. "She's great fun and not at all high in the instep."

"Ah," Martin said, nodding to Lady Berry. "She has a daughter, if I recall."

"Angela. She was a good friend of mine once."

"Was?"

"Not everything can remain as we would hope it will. Only her mother acknowledges me now." Iris fluttered her fan before her face. "Those pesky consequences I spoke of to Whitney have a way of ending friendships."

Martin glanced across the room again, frowning. When he married Iris, he would ensure a great many wrongs done to her would be corrected.

As they stood together, Iris kept up her stream of information. She seemed to know everyone he did not and that pleased him. Their marriage would gain them much if only he could hide the existence of his daughter. He was worried about how she might take the news and he still had no idea what should be done with the child. He'd always believed total honesty had its places but perhaps not before they wed. He acquired two glasses of champagne from a passing waiter for Iris and himself.

Iris refused hers. "It is not wise for you to single me out."

"Possibly so but I hate to deny you the pleasure. Do take it."

She accepted but it was grudgingly done. "Are you going to be a bossy protector too?"

"What?" He stared at her in shock. Surely she realized he'd offered her marriage rather than the disrespect of a scandalous liaison?

"There you are at last," a woman exclaimed from his left, and Martin turned quickly to see who had interrupted.

"Mrs. Ward?" It was a relief to see Helena Ward and not someone else. He took her offered hand in his and squeezed her fingers. "What an astonishing surprise to see you returned to

London."

"It's been far too long since I've laid eyes on you too." She drew close and licked her lips in a way that had once tortured him when they'd been lovers years ago. Now, however, only a pleasant memory stirred. "I arrived in Town only last week. The house has been at sixes and sevens. But I would always open my doors for you."

Her eyes flickered past his shoulder. "Do we know each other, madam?"

Martin turned to find Iris watching his conversation with Helena through narrowed eyes. "No. I am a friend of Lady Heathcote's."

"And mine," Whitney piped up, slipping her arm through Iris' affectionately. "Do excuse us. I see some friends I wish to introduce Iris to."

Martin was grateful, even if Whitney scowled at him severely.

Embarrassment filled Martin. If he had found Alexander Hedley already Iris would have described herself as his betrothed. "Miss Hedley is a very good friend of mine as well."

"Well, you do have a great many friends so I am not surprised. So that is your cousin, I take it," Helena remarked, overlooking Iris' importance to him. "I recognize her by the red hair and hostile gaze you described so well when we were together, but she is much prettier than you led me to believe," Helena said with an amused shake of her head.

"That's the one." Martin grimaced. "What brings you back to London?"

"You." She laughed a touch nervously before linking arms with his and forcing him to walk with her. "I have a proposition for you."

"Oh?" He couldn't fathom what she could suggest. It had been a long time since they'd had anything to do with each other. Helena had married well, moved to the seaside and gotten on with her life. He hadn't pined for her company.

She smiled up at him warmly. "I find myself in need of a protector."

Martin stepped back from her in surprise. "I am flattered, madam, but I cannot oblige you."

She looked crestfallen. "Wardie left me next to nothing to live on. As soon as I came back to London there were strange men calling on me, demanding payment. I cannot afford these debts so..."

Alarmed, he caught her arm and began walking the room with her again. "Mr. Ward must have died three years ago. What sort of fellows are coming around?"

"Shopkeepers for the most part. They just don't have any patience to listen to reason."

Martin sighed. "The debts have nothing to do with expenses incurred while Mr. Ward lived, do they?"

She had the wisdom to appear shamefaced. "If he'd provided better for me, I would not have this concern.

"Living beyond your means is no excuse." However, he couldn't abandon a friend. "I'll send my man of business to you to assess the problem and intercede with these men on your behalf."

She clutched his hand tight. "Oh, I knew you would still love me after all this time."

Martin quickly retrieved his hand. Helena was an exuberant creature but he certainly did not love her. "Mr. Barker will be the one to help you sort through this mess this time but you must promise to curb your impulsive habits."

"I will. I promise."

Somewhat relieved, Martin looked for Iris and found her and Whitney surrounded by laughing gentlemen, including Mr. Charles Talbot. Martin liked Talbot no more tonight that he had in the park. The fellow stood too close to his Iris for Martin's liking. His appreciative smile made Martin's fists clench. He glanced at Mrs. Ward one last time. "Do excuse me."

He hurried toward Iris.

Talbot leaned closer still. "Miss Hedley? Might I claim a dance if you have one free?"

"I believe Miss Hedley agreed to take a turn about the room with me," Martin interrupted rudely. He caught Iris' hand and tugged her against his side. "I'm sorry to keep you waiting, my dear. Come along."

Color filled her face and she dug her heels in a short distance away. "My head aches."

Martin scowled at her blatant lie. "The pain could not be too great or you would not have been laughing so heartily with that scoundrel."

"But it is now." She freed herself from his grip. "I should like to find Esme and go home."

The refusal irritated Martin. "I had intended to dance with you again tonight."

Iris gasped and then ducked behind him, using him as a shield.

Martin quickly scanned the crowd to see what had startled her, and his gaze snagged on a familiar figure across the room. Lord Grindlewood had arrived, smiling and waving to friends. The very man Iris had been betrothed to years ago. And he was in the company of Lady Heathcote. He bent his head to the countess as she whispered in his ear. His head shot up and Grindlewood scanned the crowd. Martin earned a scowl but then the man's attention moved on restlessly. Was he looking for Iris?

Martin discreetly glanced behind him only to discover that Iris had vanished, abandoning him upon seeing her former betrothed.

That was not a good start to their life together.

Chapter Ten

Society gossip sheets had once described Iris an incomparable. A diamond. The best the season could have offered were she not already engaged to marry a viscount.

The rest of society had called her undeserving behind her back, and there had been quiet joy in many households when she'd broken her engagement to Lord Grindlewood on account of her lost dowry. At the time she'd made her debut, she'd not understood her father's money had been all the appeal she'd possessed. She had laughed and smiled and believed her future to be set. Once her father's fortune was gone, her dowry used for another purpose, she had fallen far from society's good graces. She'd assumed that to be the worst sort of pain imaginable. A fall she'd never anticipated and that she could do nothing about.

Tonight she'd rediscovered a new kind of pain.

Insane jealousy.

It was very clear to her that the woman who'd captured Lord Louth's attention in the ballroom had a romantic history with him. By the way her eyes had devoured the earl, she was positive they'd been intimate. Much more intimate than she'd been allowed so far, and it wasn't fair. She had given the earl every opportunity.

Iris leaned against the stone wall of Lord Windermere's townhouse, shielding her feelings from view in the dark, and lightly thumped her head against the building behind her. She had always pitied the woman possessed of irrational hatred for women their men admired. If she had any kind of dignity, she would not have run away from Lord Louth at the first sign of competition. She was weak, spineless, and she despised those qualities in herself.

She pressed her fingers to her temple to alleviate the pain in her head as it intensified. She had made herself sick worrying if Louth would regret his decision to become her protector. Even more so than the fear someone would guess she was the robber's spy in society. Iris had been an invited guest to every single victim's home, and she was poor. Even she would suspect herself. Miss Quartermane was far too astute for her comfort and she feared where the girl's speculation would lead her next. If Miss Quartermane and her friends watched Iris closely, she would undoubtedly be exposed as an accomplice.

Seeing Lord Grindlewood again was the final straw. Her stomach had twisted into painful knots at the sight of Ethan's smiling face. He knew far too much about her real situation with her father for comfort. Her breath wouldn't come easily, so rather than risk fainting in the ballroom and drawing attention, she'd fled for fresher air on the terrace.

Those disturbing fears had passed the moment she was no longer standing in the same room with Grindlewood, Louth, or that overdressed harpy pawing at her lover. She slapped her hand over her mouth, shocked by her mean thoughts for a woman she didn't know the least about.

"Are you hiding from me?"

Ethan Hoganmire, Viscount Grindlewood, emerged slowly from the gloom, an angry expression growing on his face. Marrying this man had once been her heart's desire but now she felt uncomfortable around him. They'd talked of having children together, of visiting his southern estate during the long summers, but that life would never be.

She stared into his handsome face as calmly as she could manage. "No, Ethan. I would never do that to you."

"I know you well enough to see you are upset." He paused within reach and searched her face. "Don't deny it. Has someone been cruel to you again?"

Iris winced at how far off the mark he'd landed. He had known her once, but he didn't understand she played a part in the robberies plaguing society. She was the cruel party in this affair, pretending to be a friend while secretly hurting the hosts by setting them up to be robbed later that night. "Everyone has been perfectly pleasant tonight. There's nothing to worry yourself over."

"But you ran away at the very moment I arrived. Did you fear I will spoil your chances by making a scene, and reminding society we were once a pair?" He glanced away briefly. "If you did, I will make this quick and leave you alone before I'm noticed. Are you otherwise well, Iris? How is your father faring?"

"We are much the same."

He raked a hand through his hair. "Lady Heathcote tells me Lord Louth has become quite attentive and hinted there was a secret understanding between you."

"It is not like that." Despair filled her because it truly *was* like that. She'd promised Louth to keep their relationship a secret, but it wouldn't stay that way forever. She just hadn't imagined having to explain her eventual fall to the man she'd almost married. Louth, for all his physical appeal, was a means to an end. A way to get free of Talbot's demands. "He has always been a friend of mine and of my father's."

Ethan stepped closer. "There is still no news of our ship. I don't understand and I am so sorry my situation hasn't changed."

A few years ago, before her father's ruin, Ethan and her father had become investors in the same shipping line. The flagship was reported lost at sea although they both had doubts of the truth of that claim. They both continued to suffer for that lost cargo and still hope their ship might sail into port one day. There were other losses that had afflicted her father's finances but that ship and its cargo was of the greatest value.

"It's hardly your fault and you've no cause to worry." She forced a smile to her lips. "Everything happens for a reason."

"Does it?" He stepped back with a shake of his head. "Your father and I discussed the ship and its cargo long before I ever knew he would invest. Given everything else, I fear I bring only bad luck to you and everyone I befriend."

She reached out to him. "You are not to blame for my father's decisions. He was not a well man at the time."

"I think I'm cursed, Iris." Ethan nodded and drew back. "Maybe you had it wrong. If a man such as Lord Louth has the foresight to ask for your hand, you should accept. You are better off without me in your life."

That wasn't altogether true. If she'd married Ethan she would likely never have fallen in with Talbot's scheme for quick riches and might never have stood on the precipice of disgrace. She might have been poor, but she would have been guiltless of any crime. Ethan could have made her happy. He would have tried, at least.

She followed him a few steps and then faltered when hope sprang to his eyes. What was she doing, chasing after a man she barely cared for? She did not love him or have a future with him. This certainly was not the way to begin her new life as Lord Louth's mistress.

"Be clever, Iris, and say yes to Lord Louth when he asks for your hand." Ethan backed away. "I would only hurt you."

He vanished into the darkness so completely that she could not even hear his steps as he fled from her. And she would only hurt him, and everyone else, if she pursued him from the ball to make sure he understood what had happened to her father's fortune had never been his fault.

"Iris?"

Iris turned slowly. Lord Louth's towering bulk loomed over her. He stared down at her with guarded eyes, a question in them. Heedless of the impropriety, she set her hand to his chest and held on to him. Any lingering distress receded in his comforting presence. But how much had he overheard? She hoped he had not overheard her discussing her father's health with Ethan. "I am better now."

"You were truly unwell?" He took her arm and guided her to a stone bench. "Here, sit a moment."

Iris felt rather foolish in the wake of his tender concern. Her reactions to seeing Louth admired by other women was something she could never admit to but she would have to accept. She supposed it was a mistress' lot in life to feel on the outer. Perhaps if she could persuade him to set her up in the country, she would not care what he did in London because she would never see him bestow affection on another. "It is nothing but nerves and will pass quickly I am sure."

"It is not nothing if you're sneaking off to be with Grindlewood." He scowled. "I won't have it."

She blinked at the hurt in his voice. "I did not sneak anywhere." A blind run was a more apt description.

His eyes narrowed. "You *were* speaking to the viscount."

"Yes. But it's not what you suggest. We only talked, my lord. Nothing more scandalous than that, and please do remember that I don't belong to you yet."

"Not yet. But you will." His nostrils flared as he inhaled sharply. "A gentleman must always guard a woman's reputation and I will protect you even from yourself."

"Goodness, anyone would think I was on the brink of being seduced here on the terrace." She stroked his thigh and sighed. "I assure you that was not the case. Ethan was a perfect gentleman."

His eyes narrowed so she trailed her fingers along his thigh again. A delicious wave of anticipation swept through her. Was he all muscle beneath his fine clothes? She leaned toward him and risked brushing a quick kiss to his cheek. "Could we discuss him later?"

"Yes, we most definitely will." Louth cupped her face in his large hand and stroked his thumb over her cheek. "Are you curious about the woman I was speaking to before you ran off?"

Her pleasure in the moment vanished. "I suppose."

Painfully curious, but he would surely never like her to be possessive or reveal her true thoughts on the woman.

"We were close years ago, soon after I came into the title," he confessed with a shake of his head. He brushed his lips across hers softly then cleared his throat. "Unfortunately, she's got herself in a spot of trouble, the silly fool."

He dropped his hand and stared off into the darkness.

"I see." The minute the woman had spoken to Louth, Iris had felt insanely disagreeable toward her and it seemed her instincts were correct. Hearing the woman described as a "silly fool" eased the tightness around her heart considerably. When the lady had touched his arm, Iris wanted to scratch out her eyes. She'd been grateful to Whitney for dragging her away but now she was even more curious about their conversation. "What sort of trouble?"

"Like your father, she lived beyond her means and seeks to avoid her responsibilities," Louth confided.

A chill swept over her skin at the way Louth implied her father had been reckless. For the most part he'd been a very frugal man until the years immediately prior to his incarceration. The losses hadn't been intentional. However, Iris had enough problems of her own to wish not to hear of other people's debts. "We should return inside before anyone notices us gone so long."

Lord Louth helped her to her feet and as she stood at his side, the urge to take his arm increased. It was a possessive thought, and she quickly ignored the wish to claim him as her own. She moved toward the ballroom unaided but her heart was heavy. Just a little longer and she could cease pretending to be one of them.

Once inside, Louth led her toward Miss Crewe, where she stood in conversation with Lady Taverham beside the dance floor. For a change, the marchioness' husband was nowhere in sight.

"My dear, it's a pleasure to meet you again." Lady Taverham beamed and extended her hand. "Miss Crewe and Lord Louth have nothing but the highest praise for your character."

Iris smiled but when her gaze fell on Louth's former lover watching him from across the room with doe eyes, she did not feel herself a good character. She had detested the woman on sight, and now that she knew she'd met someone he'd taken to bed, been intimate with, she was even more anxious about the lack of contract between them. She would have to address that issue soon. "You're very kind, my lady."

When Iris glanced up at Louth to invite him to call tomorrow, he was studying Mrs. Ward as if he'd already forgotten Iris existed.

She dropped her gaze, hiding the jealousy she couldn't suppress. This would never do. She had to learn to ignore the way he might look at other women, and how they looked at him like their next affair.

She raised her chin, drawn straight into Lady Taverham's kind gaze. The marchioness tilted her head and drew Iris to her side. "Would you do me the honor of an introduction to Lady Heathcote? I don't believe I've had the pleasure yet."

"Of course. Do excuse us, my lord." She did not meet Louth's gaze before escorting Lady Taverham across the room. They passed Talbot on the way. He did not approach but given the way her skin crawled, he followed her progress.

She stopped at Esme's side and waited to be noticed. After the introductions were complete, Esme gave her a smile. "I don't think you can claim to be invisible now. A rather distinguished rogue is watching you still."

Lady Taverham glanced behind to where Lord Louth stood watching them and grinned widely. "Not a rogue but the best of men. I've never known him to be so openly appreciative of a woman before. I shall have great fun teasing him about his fall later."

That could be disastrous. Lady Taverham must think he had honorable intentions. "Oh, please don't embarrass him. He's just a friend."

"After all he has done for me over the years, I'd never dream of embarrassing him. Teasing him in private is another matter entirely. But I must correct you on one point. *I* am his friend, and I must tell you, he does not normally look that way at me or any other woman he considers a friend. You are special to him indeed."

A blush filled her cheeks as the ladies exchanged conspiratorial smiles and she glanced across the ballroom, panic filling her. This was dreadful. Both women were going to ruin everything between her and Louth. Lady Taverham would be disappointed when she learned the truth of their arrangement.

But to protest would require her to clarify what their arrangement did entail.

She wasn't that bold yet.

She lifted her chin, accepting that here was a woman she might regret disappointing.

Talbot hovered at the edge of her line of sight, waiting for her to pass word of their means of access to steal from Lord

Windermere. She was a thief's accomplice and now a fallen woman. She'd never meant to hurt anyone but it seemed inevitable no matter what she did.

Lady Taverham excused herself after a short time to rejoin her husband, and then Lady Ames claimed her company. Later Esme found her again, and around and around the room she went, apparently indispensible in every conversation. She never managed to have a moment alone again that evening. The window she was expected to open in Lord Windermere's study remained locked at the end of the night as she left at Esme's side and climbed into her waiting carriage. "What an exhausting evening."

Talbot would be furious but for once Iris was beyond caring. "It was but a great deal of fun besides."

Iris had felt included for the first time since her family's ruin and she wanted to cling to the sensation of acceptance for as long as possible.

Chapter Eleven

———— ◆ ————

Martin paced Lady Heathcote's shadowed drawing room, unsure whether to call the evening out a disaster or a success. Whitney had danced four sets more than her usual two and been much admired as far as he could tell. But his relief was tempered with exasperation. He wanted to know why Iris was sneaking off to meet her former betrothed. If she had any lingering feelings for the man, she should have married him years ago.

It might be inexcusably late to call on his betrothed but he wanted to be sure there were no impediments to his alliance with Iris. Vivian Rose had taught him the value of directly questioning everything he assumed about how women think.

The door shut softly and he faced the sound. "About time."

"Forgive me. I had not realized you were to call on me tonight." Iris stifled a yawn. "Is something the matter? Is there something you want?"

She rubbed her arms briskly, which only drew his attention to her body and the fact that she wasn't wearing the dusky-pink evening gown she'd worn at the ball but something far more intimate. A dark-hued silk robe clung to her curves and his breath caught. She'd come to meet him as a mistress would her protector, and that couldn't be further from the truth.

"Yes. You." He tried to relax, fighting the urge to touch her. "But I want to know about Lord Grindlewood first. I overheard part of your conversation."

Her brow rose at his confession to spying on her. "Eavesdropping?"

He shrugged and made no apology for spying on her. He'd been unable to turn his attention from her all night. Soon everyone, including Iris, would know what she meant to him. As the last man who would ever kiss her, his reasons for asking about Grindlewood were fair to his mind.

She tapped the back of a chair a few times and then grimaced. "Was that woman really only asking you for money?"

He stared at Iris on hearing the bite of disapproval for Helena, a woman she couldn't possibly know anything about other than what he'd told her that night. There was no need for Iris to feel slighted that he'd not introduced them. Helena was only a friend and would forever remain that way.

"To be completely honest, she initially asked for my protection, which I immediately refused of course on account of you."

"Why of course?" Iris turned away, folding her arms around her. "Lord Gandy had three mistresses at once last year, if I recall the worst accusations leveled against him by his wife."

"And he died in one of their beds, too." He laughed and drew Iris around to face him. "A happy circumstance for him I'm sure, but entirely beside the point. Do you still love him?"

"Lord Gandy?" Iris frowned. "No, I never met the man."

He gritted his teeth, hating that he couldn't stop picturing Iris and Grindlewood alone on that blasted terrace. But after his ignorance of Vivian Rose's interest in another man, he did not want to take any chances he was being used. "I meant your viscount. If he means to marry you, of course I will stand aside."

"Ethan has not the funds for a poor wife. That is why I broke with him, so he could marry someone with a dowry."

He caught her face and lifted her gaze to his. "I see, but do you love him?"

"No. I don't love him."

"Good." Martin nodded, aware of how her words had overwhelmed him with optimism. "There was something you said tonight that made me realize you'd mistaken my intent with you."

She stilled. "Have you changed your mind about offering for

me now?"

He brought his other hand to her face and gently traced her hairline. She was so beautiful like this—so honest in her emotions that they were as clear as if she'd spoken them out loud. She was jealous of the fleeting attention he'd given a past lover tonight and uncertain again of her own appeal when there was no need for concern. "Not in the least, but I fear I might not have been clear about what I do want in a wife."

Her eyes widened impossibly. "Wife?"

He nodded and smiled warmly at her. "As soon as I can procure your father's permission, I will marry you."

She eased away from his touch, staring at him in shock as if she'd never considered him as her husband. "You cannot want to marry me."

"But I do." He caught her tiny hand in his and rubbed across her knuckles with his thumb. "Why do you think I hated the idea of you taking lessons in passion from another man so very much? You will belong to me, Iris, in every sense of the word."

"Oh. Oh, I see." She rubbed her neck and spun away.

Martin watched her in confusion. He'd expected something more in response to his promise to give her his name along with his protection. "Iris? What is it? Do not say you don't want to marry me now? Not after all we've done together."

"I do want you. I do. But I never dared to dream of more." She lowered her face. "You were so against everything I wanted."

He touched her arm. "Your dreams were not high enough. I promise to do all I can to make you happy."

"That is very good of you." She turned and lifted her face to his. He was startled to see the beginnings of tears in her eyes. "I am growing concerned. Ethan has taken it into his head that he's cursed but what if *I* am the source of bad luck?"

Martin set his hands to her shoulders, astonished by her wild imaginings. "Cursed? That isn't possible. You are the most perfect woman in all of London. I've never met a lady who's impressed me more."

"No one is ever what they seem." She dropped her hands to her sides and then pressed her head to his chest. "I don't believe it's the first time Ethan has alluded to those feelings."

Martin stoked down the curve of her back. Beneath the silk

robe, she shivered. "Surely he has family to look out for him, and you will too. You do not need to worry anymore."

She moved out of his reach and shrugged. "He is, or rather was, a friend too. I cannot help but worry about my friends, even though I cannot help them any more than I can help myself."

Martin was overwhelmed by the desire to drag Iris into his arms and cease her concern for other people. A good kiss would make her forget she'd spoken to Grindlewood tonight. Removing to Holly Park and leaving London behind once they wed would keep them apart. However, he didn't want to get ahead of himself, so he held his tongue about their life after marriage. "But it was you who broke the engagement, wasn't it?"

"I did. He was very upset with me at the time and swore the money didn't matter. But it always does." She sank into a chair and placed her hands in her lap. "I had thought I had done the wise thing but now I am not so sure. He is still unmarried."

"He will find another woman eventually." Grindlewood did not lack for admirers, from what Martin could see.

She pressed her lips together in a tight line. "Are you sure you should marry me? I would have been content to be your mistress. A little home in the country is all I want, and to see you."

"Marrying is the correct thing to do and we can certainly remove to Holly Park as soon as you like, if you are weary of London." He approached her and knelt at her feet. "About what happened in the dining room. If I have made you feel uncomfortable, I apologize. I took advantage of your inexperience to prove my point that we were not finished with each other. We never will be now but I won't impose on you until we exchange vows."

She swallowed and met his gaze. "You won't?"

"I've been celibate for so long, another month or so won't harm me." Damn but he hated lying, even to himself. His cock and balls ached at the very sight of her like this. Beneath the robe, Iris was likely dressed in a thin white nightgown and nothing more. A tantalizing bow at the neckline laced the garment closed. The belted robe was thin enough that he might see her figure if she stepped before candlelight. "Unless you say you want more."

Her tongue darted out to wet her lips and his own tingled. Her gaze grew soft, and then she leaned forward and boldly pressed her lips to his. She drew back after a lingering kiss. "I do want more of you."

Encouraged, he pulled her to him, curled one arm around her back and lifted her into his arms so her legs wrapped around his waist.

Her tiny body molded perfectly to his after a little wriggle and then she settled her arms about his neck and proceeded to kiss him witless. It would be a miracle if he lasted until their wedding day before he took her to bed with him. She drove him utterly wild. Her tongue danced into his mouth, flirting with his. He groaned and sank onto the floor with her, moving Iris beneath him while he kept his weight suspended on his arms and knees.

She rubbed her hands over his chest and then tugged on his cravat, a spark of mischief lighting up her beautiful eyes and daring him to be bold too. He could not afford to lose his head. He wasn't that much of a scoundrel but giving her pleasure was a definite possibility.

Their lips parted and they both panted. "I don't know what I'm doing so you should stop me."

"No, don't stop," she whispered, meeting his gaze shyly. "You're making me mad with want. I've been thinking of you all night and I would like an end to this torture."

Relief filled him. "Was that why you couldn't hold my gaze for long?"

She nodded and removed his cravat pin, setting it aside carefully.

So that accounted for her distraction. He smiled wickedly. He'd been fighting the same thoughts too. Martin shifted his hand across her body slowly and covered her mound through her nightgown and robe. "Did you think of me touching you here?"

A ragged gasp rattled from her chest and she clutched his shoulders. "I was afraid everyone knew that I was thinking of your mouth on me tonight."

He teased her nightgown up her legs until he could touch bare skin above her knees. "Shall I end your suffering quickly or slowly?"

"Quickly. Please." She covered her face with one hand. "I can't bear it."

He shifted to his side and drew her to face him. He caressed her bare bottom with one hand before he slid around her hip and teased his way to her curls. The gentle touch seemed exactly what she wanted because she hooked one leg over his thigh and allowed him greater access to her body. He teased the seam of her sex, finding her damp and so warm his breath caught.

He parted her folds slowly, delicately touching her until she moaned in response. He grew aware of her touch on his abdomen a moment before she fumbled with his trouser fastenings, moved aside his shirt, and freed his cock.

He couldn't breathe for the anticipation surging through his veins.

"Goodness," she whispered in awed tones as she took him in hand. Martin had heard similar before with regards to his size, but experienced more satisfaction than he'd expected in hearing it from Iris. She wasn't shy about exploring his proportions.

As he ran his finger along her sex, playing with her wet heat, Iris' tentative touch grew bolder. Across her palm his length seemed obscenely large, and he trembled when she overcame her shyness and took him in both hands. With a little instruction whispered in her ear, she stroked his length firmly; long, delicious tugs that ignited his desire to dangerous levels.

He bent his head. "Iris, I want to be inside you."

She nodded swiftly and with that encouragement, he pressed a finger inside her sheath. Iris released him and moaned. He withdrew, sliding through her wetness and teasing her clitoris. When he repeated the action, she ground down on his digit then shuddered wildly. He applied pressure to her clitoris as she surrendered completely to desire. She clung to his shoulders as she climaxed, buried her face in his neck and muffled the sound of her panting. As her body grew limp, her hold on him loosened.

He eased away onto his back, intending to end things there, but she followed him up and sat over his thighs, trapping him beneath her. Her nightgown bunched high on her thighs, her robe half off. When she wrapped her fingers around his length and stoked him, he arched his back.

Iris glanced along his body and smiled. "I like to see you this way."

"I don't need it."

Her eyes narrowed. "Yes you do. Otherwise, it would not be fair. I would not be able to sleep a wink tonight if I disappointed you."

"You never have." He grinned. "Shocked, surprised, and tempted unbearably every other moment, yes, but not disappointed. I don't know what I was thinking to say no to you."

Her expression grew serious as she stoked him and he lay back to enjoy the pleasure her touch brought. He placed both hands on her thighs and closed his eyes to savor the sensation of her hands bringing him ease. He'd had no idea she had such a talent or interest but he wouldn't deny her wish to pleasure him. He was too close to stop anyway.

Martin dug into his pocket for a handkerchief and when he was ready, fit to burst, he covered the head of his cock with it, covered Iris' hand, and together they brought him off. When his mind cleared, he glanced down at the soft bundle of curves covering him. Iris had toppled forward, her head rested over his heart, her legs spread on each side of his thighs. She embraced him firmly. Possessively.

It *was* nice to be held by a lover. Especially a woman of Iris' honesty. He teased the skin of her neck and grinned in the dark. To think he'd resisted claiming the woman for his own on the flimsiest of reasons. He'd never imagined such honest desire could be his and he would do everything to protect her from harm.

He rolled Iris to her back, settled his bare hips between her legs and brushed a light kiss across her lips. He inhaled the sweet scent of her skin and sighed deeply, content at last that everything was settled between them. "I will be the most fortunate man in London to have you as my wife."

"I hope so," she whispered sleepily. "I hope I never give you cause to regret."

Chapter Twelve

———◆———

"I did not have the opportunity, I swear," Iris sobbed as Mr. Talbot squeezed her hand so hard tears sprang to her eyes.

"Liar," Talbot hissed.

She whimpered as the tendons and bones in her hand were crushed almost to the breaking point. She had underestimated Talbot's fury over last night's failure to gain his men access to Lord Windermere's home. She'd not truly tried sneaking away and unlocking the expected window. It was her own fault she suffered now. She'd been too busy fretting that Louth was about to be stolen away from her by his former lover.

Talbot tossed her aside like a doll made of rags and Iris slammed into the wall so hard her teeth rattled. She quickly regained her balance, shifting closer to the locked gate of the Marshalsea, but there was no hope of escape. Talbot continued to block her exit from prison.

To think she'd walked through that gate this morning with hope in her heart because she'd one day become Lord Louth's wife rather than an easily discarded mistress. It had only been a short-term happiness. The moment she'd left her father's side, Talbot had pounced on her for an explanation.

She glanced toward the deserted prison yard desperately. Mr. Fitzhugh was making himself useful and keeping anyone in the barracks from approaching the prison gate. She couldn't be seen from the barracks rooms in this spot. No one would come to her aid. Not even her father would be a match for Talbot, should he discover what was happening to her.

"I had plans for Windermere's jewels," Talbot growled menacingly. "Buyers were waiting and now I have nothing to sell them."

She bent her head in pretend shame and contrition. She had been very glad to spare the earl the robbery until now. "I am sorry. I could not get away."

He moved over her, reminding her of her fragility. "You will not fail me again."

Terror filled her as she whispered, "Lady Heathcote has no plans to attend any large entertainments in the coming week."

"Then what else has she been invited to?" he screamed directly into her ear.

She backed into the nearest wall and risked a peek at him. His black eyes were cold and unyielding and she shivered. "You cannot steal from the smaller gatherings I attend. I'll be an immediate suspect in any investigation. I don't know where every safe is located."

His palm slapped against her cheek and with an effort he held back a second strike. "Then choose better marks."

She pressed her palm to her stinging cheek and stared at Talbot's red face as comprehension dawned. She would never end this mad pact without going to prison. It was already too late. She had to make him see reason. "I cannot do any more for you than I already have."

He caught her by the throat and pushed her hard against the wall. Her skull exploded with pain but she heard his threat regardless. "You'll do as I say or he'll pay the price. You know what I want to hear next, don't you?"

"Yes, sir." She quaked and dug her fingers into the bricks behind her, scrambling for purchase where there was none. Talbot would hurt her father if she didn't comply.

There was only one gathering she knew of. A private dinner in the Marquess of Ettington's London residence. She did not want to put the Ettingtons in harm's way if she could help it but there was no other option unless she wanted to die here and now.

She dug her fingers under Talbot's around her neck and he

loosened his grip a little. "We will be attending a small dinner at Lord Ettington's on Friday," she croaked, "but that is the only engagement I know Lady Heathcote will be attending at the present time. She's very unpredictable."

Talbot squeezed her throat again and desperate panic filled her.

"I swear it's the truth." She thrashed to be free of his grip, to no avail. "If…You can't kill me…you need me to get into the Ettingtons' townhouse."

Talbot released her with a shake that rattled her teeth and she fell to her knees on the cobblestones, gasping for air.

"Get up," he barked.

Iris scrambled to her feet even as her knees stung, keeping her eyes lowered so as not to provoke further anger. When the silence lengthened, she risked a glance. Talbot raised his hand. "You will send word of any other accepted invitations or by God, I will make him suffer for your disobedience. Don't think I won't be watching you still. One of my boys will bring your message to me about the next ball. Just wave a piece of paper as you walk along then drop it. I'll be waiting."

He stepped back and, taking that as a sign she was free to go, Iris bolted out the gate and ran as fast as her legs would carry her to the lane behind her former home. She found a quiet corner and fought to get her emotions under control.

She was doomed. She covered her face as her eyes filled with tears. She'd never be free of Talbot and everyone would soon know what she'd done. Her remaining friends would despise her. Louth would hate her for entangling him in her problems.

She dropped her hand to her throat, rubbing at tender spots along her skin. If he'd bruised her, she'd have no hope of hiding the marks. At least then she might have to stop. Give up and allow fate to run its course.

But that would leave her father vulnerable.

Her eyes stung at the pain of abandoning him to an ugly future. Talbot would kill him, and she'd long suspected it was only a matter of time before he made good on his threats. He'd likely kill them both if she gave herself up for justice. But she couldn't live like this anymore, afraid and loathing herself every waking moment.

She wouldn't.

She would stop Talbot one way or another.

Iris dried her eyes and quickly ran her fingers over her hair, repinning that which had fallen down. She must look a fright. Anyone would see her guilt when they looked at her but she suspected she was beyond hope now.

Once she had caught her breath, she slipped back onto the street as if nothing had changed. However her mind churned with how to achieve her aim of stopping Talbot. It was time she took control of her life and stopped being so pitiful and weak. She had to confront the problem head-on and leave nothing out.

She had to tell Esme first.

Instead of taking the servants' entrance so no one noticed her return in these shabby clothes, she knocked on the front door of Esme's home.

The butler's eyes widened in surprise at seeing her on the front steps. "Welcome back, Miss Hedley," Higgins whispered. "My lady and Mr. Meriwether are in the drawing room. If you are quiet, you could sneak upstairs without being seen and change."

The warning was unnecessary. Mr. Meriwether was exactly the man she *had* to see before she lost her courage. The man investigating the robberies needed to know the truth before it was too late. "Would you announce me, Higgins? I need to speak with them together."

Higgins was gone a few moments then opened the door to admit her. Esme and her lover were settled comfortably enough on the settee, however, Esme's slippers lay across the room and Meriwether's waistcoat buttons were misaligned.

"Darling," Esme cried out warmly.

Iris cringed inside at how hurt her friend would be after this uncomfortable confession. "Lady Heathcote. Mr. Meriwether."

She stood before them and clenched her hands together as Higgins closed the door.

Meriwether tilted his head to the side. "Is something amiss?"

Iris swallowed the hard lump in her throat and then nodded. "Yes. I've come to confess."

"Confess," Esme said with a little laugh. "Have you spent the morning with Lord Louth again? I swear I must press for the wedding before the week is out at this rate. You will have tongues wagging."

Iris quickly shook her head. "No. I mean to say I'm responsible for Lord Hazelton being set upon in his home."

There was silence a moment then Meriwether rose in one fluid movement. His stare was cold as ice. "How could that be?"

"I opened the window in his home. And in many others before that night."

He gripped her arm, one that had already been abused by Talbot. "What others?"

After suffering Talbot's threats and treatment, she wasn't the least bit afraid of this man. "All of them. I had no choice."

Esme crossed the room and removed her from Meriwether's grip. "Don't say another word."

"I have to. It won't end unless I do something to stop it. If not for my father—"

"Yes, your father," Meriwether mused, his gaze holding hers. "Is he behind it? Attempting to cover his losses by stealing from those who slandered his name?"

Iris blinked in surprise, never considering someone could believe that of her gentle father. "Of course not. My father scarce remembers where he is, let alone has the wits to mastermind revenge against any detractors. This is Talbot's doing. Mr. Charles Talbot."

"That is a very severe accusation, young lady. I hope you have proof."

She had no proof at all but her word. "He threatens my father's life if I do not help him gain access to the homes in society and tell him where a safe might be located. I have no choice but to help him."

Esme gasped and wrapped an arm around Iris' shoulders. "Perhaps we should sit," she murmured. "And discuss this calmly."

Iris leaned into the comfort, fearing it would be the last she'd ever have.

Meriwether scowled and shook his head. "It would be best if you left us alone, Lady Heathcote. If I am expected to make sense of Miss Hedley's accusation then she has many questions to answer."

Esme ignored the dismissal and smiled instead. "Then I'll send for tea, but for propriety's sake, I will indeed stay as a chaperone to my dearest Iris."

Meriwether rolled his eyes at the idea but followed them when Esme settled Iris to the settee with a gentle push. She requested tea, took a place beside Iris, and when Meriwether moved a chair to sit directly before them, she held Iris' hand. Her smiling encouragement helped her unburden herself of everything.

She told Meriwether how it had started, naming victims, most he knew, and when she confessed who the next target would be his brows rose. "Good choice."

Iris started. "How can you say that? Hazelton was assaulted in his own home. Ettington could fare just as badly."

Meriwether shrugged. "Ettington is a relatively easy man to deal with. With luck, he can be persuaded to help us catch these criminals."

"But you will only catch the men who work for him, not Talbot himself, who is behind everything. He is the one who needs to be caught. I am sure Ettington hasn't invited him to sit down to dinner."

"Not in his class," Esme murmured in agreement. "And assuredly not already invited. The guest list is modest, as common for the marquess' style. To press him to invite Talbot at this late a date would raise considerable suspicion."

Meriwether's brows drew together. "Then we must set a better trap."

The pair lapsed into silence. Esme with her thumb to her lips, Meriwether pursing his.

"What we need is another ball," he said suddenly.

Esme frowned and glanced at him keenly. "And a good reason for it, to avoid any suspicion of a trap. Perhaps Iris' wedding breakfast could be a grander affair than I'd first envisaged."

"I cannot marry Lord Louth now." Iris shook her head. "Given what I've told you, it is only fair to break the engagement and spare him the embarrassment of being associated with a criminal. I fully expect to pay for my actions. I knew it was wrong from the beginning. I only wanted to protect my father."

Esme's arm tightened around her protectively. "She never stole from anyone, or took a shilling in payment. She simply opened a window and failed to latch it properly. Surely you agree, Mr. Meriwether, that she should avoid punishment."

"And what of her disclosure of the locations of the safes?" He scowled. "Searching other people's homes for the locations of their valuables isn't something I can overlook, no matter whom the party is."

"I never had to search for any safe," Iris admitted quickly. "The victims actually told me themselves, and many others in fact at the same time, several weeks before the robberies occurred. It was then simply a matter of waiting for an invitation to enter their homes and a large enough event to hide what I did. When they hosted a ball, no one ever noticed me admiring the view outside their windows."

"And that's why you believed yourself invisible? Oh, my darling. What a nightmare you've lived under my very nose." Esme pulled her head close to hers, as protective as a mother of her young. "You must help her, Meriwether."

Meriwether remained silent for a good long while as he considered her fate. His eyes narrowed and he rose to his feet. He bent over them and touched the skin of Iris' neck, a light caress immediately over the spot Talbot had held to shake her. "How did you come to be injured?"

Iris covered the marks. "Talbot wanted the contents of Windermere's safe very badly. He'd made promises and I had failed to open the window for his men last night. He was very unhappy with me that his buyers were to be let down."

Meriwether met her gaze. "How badly are you hurt?"

"It's nothing more serious than a few tender spots." Iris touched the back of her head and winced. "Perhaps a graze."

Esme gasped and carefully checked the back of her head. "My God, she's bled? That beast! I'll make him pay dearly for this."

Meriwether shushed Esme. "Did Talbot ever mention who handled the gems after the robbery had taken place?"

"No, not once. I'm sorry I don't know anything else to help recover what has been stolen."

Meriwether resumed his seat with a sigh. "Consider yourself

held under extreme suspicion, Miss Hedley. You are not to leave Esme's side for even a moment."

"I have to see my father tomorrow. I always go. If I don't, Talbot will become suspicious and he might harm him. He's in no state to protect himself."

"And don't forget, she was to be watched," Esme cut in quickly. "She must pass along word of our engagements to these shadowy figures who follow her. She cannot simply hide away and give up her usual routine of going out."

"Very well." Meriwether bit his lip and then nodded. "This is what we shall do, Miss Hedley. You will go about your usual business and relay any further excursions with Lady Heathcote directly to Talbot, careful not to provoke him to anger again. Leave nothing out and do what he said to do. You will be in danger but it is imperative you do nothing to spook Talbot and give the game away. Your engagement to Lord Louth, when it is announced, will most certainly provoke a flurry of invitations that will be to our advantage."

"I don't want to lie to him anymore." Louth would be in harm's way the moment their engagement was announced. "He needs to know he isn't expected to marry a criminal."

"I will explain as much of the situation to him as needs be." Meriwether rubbed his jaw. "If it can be arranged at such short notice, there will be a trap laid at Lord Ettington's home and we will ensure a successful robbery takes place. Think nothing of it and go about your engagement in the normal fashion, shopping and house calls, etcetera. The frivolous activities any young woman would undertake prior to her marriage. The valuables stolen will be paste gems, a fine setting but of lesser value than the real thing. By the time the ball is announced, Talbot will be quite desperate. It is there we will catch him."

Esme leaned forward. "What if he doesn't receive an invite to that event?"

"Oh, I can safely predict he will." Meriwether raised a brow, suggesting Esme should know better. "I'll be calling in a favor."

Chapter Thirteen

◆

Mr. Richard Barker waited at the open door of the carriage and wasted no time in speaking up once Martin's feet hit the footpath. "Thank you for coming at short notice, my lord."

Martin glanced at the façade of Mrs. Ward's home as his carriage pulled away. "You did say it was urgent. What seems to be the problem?"

The usually unflappable man of business raked his hand through his ginger hair as if he was at his wits end. "She told her butler to turn me away, saying my services are no longer required. Yesterday, when I suggested a modest reduction in her expenditure at the dressmakers, she threw a vase at me and then fell to pieces. I couldn't stop her tears and she begged me to leave."

Martin shook his head and surveyed the street. "Sounds like Mrs. Ward has not changed. She once threw an entire dessert at her late husband, if I recall, because he mentioned a woman who had slighted her in glowing terms. Poor fellow hadn't known what to do either."

Barker gaped. "And you do?"

"Oh, yes." He ran up the short flight of stairs and knocked. The butler was unfamiliar to him and clearly suspicious of a strange man at the door, so he handed over his card. "If you'd be so kind as to ask Mrs. Ward if she might have a moment to see me."

The door closed in his face and Martin turned to his man of business. Damn Helena for being difficult. The reason he'd sent Barker was to lessen the demands on his time. He already juggled three women—Whitney, Iris and the infant. He didn't need a fourth. He had a dinner to host tonight and handing the responsibility over to Whitney had not been his intent. "Aside from the current difficulties with Mrs. Ward, you're keeping well, I trust?"

"Yes, my lord." He winced. "My sister recently had a babe, so it seems I'm an uncle to a little girl now."

"Well, congratulations."

Barker frowned. "I'm supposed to be impressed of course but it's hard to be excited over something small enough to fit into a desk drawer."

He grinned at the pleasant fantasy of placing his daughter in the drawer of his study desk at Holly Park while he worked. She could sleep while he managed the estate business. "You would feel differently if you were talking of your own child."

"I don't know about that." Barker scowled and drew close. "Given the way my sister has carried on about being indisposed, I'm of a mind to skip marriage, and women, entirely."

The butler invited them inside and took his hat. Martin faced his companion. "Mr. Barker, would you mind waiting here a moment. I'll see Mrs. Ward alone first and try to sweeten her temperament."

"Thank you." Barker plunked down on a nearby chair and made himself comfortable.

Martin was led to a room he remembered well, a sitting room so cushioned that even the floors could be made very pleasant for an afternoon romp. Helena moved to greet him, her gown swishing about her legs. The diaphanous creation revealed her curves and hinted at the bounty that lay beneath. She had dressed for seduction.

Martin accepted her offered hand and kissed her knuckles perfunctorily. "My dear, you look beautiful."

"Thank you for calling, my lord." She fluttered her lashes at the compliment. "Do sit down?"

She indicated a spot next to hers and he took it. "Thank you.

Are you happy to be in London again?"

"Oh, yes. The social whirl has me quite in its grip. Isn't it terrible about these robberies?" She grasped his arm. "Makes a woman long for a man at her side to offer his protection."

He shrugged off her touch. "I think you are safe. In all cases, the victims hosted large gatherings the same night as the robberies took place."

Her smiled widened. "Yes, but I do have a safe."

"As do many homes, I'm sure." He studied her. Her fears were understandable but entirely for naught more than attention at the moment. "What game are you playing with poor Mr. Barker?"

"That man." She shuddered. "I tell you, I've never encountered such a beastly fellow in my life."

"You threw a vase at him."

She grabbed a fan and fluttered it before her face. "What else is a poor widow to do to defend herself?"

Barker was an even-tempered man. The most agitation he'd ever displayed had been outside. He couldn't believe her description of him. "So you are saying he provoked such an attack?"

She sniffed and turned her face away. "It's over now and forgotten."

"Good, because he is waiting in the hall to continue the discussion of your finances."

She spun about. "You brought your man of business into my home after I expressly told Peters to deny him? He's as bad as the shopkeepers demanding money. He will want blood next. I will not have him in my house telling me what I must do or not do. I am not a child."

Martin had not missed Helena very much at all he discovered then, especially her habit of blowing a confrontation out of all reasonable proportion. "But the reason he was sent to you is to make sure you could keep the roof over your head that you love so much. You came to me and asked for my help. He is the extent of my offer."

"Never mind the past." She moved toward him. "I'd hoped you'd come to talk as we used to do."

"Barker is the only reason I am here. He sent for me because you would not let him do his job." Martin scowled. Helena was not above playing the victim to get her way and they both knew it. "He is not used to suffering a lady's theatrics so I must ask that you deal fairly with him."

Helena's lower lip trembled and she lifted her hands to cover her face. "How can you speak so cruelly to me?"

"The truth isn't cruel, just as those tears aren't the least bit real. Stop this nonsense or you will see the last of me."

Her hands fell. "We were so good together. We could be together again, and I promise I will learn to curb my spending to make you happy."

She leaned even farther forward, presenting him with a direct view of the crests of her lush bosom.

Martin was unmoved. "What you want is not possible."

Helena slipped her gown off her shoulders and pressed against him, pinning him to the side of the settee until her bosom was quite squashed against his chest. "I can make you feel so very good. I know you remember how it was between us."

He did remember, but that was beside the point. "I don't agree that married men should keep mistresses any more than you do."

Her gaze grew a touch uncertain. "Well, neither of us is married now."

He hadn't planned to tell anyone about Iris until he was assured of her father's agreement to the marriage, but clearly he had to say something to convince Helena of his disinterest in a way she would understand. "But I am going to be married soon, so an affair is entirely out of the question."

Helena's eyes narrowed to slits. "Who is she?"

"Someone I admire very much." He pushed her away gently. "Our union is not public knowledge as yet, so I would appreciate your discretion in the matter."

"I see."

"To tell the truth, I feel uneasy even being here. I told her Barker would handle your financial muddle without my involvement in the matter. My future wife's behavior suggests she's not the sharing type."

Helena dropped her gaze, a smile curving her lips. "Your secret is safe with me, my lord."

"Thank you." He rubbed his hands together. "Now, over the years I've learned to trust Barker's advice implicitly. I would not have sent him to you if I didn't think he could be of service. Might I call him in now to hear for myself his beastly suggestions?"

She smiled but it wasn't the genuine smile he'd hoped for. "If you insist."

"I do." He stood and returned to Barker where he was cooling his heels in the hall. "Helena and I have had a discussion about her situation. If you'd be so good as to follow me and show me what you've suggested, I can be on my way. I don't wish to be late when I'm hosting my own dinner party tonight."

Barker nodded but the moment he crossed the drawing room doorway, he froze, gaping at Helena like a starving man would look at a banquet. His gaze swept over the lush woman and two bright spots tinged his cheeks. At a guess, Helena hadn't dressed this way for his prior visit.

Martin snapped his fingers before the man's face. "Barker, pay attention, man," he hissed.

"If she'd been dressed like that when she threw the vase I would have welcomed the pain." He swallowed hard, adjusted his cravat and then moved to set his papers over a nearby table.

Martin met Helena's gaze and saw a satisfied smile now graced her lips. She knew the affect she had on men, even if it had failed to work on him. If she ever turned her seductive skills on Barker, he'd be putty in her hands.

Martin picked up the first of his papers and scanned the sheet. Barker's notes were thorough and to the point. Helena was living well beyond her means and the only way to delay the creditors was to curb all impulsive spending. He glanced at his man of business to show his approval of the fellow's findings but Barker's attention was again glued to Helena Ward's lush figure.

He coughed to gain his attention. "Barker, do you remember what you said to me outside about avoiding women? Keep that firmly in mind when dealing with her or you might end up footing her bills out of your own pocket."

Chapter Fourteen

———◆———

"**D**id I mention how lovely you look, Iris," Louth whispered as he took a place at her side on the settee after dinner.

"Yes," she replied. "Several times, I believe."

"Well, it's as true now as the first mention," Louth insisted. "I'm glad you could come at short notice."

They'd enjoyed a lovely dinner together but all Iris could think about was Talbot's men lurking on the street outside. She'd seen them. They were waiting for her to open a window to Lord Louth's home so Talbot could steal from him too.

She glanced around the exquisite drawing room. Esme was engaged in conversation with Whitney, continuing a heated discussion begun at dinner. The pair couldn't agree who was the most fashionable gentleman in London at present—Lord Ettington or Lord Acton.

She bit her lip as she waited for him to mention the trouble she was in because of Talbot. Meriwether had promised to speak to him and spare her the pain of confession but so far Louth had said nothing on the subject. "You are very kind."

He leaned close. "Am I boring you tonight?"

Her eyes widened and she spun to face him. "Of course not. It is a little difficult today to pay attention under the circumstances."

He appeared puzzled. "How so?"

His expression was open and friendly. He did not appear a

man who'd just learned an unpleasant truth about his future bride. Her heart sank. She'd enjoyed a wonderful evening believing herself forgiven for her part in the robberies but Meriwether must not have found the time to mention her troubles to the earl yet. She scrambled for a sufficient response that would make sense. "You are an attractive man, and the things we've done together. I…"

"Are you embarrassed?"

"No, but shouldn't I be?" She shook her head. "I do not understand myself anymore."

"There is nothing to worry about. The best pleasure is mutual." He smiled warmly. "If given the opportunity, I would have already dragged you into my arms. I wanted to kiss you when you arrived."

"I thought of that too. You are very distracting." Her tension eased a bit. If they were equally afflicted by desire then her situation wasn't quite so bad, but her problems with Talbot were always in her mind.

She would give anything to feel Lord Louth's arms wrap around her and to hear everything would be all right. Would he understand how conflicted she was? The brief interlude on the rug in Esme's home yesterday had proved what a very wicked woman she could be. She wanted experience more of that feeling.

Louth smiled and warmth spread all over her body in a disconcerting rush. "That fichu covering your bosom is entirely too modest for my taste and I will insist you be rid of them the moment we wed."

She glanced down at the white scrap of lace covering her upper chest as her breasts grew heavy at his mention of them. She'd pinned the lace as high as she could to cover a bruise that proved troublesome to hide with cosmetics. "I thought you would approve."

The look he sent her suggested she should know better. "You didn't used to wear one until recently."

"Well, I'll be a wife now rather than a mistress." She blushed and lifted a hand to her face as her skin heated. "I thought I should look the part."

"So I'm to be denied a delightful view just so you might be an unnecessarily modest wife." He glanced sideways. "I truly don't mind what you wear, so long as I am the only one enjoying the hidden parts."

She gripped the settee cushion as her blush grew hot enough that she wished for a fan. While she had been intimate with him, they had never truly spoken of it when others were around. She kept her gaze on her friends as she answered, "I would prefer to be the only one seeing your private parts, as well."

"I can agree to that very easily." His skin darkened. "In fact, I can assure you I'll be the most faithful of husbands. Home before my bedtime every night."

She frowned, skeptical of such a claim. No gentleman kept to a bedtime. London was for pleasure. "You're teasing me?"

"I am a little about the bedtime, but I'll never stray, I promise. Too many people never keep their promises." He shifted closer. "Press your hands down into your lap a little farther, until you feel your body stir."

"Stir?"

"Until your sex clenches at the anticipation of my touch between your legs."

Her lips parted in shock at his suggestion but her body reacted with a rush of moisture between her legs. He couldn't mean to do it here or now. "But there are other people in the room with us."

"A little danger can add to the excitement and spur pleasure to greater heights, especially in a crowded room. Imagine finding your release in a ballroom with no one the wiser. Press down now."

Iris swallowed. She rarely touched herself, and then only in the privacy of her bedchamber had she ever dared truly explore her body. The idea of Louth knowing what she did alone titillated, but she was afraid too. What if she was caught? Oh, how she would blush then.

She adjusted her hands a little higher in her lap and pressed down over her sex as he asked. A small tremor of desire fluttered between her legs and she gasped. There, that ought to be enough. "Satisfied?"

"Not yet, but you will be first." He reached over the side of his chair and she was surprised to find him holding an embroidery hoop before him. "What do you think of Whitney's work?"

She winced. The work was poorly done, uneven and lumpy stitches, but she shouldn't really say so out loud or to him. "I was embroidering a cushion for Esme with similar colors."

"She started this when she arrived to pass the time, I think, but her heart really isn't in it. She loves to paint above all else." He held the piece over her lap and she grabbed the left side while he held the other.

The hoop touched her thighs. "Press down again between your legs and rub yourself. No one can see what you do now. I want you good and wet for later."

Warmth gushed from her at his brazen words. She pressed down a little harder, pushing her skirts between her thighs and rubbing her fingers in an awkward manner to stimulate herself. It wasn't much, but her behavior, and his scrutiny, excited her unbearably.

"That's it," Louth rumbled with obvious approval. He pointed to the design. "This is thistle and holly, correct?"

How could he talk of embroidery at a time like this? "Yes, I think holly is very appropriate, given the townhouse name."

He was silent a long moment, but his gaze flickered to her secret activity between her legs. "I doubt this is meant as a gift."

She nodded at Whitney, glad of the distraction. "Perhaps it is a small token of appreciation for all you have done for her."

He smiled wickedly. "I'm going to keep you in my bed all night when you're my wife."

She trembled at the idea, wishing for the privacy of a bedchamber now. Everything they had done so far had been done in rooms best meant for conversation rather than pleasure. She would like nothing better than to spend the whole night alone with him. She was learning so much about desire and her body's need for stimulation.

He slid his fingers down the embroidery and behind the shield of the hoop; he touched her thigh and then covered her fingers.

Under the pressure of his hand, the thrill grew torturous. If not for her friend's and Whitney's presence, she would climb onto his lap and beg him to slide inside her body. Her eyes fluttered closed as her sex clenched at the very idea. Anticipation made her breath churn, her body throb. She wished to spread her legs here and now and have Louth's fingers teasing her to completion. Only his touch on her bare sex would settle the anxiety in her heart that she could keep his interest after the truth was known.

"Not yet," he murmured. "Come back to me."

His touch trailed away as Esme and Whitney laughed together. Iris snapped her eyes open and withdrew her hand from where she'd been pressing. She'd been on the verge of exploding without a thought to the consequences of being discovered.

Esme faced her a moment later. "Do excuse us, my dear. I simply must inspect Miss Crewe's latest work of art and I believe it is upstairs. I won't be long."

The pair departed immediately, leaving her with flaming-hot cheeks and unfulfilled need.

Louth stood, crossed to the doorway, and quietly closed up the room. He shook his head and grinned. "Continue," he whispered.

She shivered at the heat in his eyes. "Without you?"

Surely tonight he wanted her body to ease his own passions? It might be the very last chance she had.

He knelt at her feet and drew her to the edge of the settee. When he lifted her skirts slowly up her legs, her body quaked in anticipation of his touch. He lifted a brow as her hands fluttered at her waist but when she boldly lowered them to her bare sex, he grinned widely. "Yes."

She pushed her fingers lower and into her curls.

Her sex was so wet she was embarrassed, but when Lord Louth unbuttoned his falls and took himself in hand, she lost any shyness over it. She teased the aching bud at the apex of her thighs, and slid her fingers down again into her wet heat. He eased closer and set the tip of his erection against her slit, so warm and hard he took her breath away. While she fondled herself, he teased. The friction of his erection against her body made her restless and even more needful.

"Make love to me," she whispered as she stretched her fingers to stroke him once.

"I am. We are. There are as many ways to make love as there are days in the year, but we have little time alone so this moment must do." He pushed into her, not breaching her but making her anticipate the feel of him. The pressure of his size hastened her touch on her sex and before too long, her legs were wide apart and she was lost.

She arched at the strangeness and the sharp longing to be one with him. As he slid along her wet sex, her hand fell aside. His cock was soft as silk against her bud and she began to tremble uncontrollably. He clamped one hand over her mouth as her body shattered and she came apart just from imagining him finally pushing into her.

She fought for breath and lost, staring at the wonderful man who'd claimed her for his bride and brought such feeling into her life. He'd been correct. She'd never understood what making love would be truly like. She'd never imagined she could crave his attention so badly. Could love him so easily for bringing her ease without taking.

And tomorrow she'd have to hurt him by telling him the truth.

She reached for him as he climaxed. His seed splattered her palm as he groaned darkly. He bowed his head low and drew in heavy, uneven breaths. Iris examined her hand, but he grabbed her and wiped his seed away. "I apologize for the mess." His expression grew troubled.

"Don't," she whispered. "I like what we do together far too much to protest about a little soiling. Besides, it's nice to have proof you're as affected by me as I am by you."

He lowered his face and licked along her slit, tasting her with unhurried enthusiasm. "More," he whispered and then kissed her there.

The touch of his mouth after such a release startled her but as he lapped at her, she grew accustomed to the sensations and found herself growing warm again. "If all the days of marriage can be as pleasurable as this, I would be a fool to refuse you."

He pressed a lingering kiss to her sex then pulled her skirts over her knees. "Have you ever denied me?"

She smiled. "Well, I haven't been properly asked to marry you yet, so how could I."

His head shot up and he blinked at her. "Tell me if you have some idea of where I can find your father so I can."

She touched his face gently and steadied herself for the lie she had to tell. "I don't know where he is right now."

Louth climbed to his feet slowly, redressed and, after a quick glance at her to make sure she was relatively decent, opened the drawing room door again. "No man should be this hard to find."

Iris stood, adjusting her skirts and then moving to check her reflection in the mirror above the fireplace. Not a hair out of place but a slight flush to her cheeks. She hardly looked like a wanton girl, but then again, she didn't look like a thieves' accomplice either.

"Would you care for a sherry?"

"No, thank you." The moment Louth turned his back to set the decanter down, she eased to the side, peeking through the nearest uncovered window. All seemed quiet outside, but she had no doubt Talbot's men were still watching every window of the house. She couldn't allow an innocent man to be harmed. The window was already locked, and the head of a new nail revealed both window frames had been joined together. She breathed a sigh of relief that Louth had taken extra precautions to protect his home. Short of breaking the glass panes, the window couldn't be opened easily. She resumed her inspection of the exotic fire screen. "This is so beautiful."

"I'm glad you like it." He drew close and pressed against her back, his head close to hers. His voice dropped to a seductive tease. "Would you like a tour of the rest of the house before we seek out my cousin and Lady Heathcote?"

"I should like that very much." She curled her arm about his and strolled through the lower rooms, memorizing the layout for her future dreams. No matter what Meriwether promised, there was always the lingering worry that she'd go to prison along with Talbot. No matter what happened, she would always remember this house, and the man who'd tried to protect her.

Chapter Fifteen

———————•◆•———————

Whitney was still at breakfast when Martin found her the next morning, her head bowed over the paper and the tip of her fork pressed to her lips. For a change there was no oil paint under her nails. She seemed so fascinated by what she was reading that she didn't notice his presence at first. "Any news?"

"Nothing so far about further robberies," she said as she turned the page. She pointed to his place setting and a pair of letters. "There are, however, several personal letters for your attention."

He picked up the first and recognized the hand immediately. *Helena.* Since they'd spoken just yesterday, he'd no idea why she'd be writing to him. He'd thought the matter of Barker had been addressed. The other was also from her.

"Cousin, is there a reason you're getting love letters from a woman other than the one you're obviously pursuing?" She scowled at him. "Because I am almost certain you and Miss Hedley made love last night in the drawing room."

"They're not love letters," he scowled. It annoyed him that Whitney was so observant and outspoken about her uncomfortably correct instincts. "I'm merely helping Mrs. Ward with a problem."

He ripped one open to prove it and rose petals dropped onto his plate. The note contained an eloquently worded invitation to a late supper that night. He shoved the note and the remaining unopened one into his coat pocket and swept the rose petals into his hand. He deposited them in a nearby vase. Martin was astonished she had not believed he was involved with another woman and would still pursue him for an affair. He would decline her invitation and any other like it.

"You're just like every man." Whitney sighed. "How tragic. I thought you were different from the others."

He glanced up from his plate, scowling. "Whom are you comparing me to?"

"Why, the men who dabble with decent women and then run off to meet, shall we say, a woman of lesser delicacy. I'm sure Miss Hedley by now believes you to have honorable intentions toward her. As did I and her chaperone, Lady Heathcote, last night, when we left you two alone so you might progress your suit."

He gritted his teeth at Whitney's concerns. He was for Iris and no one else now. In fact, after receiving and declining Helena's seduction yesterday, he'd felt rather relieved the days of casual flirtation were far behind him. He knew what he was getting in Iris. A woman who was not afraid to ask for what she wanted most.

"Mr. Lynton Manning is in Town." Whitney sipped her tea, watching him over the rim. "I passed him in Bond Street just yesterday and he was so obliging and sweet, as always. It is a pity he left the church. You could have asked him to perform your marriage ceremony when you do wed."

"I had always intended to." Martin met his cousin's gaze and gave up trying to hide his decision from her. "Stop fishing. You've won."

Her brow rose.

"Yes, I have asked Miss Hedley to marry me, and yes, she has agreed. As soon as I gain her father's approval we will make an announcement and be wed."

Whitney's smile was radiant. "My dear cousin, I couldn't be more pleased with you than if you'd flouted convention and run off to Scotland."

"You'd like a touch of scandal, wouldn't you?"

She pressed her hand to her chest, fingers spread wide in mock horror. "I'm crushed by your accusation."

He sat at the table and considered his cousin. She was utterly incorrigible. No doubt she would run off to Scotland to wed for the fun of it. "I'm glad you like Iris."

"She likes you, and that is all I'd hoped to see from your wife. Once you're married, I should like very much to paint your portraits. It's high time the one covering your safe was replaced. Our grandmother's expression gets on my nerves every time I look at her."

He laughed. "Only because she looks as if she knows you're thinking of wearing her gems. I would like a smaller portrait of Iris for my pocket watch one day, if you will oblige me."

And a portrait of his daughter, too. But he couldn't ask Whitney to paint that. The pair would never meet if he could help it.

Whitney frowned. "If you'd rather engage a gentleman for the task, with a fine hand for detail, I can recommend several."

"After all the coin I've spent on paints and canvas?" He snorted and snatched the newssheet from her hands. "I should gain something in return for putting up with you, hoyden."

Whitney set her hands to the chair beneath her legs. "About Miss Hedley. Would you like me to return to Holly Park when you marry or remain behind in London so you might have time alone? I can understand if you'd rather me out of the way."

He glanced around the paper, astonished by her kind offer. "There's no need to part company when we marry, although… Miranda mentioned last week that she was thinking of inviting you to stay with her in the country."

Whitney stilled. "Go to Twilit Hill?"

He nodded. "You could paint to your heart's content. It's very lovely there and I'm happy to send you along with all the supplies you'd ever need for a comfortable stay."

"So you do wish to be rid of me?" She sighed. "As much as I would like to oblige her, Acton lives nearby so that is one strike against the idea of a prolonged visit."

"But not his sister, and for that you should be grateful." He put the paper aside without having read any of it. "Tell me, what exactly is it about Acton that bothers you?"

Whitney rolled her eyes. "Would you like a list drawn up?"

"Yes," he agreed. "I find myself uncertain if this has anything to do with his past disagreements with Miranda or something else entirely. Has he been rude to you?"

Whitney drew in a long breath.

"He seems to ignore your snippy remarks easily." He leaned toward her. "And yet you still continue to sting him whenever you meet."

Whitney laughed. "You've a fanciful imagination. Are you going to see Miss Hedley today?"

"Don't change the subject." He caught his cousin's hand in his. Since they rarely touched without the benefit of gloves, he was surprised to find her hand ice cold. He lowered his voice. "Has he done something worse?"

She shuddered and slipped from his grip. "Why ever would you think I'd encourage that man?"

"I don't know but if he's ever bothered you, I promise I will deal with him."

"Don't you dare." She shook her head. "Besides, there is nothing to deal with. He's a disagreeable man with an overly inflated notion of his appeal."

He didn't like her answer but he couldn't very well force her to be honest with him. "Very well, perhaps the visit to Miranda's isn't feasible but do think about it. With the anniversary of her wedding approaching, she's eager for company. And as for your earlier question, I'll see Miss Hedley at dinner tonight. Remember to be on time so we are not late for the Ettingtons."

"Yes, about that. Given the robberies going on, shouldn't one of us stay at home just to make certain we are not a target? I'm happy to volunteer to stay behind and keep the lamps lit."

"What would you do? Catch them and paint their faces until they confessed?" He laughed. "We will not cower at home. I won't give the thieving bastard the satisfaction of keeping us from going out."

Iris inched closer to Lord Louth as they entered the Ettington dining room side by side, more than a little afraid of her surroundings. After the elegance of the drawing room, she was rather astounded by the view. "Is there a reason behind Lord Ettington's collection?"

She glanced up at the walls of the Grosvenor Square mansion and did her best to hide her dismay. Broadswords and stuffed animal heads lined the walls of the dining room that should have been elegant, considering the marquess' distinction, but were certainly not.

Louth laughed softly as he held out a chair for her to sit in. The tips of his fingers slid across her back as she settled in the chair. "A distraction left over from his days as a bachelor. He never wanted female guests to become too comfortable in his home. His wife doesn't care for them either but hasn't pressed for their removal. Not yet at any rate."

They were positively grisly. She lowered her voice further. "I'm sure his plan worked amazingly well."

It was still working. She wasn't sure how she would manage to eat a bite with the blank accusing stares of those creatures on her as she ate their brethren. However, she did not know which was worse—the stuffed heads or the marquess' cold regard. His welcome upon her arrival had been decidedly chilling to say the least. He knew what she'd done and what she was here to do.

Ettington had agreed to let her leave an east drawing room window unlocked tonight.

So far, she'd been too terrified to move in that direction and had already missed one obvious opportunity to slip the latch open. She didn't want to do this to Ettington. She'd never wanted anyone to be stolen from or put in danger. But for her father's safety, in order to catch Talbot in the act so he might be stopped, she had no choice but to go along with Meriwether's plan.

Her stomach churned and Lord Louth drew near. "Try to ignore them."

She nodded and glanced at Esme. Her friend offered an encouraging smile from her spot across the table but it didn't comfort Iris in the least.

She glanced at Lord Louth and forced a smile. Meriwether had decided not to confide in Lord Louth after all. Meriwether insisted that the least number of people aware of her business, the better the chances of success. Her intended still had no idea what she was about to do to his friend. So she was still lying to Louth and hating herself even more.

She peeked at the man seated on her left.

Her hosts had seated her between Louth and Lord Acton around a large mahogany table covered in gleaming flatware and crystal. A thief's palace. Although she had dined many times amid such elegance when her father had been at the height of his popularity, she was rather overwhelmed by this extravagant display. The silverware alone could likely pay off her father's debts.

There was something about Lord Acton's attitude tonight that set her teeth on edge. He watched her but said little, a constant frown appearing and disappearing on his face. Iris would be a little more comfortable around him if he said what was on his mind rather than holding back. She was tense enough as it was.

Louth leaned close. "What the devil was Pixie thinking to place my cousin so near the duke? Exeter appears out of sorts already and we've only just sat down to dinner."

Iris risked a peek in that direction, as did Acton, and swiftly back at her plate. The duke had not spoken directly to her. And he'd looked very surprised to see her. The moment of recognition had quickly shifted into disapproval. She was very glad to be seated far away from him. "I'm sure the marchioness knows what's best."

"I'm sure, in this instant, she's playing with fire," Louth grumbled.

Iris chose to think the best of Lady Ettington. Whitney sat at the other end of the table, close to the Duke of Exeter but not directly beside him. Their hostess seemed a bubbly sort of woman and not at all the marchioness society had once expected for Ettington to have. Lady Ettington lacked the reserve often favored by the noble born and had even winked at her husband when dinner was announced. The marquess could barely stop smiling when the his wife was around too.

She let her gaze drift along the table as she heard earnest laughter. These people were so lucky. So happy. And she was about to ruin everything.

Louth's shoulder brushed hers as he leaned close again. "Try not to look up too often. I've heard that helps tremendously."

She smiled brightly and caught the napkin the footman tried to lay in her lap. "I'll do my best."

His lips quirked into a smile and she trembled. A future with Louth seemed so far away right now. She shook her head. She should have come clean about her problems as soon as she'd had the chance.

Lord Acton cleared his throat a few times before he faced her. "How are you enjoying the season, Miss Hedley?"

"I am enjoying it very much, thank you."

He sipped his wine and set the glass down carefully. "Have you attended many events this year? I don't think our paths have crossed."

"Several." She had seen him at many, but clearly his mind was elsewhere when they'd met. She didn't bother to educate him as to the number time he'd looked over her head in search of someone else.

He turned his glass on the spot. "Did you attend the Fairmont ball, by chance?"

Her mouth grew dry. That had been the first robbery she'd aided Talbot in. "I did but left early with a headache."

A headache brought on by utter panic and disgust by what she'd done.

His gaze snagged on her face. "Early, you say?"

She nodded. Riddled with remorse, Iris had later read every word printed about the masquerade and listened to every spec of gossip. She'd been terrified that her name would be linked to the theft of the Fairmont parure, a set of five perfectly matching emerald and diamond pieces. The gems had not been recovered. "Yes. But I don't recall seeing you." She swallowed as the fear she'd experienced that night returned. "Esme saw me home and to bed by eleven. She returned to the ball without me once I was settled. I hear it was great fun though, and truly scandalous. Did I hear some poor fellow lost his trousers that night?"

He surveyed the guests around him and after a long moment spoke quietly to her. "Yes."

She glanced at him quickly. "No. Did you know him?"

"We have a slight acquaintance, though I'm sworn to secrecy about who he is." He frowned at his white soup and winced.

"I've been commissioned to aid the poor fellow recover his belongings. However it is a difficult topic to broach."

"I'm sure it must be. Poor man." Iris sighed as tension left her. There had been wild speculation that whoever had stolen the fellows trousers had done so on a dare, though what they were doing off the gentleman's lower portion so they might be stolen boggled the mind. The trousers had never been recovered, and the gentleman not identified save for his white bum fleeing the masquerade on foot into the night. "There's been many a scandal begun at that ball I've heard. Your acquaintance has nothing to be ashamed of," she promised.

She glanced at Acton and detected acute embarrassment. Was he really investigating the matter for a friend or had Lord Acton been the man to lose his trousers? "There's been many a scandal begun at that ball I've heard. Your acquaintance has nothing to be ashamed of," she promised.

Iris quickly turned her attention to her soup, puzzled by why someone would seek to embarrass Lord Acton of all people. He was handsome, many women admired him. Had he tried to seduce a lady at the ball and come off second best in the exchange?

Lord Louth settled his hand on her spine. "Is there a problem, Acton?"

"A harmless query, nothing more," Acton said with a smile that did not reach his eyes.

Iris agreed, determined not to add to the man's discomfort.

"Was that a new horse you were riding in the park the other day?" Louth asked of Acton.

Acton pursed his lips and exhaled slowly. "Not exactly."

He glanced along the table as Whitney burst out laughing. He clenched his jaw and shook his head. "I am training the brute for London traffic for a friend."

Louth nodded. "How is it coming along? Seemed a fine-looking animal."

"The beast was difficult at first but he's finally doing what he should as long as I'm firm. Another few weeks and I hope I'll be able to send the horse back to its owner." The men continued to talk over her head about the training of horses and when she finished her soup, she sat back in her chair and merely listened.

Louth appeared very interested in the topic and comfortable with Lord Acton. Iris wished she could feel the same. She might not be the focus of attention tonight but with every word or movement she made, she felt as if she were being judged.

Louth stroked her leg before leaning away and resuming his meal. Iris struggled to breathe properly. She would miss how his touch made her feel powerful, beautiful and, above all else, wanted.

Across the table, Lady Hallam and Lord Daventry began to whisper, casting the occasional glance in her direction. Iris adjusted her napkin in her lap and pretended not to notice she was being spoken of.

She cast a speculative glance along the length of the table as the meal progressed at her fellow diners. Esme and Lord Windermere were engaged in an animated discussion she could not make out. For a pair that constantly squabbled, they never lacked for topics to discuss and could do so for hours on end. The older man appeared well entertained by Esme's conversation though, so all seemed well there for the time being.

She caught Whitney watching Acton once. The corner of her mouth turned down and she then turned her attention to charming the duke into laughter.

When half-dozen footmen trouped into the room to clear the last course, Iris regarded their arrival with considerable relief. She couldn't stay in this room another moment.

The Ettington drawing room was a large space that suited the marchioness so much better than the dining room. Filled with comfortable chairs and hothouse flowers, Iris was instantly at ease. She glided between the guests and took a cup of tea from a waiting servant.

"My dear, I must thank you."

She turned to find Lady Taverham smiling down upon her. "Oh, how so?"

"You proved me correct, and of late that has been very rare." She grinned. "I know it's not been announced and my timing is always terrible, but I just want you to know you're always welcome to visit."

"Thank you."

She linked her arm through Iris' and guided her to a settee

apart from everyone. "I've known Martin since before I was married and his obvious happiness makes me very glad he's finally ready to settle down. Many have tried to capture his attention before."

Iris grimaced at the mention of former rivals.

"There," Lady Taverham crowed in triumph. "That is how I knew you loved him. It is a horrible sensation, isn't it?"

Iris stilled. "What is?"

"Loving someone that someone else wishes to have too." The marchioness accepted a cup of tea from a footman. When he went away, she continued, "I have spent most of my marriage feeling the same way."

She stared at the woman next to her. "How do you bear it?"

"I didn't." She grimaced. "I ran away from the situation, which I now know was a mistake. I can never change the past but I can help you. Don't doubt him. If Martin has offered, he means it. If you listen to gossip and start to wonder how deep our friendship goes, I promise you our admiration is nothing stronger than that of a brother or sister. He's fallen for you."

That was the worst news she'd ever heard. He'd be even more hurt by her betrayal if he loved her. "Oh, my lady."

"And do call me Miranda when we're alone. Please. I find my title an encumbrance at times to forming honest friendships at my age."

"Attempting to avoid the conventions again, Merry?" Lady Ettington joined them with a laugh. She wagged her finger. "As my sister-in-law always warns us—you can never truly belong in society unless you adopt your haughtiest mannerisms with everyone you meet, and heaven forbid you show any hint of real friendship."

Miranda rolled her eyes in a very unladylike manner and laughed. "You were always an unruly child, Pixie, and it gladdens my heart that Virginia's nonsense warnings have fallen on deaf ears. Besides, we all need someone to rebel against the conventions with."

Iris grew uncomfortable as the pair bickered over their natures with mock ferocity. They were friends, and judging by the topics discussed, it seemed they'd forgotten her presence. She set her cup aside and excused herself for the retiring room.

She needed a moment alone before she carried out tonight's plan. When she returned to the drawing room, she would remain on her feet, circulate through the crowd and open the window.

Then tomorrow she'd break with Louth and cry herself hoarse.

She might feel comfortable with him, but was never part of her future.

Chapter Sixteen

Martin had eaten far too much to be considered good for him but he was so exceedingly happy with the evening and his life that he didn't care for a change. The women had retired to the drawing room for tea and only the men remained in the dining room, drinking port and smoking cigars. He was confidant Iris was enjoying herself tonight, aside for the shock of their host's dining room decoration. "Excellent dinner, Ettington. But when are you going to rid yourself of the grim beasts overhead?"

"Never." He grinned. "My wife is of the opinion they should stay exactly where they are, and for the very reason I had them placed on the walls in the first place."

Martin shook his head at the news. "They do also deter women with no designs whatsoever from thinking well of you too," he warned.

The marquess handed out refills and raised his glass. "To my wife."

"To Pixie!" the gentlemen agreed en masse, laughing with good humor. The marquess' wife, known as Pixie among intimate acquaintances, had brought many changes to the marquess' life. Not the least was more frequent parties with friends when they were in London.

Lord Acton joined them. "I've been meaning to ask, why Pixie?"

Ettington sat forward, rubbing his hands together. "Trouble always seemed to follow my wife when she was younger and the name stuck. I imagine she's planning to lead Miss Crewe into another of her mad schemes that I'm sure to regret not stopping later."

Martin tossed back his port. "My cousin doesn't need help. She can get into trouble all on her own."

"I am sure you are correct," Exeter agreed, joining them after refilling his glass. "Quite outspoken for someone so young."

Martin winced. He'd been watching his cousin at dinner and had tried not to groan every time she'd addressed the duke directly. He'd hoped she'd behaved but perhaps she'd fooled him. "I apologize if she's given offence, Your Grace."

The duke waved his hand. "None required. It's not every day that a young lady is brazen enough to suggest it is high time I stop mucking around and found myself a wife."

His friends chuckled with varying degrees of mirth at the idea of the duke taking on a wife. The duke was a bachelor, well over fifty, and had been firmly pointed away from matrimony all his life. Martin could not imagine him wed, nor even courting a woman. Was Whitney after the duke for a husband?

He could barely believe she'd consider someone so old but who knew with that girl. He'd have to watch his cousin closely. A scandal involving the duke that did not end in a marriage could ensure he might never get her off his hands.

"I'm cursed," he murmured to the duke.

Exeter smiled benignly. "There, there. Why so glum when you have the undivided attention of a pretty woman hanging on your every word at dinner?"

He liked the idea that Iris yearned for his attention very much but he tried to keep his smile within reason. "Did she?"

The duke set his port aside. "She did indeed. Her father and I met at school you know, and I recall he spent one summer at my estate because he had nowhere else to go. No other family unfortunately. Pleasant sort. Brilliant at one time. A shame what happened to him."

Martin glanced around them carefully to see who was nearby. Acton had retreated while they'd spoken of Whitney, and Ettington was pouring refills for their friends. Martin was dying to know what had caused Alexander Hedley's disappearance from society so thoroughly. He'd begun to fear the man was dead. "What happened to him beyond having pockets to let?"

"Lost the lot. Home. Second wife ran back to her family. A string of bad investments ruined everything."

Martin nodded. That much he already knew. "So he fled his creditors?"

"My dear sir, Alexander is a man of his word, or was at one time." The duke declined another port and waited till his nephew had gone away before speaking again. "It is kind that you've taken an interest in Alexander's daughter but remember you are a bachelor of means, and must guard your wealth and reputation. Alexander was particularly obstinate about accepting help when it happened, and I am ashamed to say I took him at his word that he would recover on his own. Their situation slipped my mind until I saw her tonight, but a man rarely ventures to such a place to be reminded."

Martin stilled as a sinking feeling overcame his happiness. "What place?"

"My good man. Do you not know?" The duke drew back in shock. Then shook his head. "Dear God, you must not or you would not ask. I am afraid to tell you that Alexander Hedley is a guest of the Marshalsea Prison. He's been there a year or more I think it must be now."

"That could not be. She never said a word about her father being in England." He shook his head to deny the claim. "Why would Iris not tell me the truth about her father?"

"It is not at all surprising, when it must have seemed there was a chance to make a match with you." The duke winced. "Now though, I'm sure you've come to your senses and can make an escape from any understandings that might exist. I've no idea how she came to be mixed up in it all but it's assuredly for the best. Alexander will be ashamed that his daughter has fallen in with a rough crowd, despite Lady Heathcote's best efforts to shelter her."

Martin reeled. "What rough crowd could you possibly mean?"

The duke tilted his head. "Why, the robberies plaguing society this season. Surely Meriwether alerted you that she was in league with them, acting as an accomplice inside the *ton?* That is why she is here tonight. I am against the trap being set but my nephew is determined to lend his support to prevent anyone else being harmed."

Rage filled him. Fury. He took a step toward the duke, fists clenching. Dear God, the woman he wanted to marry, the woman he'd fallen in love with, was considered a felon. He could not believe it. "Nothing could have induced Iris to agree to such a situation but the worst kind of pressure. She is too good to play a part in any robbery. You must be wrong. I cannot imagine Iris agreeing to rob anyone," he protested.

"Steady man, you will draw attention soon," the duke warned.

Ettington knocked on the tabletop. "I think it's time we rejoined the ladies?"

Damn right he would.

Iris was seated at the rear of the room when the doors opened to admit them. She perched between Ladies Hallam and Daventry, and appeared extremely uncomfortable.

When the countesses rose to greet their husbands, Iris remained behind. Her shoulders tensed. He nodded to her but kept his distance, not trusting himself for the moment to blurt out his questions in front of his friends.

"She is lovely," Miranda murmured at his elbow.

Martin squirmed. Lovely, but a thief? "Agreed."

"And I understand you've been calling on her daily."

"Not every day," he corrected. He'd been on a fool's errand in search of Alexander Hedley all week. The man was in the Marshalsea, a place he'd never considered finding him. Why had she let society think her father had abandoned her? He risked a glance at Iris. Did she visit her father? Did they speak?

"Of course she does," he muttered out loud. She went out every day and he'd accepted her silly little explanations of running errands for Lady Heathcote at face value.

Miranda grinned at him. "Look at you, barely able to take your eyes from her even in company. A lucky find indeed, my friend. By the way, the other wives are firmly of the opinion you should not let her get away. If you are not careful, you'll find yourself leg shackled before the week is out."

"It's not like that." Martin wasn't sure now what to think of Iris now, but there was no way he could marry a felon. In a way, he could understand why she might have lied to him about her father. Embarrassment. Concern he'd turn away, as so many had done before. "How do you know a person well enough to be sure you're not making a mistake?"

"Trust that feeling in your heart. The voice that won't let you sleep at night, wondering where they are and what they're doing. I've never met a man, or woman for that matter, who wasn't afraid of making a mistake until the last moment of giving up his freedom, and I'm sure you are no different." Miranda sighed. "So it's the altar and life starts anew."

"I don't know if I can," Martin warned, glancing around. "Now really isn't a good time for this conversation. I need to think."

His friend laughed softly. "Just don't take too long. I think she's as uncertain of you as you are of her. It's clear she likes you very much, and don't deny you like her too."

He *had* liked her. He'd fallen in love with her dignity and honest desire of a better life. Only now, after speaking with Exeter, he wasn't sure he had ever known her. While he'd been speaking to Miranda, Iris had stood and moved restlessly through the room, never settling in to converse with anyone for long. No one else but him seemed to notice where she went. She paused to glance out the east window, where rain was pattering against the glass, lost in her own thoughts.

She was lovely but he didn't know whether he could marry her if Exeter's claims were fact. He'd thought the existence of his daughter might tarnish the family name. Marrying a felon would be an undoubtedly worse scandal if her double life was ever exposed.

He moved toward her. "Is the view remarkable?"

She spun about to face him and pressed her hands to her chest with a soft shriek. "Oh, you startled me."

He stared at the window and his heart stopped. The catch was open. It had been locked earlier in the evening. He'd seen that for himself. His mouth tasted of ashes as he realized Exeter's claims were all too true. She was the thief in their midst. "I apologize."

She seemed confused by his short reply but then smiled. "I like your friends."

"I like them too. I would be very concerned if something or someone intended them harm."

Her cheeks drained of color and she glanced across the room toward the marquess. "So would I. They are kind people indeed."

She couldn't mean that, given what she'd just done. "You should return to Lady Heathcote. I believe she was about to leave."

"Yes, of course." She dipped a curtsey, a frown creasing her brow. "Good evening, my lord. I hope to see you soon."

"You will." He didn't want to talk to her tonight but tomorrow was another matter. He wanted her to go so he could sort out his conflicted feelings. He did not like being lied to.

She fled to Esme's side and after a flurry of whispers, the pair eventually departed. That left him standing near the unlocked window that would ensure his closest friend was robbed.

A hand clamped on his arm. "We need to talk," Ettington hissed, and dragged him toward the nearest doorway and down the darkened hall before he could lock it again.

When the study door closed behind their back, the marquess swore. "Devil take it, do you want to get her killed?"

"Excuse me?"

"Miss Hedley, you fool." Ettington shook his fist. "If you'd locked that window after she'd finally worked up the courage to accomplish her goal, you could have put her life in peril. And her father's."

The marquess raked his fingers through his hair and strode to the sideboard to pour himself a drink. "Damn frightful business, I don't mind telling you. I've never been very good at keeping my wife in the dark."

"You'll be robbed."

The marquess spread his arms. "I *need* to be robbed tonight."

"What?" His heart sank. "Why?"

"These robberies are getting out of hand. They've grown even more cocky and dangerous after every success. Tonight someone is going to steal some very good paste gems from my safe. Gems planted there to avert suspicion falling on Miss Hedley ahead of the *real* trap being set for the next ball. In the meantime, Miss Hedley must play her part without any interference, as much as we all dislike the situation. She is the inside spy, finding targets and ensuring access to the best homes, and all so her father's throat won't be slit. You almost spoiled our one chance to set everything in motion."

Martin sank into a chair in shock. "Who is we?"

"Meriwether. Lady Heathcote. Miss Hedley confessed to them a few days ago after being attacked." The marquess shook his head. "Despite the potential risk to herself and her father if they suspect her of duplicity, she wants it all to stop."

Martin stood. Dear God, what had he done? He'd sent her away without letting her explain herself. "I should go to her."

Ettington shoved him back in the chair roughly. "Sit down. You cannot do anything to stop this now. And you certainly cannot help her without giving the game away."

"She has no idea of what she's doing or saying." Martin covered his face. He'd judged her and found her wanting just as everyone else had done since her father's ruin. "She'll be sent to prison," he whispered.

"Most likely. The woman has had ample time to consider the consequences of her actions but she came forward nearly too late. The attack on Hazelton scared her into hesitation at the next opportunity and she was threatened very badly." The marquess pressed his lips together in a tight line, his expression filled with compassion. "I don't know if she can escape judgment, but if not then let's hope sensible heads prevail at sentencing."

"Thieves are transported. Dear God, I cannot lose her." Martin closed his eyes as horror and guilt brought tears. He brushed them aside with the back of his hand. "I might never see her again."

Ettington's hand settled on his shoulder. "She's more concerned for her father than her own future, I'm told. He's vulnerable and she knows he might not last long in the Marshalsea without her."

Martin stood. "Then that is what I can do. All I can do. I've been looking for him for some time to ask permission to marry her and now I know where he is."

"You cannot marry her. Not now."

"I have already promised to do so, and once Alexander Hedley is free and gives his consent, we will be wed by special license. Everyone expects us to marry anyway and if I don't follow through, there will be too much speculation over why I did not."

"You'll ruin your family for no good reason when the truth comes out."

"No, I won't." Martin smiled. "I'm doing this for the right reason. I love her."

Chapter Seventeen

———◆———

At the door to Lady Heathcote's London townhouse, Iris almost broke down in tears. Her visit to her father that day had been horrible and had broken her heart. When she'd first spoken, he'd looked at her blankly and Iris had needed to remind him of her name. He'd shrugged off the incident but upon her leaving, he'd looked at her so strangely again and only pressed a courtly kiss to her hand rather than his usual buss to her cheek.

She rapped the knocker and almost fell inside as Higgins admitted her. "Miss Hedley, are you all right?"

She nodded, keen to hide her distress from the servant. "Simply exhausted after my long walk."

Higgins knew where she went but they never spoke of her destination. Today he seemed troubled. "You should not go so far on foot next time."

She had no choice but to keep up the ruse. Esme's butler was a kind man and she liked him very much, but she didn't want to inconvenience the staff, and she could not change the method of her travel without being noticed by Talbot. Everything depended on her keeping up the charade just a bit longer. She removed her bonnet and handed it to him. "Is Lady Heathcote at home?"

"She is," he glanced around, "and somewhat impatient about

your return."

"Oh." Iris nodded. Had Esme taken Meriwether's fears to heart and believed she would flee the consequences of her actions? "Then I should not keep her waiting."

"No, you really shouldn't," Esme said irritably at her back.

Iris spun around. "Good morning, my lady."

"It is *now*." Lady Heathcote glanced at the butler. "We will take tea in the parlor as soon as it's convenient."

"Faster than that." Higgins nodded and rushed off to do his mistress' bidding. Esme embraced her and led her into the parlor one flight up. In this private domain where Esme always led her closest friends, Iris felt most secure.

Once the door was closed, Esme caught her chin and stared into her eyes. "You don't look very well today."

"I could not sleep a wink, worrying that someone would be hurt." She drew in a deep breath. "Is there any word about last night in the papers?"

"The robbery took place and the papers say the marquess is furious. Meriwether's men followed the thieves but he would not say to where." Esme led them to a cozy pair of chairs and pressed her down. "How is your father today?"

Iris bowed her head as tears spilled down her cheeks. "Oh Esme, he didn't recognize me when I got there. I had to remind him that I was his daughter."

Esme embraced her and rocked her back and forth.

"It hurts so much to see him like this. What am I going to do? I feel as if I'm being pulled apart."

Esme stroked her back. "Your father loves you."

"He's not himself anymore." She sniffed back her tears and dabbed at her eyes. "He is so changed I don't think he'll ever be the man I remember. Even if he were free again, if I can escape imprisonment and Talbot, he couldn't move about in society like he once did."

"Oh, my dear girl. Now is not the time to worry about the future. There's little we can do but wait. I suspected Alexander was headed for Bedlam a long time ago. Why do you think I've pressed you to make a match? Louth is a good man, sensible, and he will not judge you for your father's odd behavior."

"Did the earl call today?"

"Not yet?"

Iris closed her eyes, remembering her last words with Lord Louth. "He must hate me."

Esme kissed her brow. "He will understand."

"No he won't." Iris burst into fresh tears and let Esme soothe her like a little girl. "I saw the disappointment in his eyes when he'd saw proof of my involvement. He saw the window was open. Why else would he suggest we leave the party so abruptly?"

"To make sure you were safely away before any trouble started?" Esme's suggestion sounded so reasonable, but Iris couldn't quite believe that was the reason. She wished he had said something more last night. Left to her imagination, she had conjured up all forms of horrible ends to their relationship.

A knock sounded on the door and Iris collected herself, grateful for the interruption that forced to think of something beside her own troubles. Higgins brought tea and said nothing regarding her tear-stained face before he went away again.

The pouring of tea proved enough time for her to lose her depressed spirits and attempt a smile as she accepted her teacup.

Esme bit her lip. "Have you settled on a date to become Lord Louth's wife?"

Iris' cup rattled in her hand and she set it aside before she spilled the hot liquid. "No. He wanted my father's permission first. Of course, I've not dared to disclose his location. He will hate that I have kept that a secret from him too."

"Everyone has secrets." Esme blew lightly over her tea.

"Not Louth. He is the most open man I've ever met."

"Hmm, I wish that were true." She set her cup down. "My dear, I have discovered a disagreeable situation that I must warn you of concerning Lord Louth's affairs. I—"

Beneath them on the floor below, male voices rose in argument drifted up from the entrance hall. Iris frowned at the sound and when the parlor door burst open, Lord Windermere was framed in the doorway. "What the hell did you mean by that remark last night?"

Iris shrank into her chair but Esme rose smoothly and approached the angry man without any apparent fear of his temper. "We should speak in private. Excuse us, Miss Hedley.

This might take a little while."

Esme pulled Lord Windermere from the room by his arm. Although Esme pulled the door shut after her, it didn't catch and slowly swung open again. A few moments later, Windermere's voice bellowed through the house as clear as day. "You expect me to believe *you*, of all people?"

What Esme might have replied was too low to be heard but Lord Windermere's next words were painfully loud. "I don't give a damn what you heard, you meddling bitch. How dare you interfere in my life?"

A pause.

"You're wrong," he bellowed again. "And I'll prove it."

The front door slammed and the house grew silent once more.

Iris jumped to her feet and peeked through the front curtains in time to see Lord Windermere stride angrily away from the townhouse, riding crop swinging wildly beside his leg. Higgins chased after him, towing a fine horse missing its rider. She let the curtain fall when they were out of sight. Esme had a knack for discovering unpleasant things. It must have been quite the secret to make the earl behave in such a brutish manner.

It was a while before Esme returned and Iris had time enough to pour another tea for herself while she waited.

Her friend smiled weakly when she returned but her eyes were red-rimmed. "It's for the best."

The words were lightly said but it wasn't hard to see Esme was unsettled by her encounter with Lord Windermere. Iris caught her hand and squeezed. "I'm so sorry for his unpleasantness."

"It's my own fault, but I just couldn't stand to see him made a fool."

Curiosity got the better of her. "I couldn't hear what you said to make him explode like that."

"I tried to be subtle with him and drop enough hints but he simply wouldn't listen. Windermere was about to be duped into marrying a woman because she claimed to be with child. Only there is no child. There never was. He is understandably angry with me but he will discover I spoke the truth soon enough I hope." She sucked in a sharp breath and glanced around. "Now that *that* unpleasantness is in the past, I have a mind to take an outing with you. As much as it pains me, we must expose another secret today."

Iris gaped. She didn't understand what the other secret could be, and when Esme stepped into the adjoining room to fetch her things, she had to admit she was curious. She hurried to her room to change then followed the woman down the stairs. Esme's carriage stood at the ready at the front of the townhouse by the time they stepped outside.

There was also an obvious crowd staring at them from the footpath and at nearby windows, or more particularly at Esme. Had Lord Windermere's outburst carried outside the house? She drew close to Esme to lend her support if it had.

The countess ignored the gawkers with a proud lift to her chin and entered her carriage. Iris, not quite so certain what was going on, or how to react, followed a bit more slowly and overheard a whisper that Esme must have turned down an offer of marriage to have so angered Windermere.

Iris closed the carriage door firmly on the whispers and faced Esme to see her reaction. The lady had closed her eyes and Iris reached for her hand and squeezed. That story would be circulating all through society by nightfall, and in such circumstances it was always the lady's whose reputation was torn apart unfairly.

Once the carriage had moved off, however, Esme burst out laughing and carried on for a good long while. Tears streamed down her cheeks by the end and Iris could only watch in astonishment.

Esme pulled a handkerchief from her pocket and patted her damp face. "Oh, I needed that today. The imaginations of some people never fail to surprise me. As if we would ever want the other in our bed."

"So Lord Windermere didn't propose to you?"

"Oh please, not you too. I couldn't bear it." She held out her hand for silence. "That man will never be my lover, much less a husband. He's much too sure of himself and much too certain about me."

Iris admired confident men, personally, but she supposed another woman might have a different view of them. A widow of Esme's experience and temper might just have an entirely different set of standards she measured men against. "Esme, where are you taking me?"

Her friend squeezed her hand. "As I've just discovered in Lord Windermere's case, seeing is quite often a necessity to believing. It's not far."

"You are being very cryptic again. I do not like that trait in you."

Esme patted her hand. "As time goes on, I'm sure I will confide in you more often but I want to make it clear that I do not like this situation one bit. Ah, here we are."

The coachman had stopped the carriage on Pollen Street in an area Iris was largely unfamiliar with. A groom hurried forward to drop the step and once on the street, Iris glanced around. As far as she could recall, Esme had no acquaintances living nearby. It was actually only a few blocks away from Lord Louth's townhouse. She could easily walk the distance in a few minutes.

"Iris, this way." Esme caught her arm in a tight grip and whispered, "Whatever I say, please play along. We must get inside without a fuss or delay for your own good."

She hurried them up the shallow flight of steps of an unexceptional townhouse and rapped long and hard on the door. After a few minutes, the door opened a crack and an eye peered at them through the gap.

"Please, my friend needs help desperately," Esme pleaded, wringing her hands ineffectually.

The door swung wide and an older woman with a kind face was framed in the doorway. "I am Mrs. Hughes. How can I be of assistance, madam?"

Esme barged in, towing Iris with her into the house before she could protest. When Iris glanced back, she squinted at the woman who'd opened the door. If memory served, she was the nice woman she'd met in the park when she'd been walking with Lord Louth and his cousin. The one with the tiny babe in the fancy wicker perambulator who Iris had stopped to admire. "We are so sorry for disturbing you."

Esme finally stopped and glanced around. "Could my friend have a glass of water, perhaps? She's taken a giddy spell and I'm quite concerned."

"Certainly." The woman bustled off to the rear of the property.

Iris wasted no time to lean toward Esme. "What do you think you're doing, barging into a stranger's home like this? Are you mad? The house is in mourning."

She winked. "It's not her home."

"Well, no matter whose home it is, you're being very rude." Iris crossed her arms over her chest. "You will have to apologize for your behavior. Do you even know the family that lives here?"

"No family lives here. Until recently, this was Vivian Rose's home. Her protector provided her with lodgings during their arrangement."

Iris frowned at that. Many men kept mistresses in London. She didn't need to invade their homes to know it. "And what has that to do with anything or either of us?"

"It may matter a great deal to you in the future." Esme paced the lower room and then smiled. "Would it surprise you to learn that Lord Louth owns this house?"

She glanced around swiftly in shock. "No!"

"Oh, yes. He's the reason we are here. I will not have a friend cruelly disappointed if I can help it. Especially not now, with the stress of your father bringing you so much pain."

Iris' palms grew slick. Louth had kept his mistress so close to his home even after they'd ended things? I tight ball of disappointment filled her chest. He'd promised he had no attachments. "We should go."

"Not until you see what he's hiding from you. You have put him upon a pedestal and yourself in the gutter when neither of you are exactly the model of propriety. You can make up your own mind about whether you have a future with him after this." Esme moved to a wall and slammed her palm against the papered surface three times. Very loudly. Then, calm as can be, she took a chair.

The servant returned in a hurry, a glass of water slopping over the rim to drench her hand, her eyes wild. "What was that noise?"

Her words trailed off as a child began to cry close by.

Esme smiled tightly. "I've no idea."

The wailing continued while the woman dithered. Iris took the glass and set it aside. "Perhaps you should attend to the little girl."

Esme's eyes rounded. "You know about her?"

"Yes. We met in the park, when I was with Lord Louth and his cousin. Mrs. Hughes, isn't it? The child she cares for is very beautiful."

Esme's eyes narrowed then she stood and faced the other woman. "I see. Then perhaps you could introduce me as well?"

"I don't know about that." Mrs. Hughes wrung her hands as the child's wailing intensified.

"Well, I do," Esme insisted. "I'm no authority on the rearing of the young but I cannot imagine it is good for any child to cry in that fashion for much longer."

Mrs. Hughes nodded slowly then hurried from the room. Esme followed her and Iris did too, puzzled by Esme's insistence on seeing a baby. The other woman scooped up the protesting bundle and attempted to calm her.

Dark eyes, dark hair.

And then it hit her, so hard she had to grip the cradle edge for support. This was Lord Louth's property. He kept a mistress here. And the child?

Must be his.

Iris had misjudged Lord Louth indeed. She glared at Esme. "I would have believed you. There was no need to drag me here."

That she had to raise her voice a little at the last because the child appeared inconsolable was a testament to the child's temper.

Mrs. Hughes attempts to chivvy the child into better spirits wasn't working either, unfortunately. She patted the babe's bottom ineffectually. "I'm so sorry," she said loudly in the end. "My mistress' death has been a difficult time. I never had children myself. I am only the housekeeper."

All the air rushed from Iris' lungs. The mistress had died? Dear God. The infant wasn't just illegitimate but an orphan too. Her chest squeezed painfully at the injustices often served to those too innocent to protect themselves.

She squared her shoulders and held out her hands. She was

well enough acquainted with children to feel confident she could be of use. "Give her to me."

Mrs. Hughes gaped and Esme gasped out loud. "It's not your problem."

"She's a child, and upset because of our arrival." When Mrs. Hughes hesitated, Iris took the child and brought the squirming bundle close to her chest. It took a while but eventually the girl calmed enough to hiccup.

Iris arranged her more comfortably on her shoulder and the child burped loudly in her ear. "Ah, so that was the problem, sweetheart. There now, I'm sure that feels better."

Now that the house no longer rang with the child's cries, a silence so complete engulfed her. She glanced at Esme. "What are we really doing here?"

"Visiting Lord Louth's daughter," she replied softly.

Iris glanced down at the child in her arms. Dark like her intended, rounded face so sweet once she no longer wailed. The resemblance was quite obvious to Iris now and her heart broke. He already had a daughter. But why was he so against her carrying his children?

She paled, remembering his earlier concerns about becoming her lover. He'd claimed his size was a problem and she did not believe he'd only had concerns about intimacy. She faced the housekeeper. "Why did the child's mother die?"

Mrs. Hughes sighed. "The birth was too much for her delicate constitution. The child too large for her to bear."

Iris held the babe a little closer against her chest and swept her fingers across the soft dark hair. No wonder Louth believed they wouldn't suit at first. It also explained why he didn't want her to become pregnant with his child. He feared she'd not survive a birth. He blamed himself for this situation. "I never suspected he had a proper reason for his hesitation."

Mrs. Hughes wrung her hands. "He has been very concerned for how this situation would impact his cousin's chances of making a match."

"Yes, of course." But that wasn't what she had meant. He'd said he didn't want to lose her.

"Not to mention protecting his own reputation, I should think." Esme held her hand out for the child. "Well, I think that settles that."

Mrs. Hughes appeared embarrassed. "It wasn't his fault. My mistress concealed the pregnancy from him. He would have married her I think."

That explained a great deal of his behavior, especially his dislike of her intentions to become a mistress. He knew first hand the problems she might have faced. She was holding the one complication he'd harped on about the most. "You are wrong Esme. This changes nothing as far as I'm concerned."

Esme met Iris' gaze, her expression startled. "You know what society will say of the girl's existence better than anyone. If you thought your father's bad decisions made your life difficult, imagine hers if you can when she is old enough to understand."

"Yes," Iris sighed and rocked the child, noting she was falling asleep in her arms. "She'll be a pariah, sneered at behind her back."

Mrs. Hughes clucked her tongue and stretched out her arms for the babe. "Her father will take care of her. I should return her to bed. She prefers a routine."

"Thank you, Mrs. Hughes." She grazed the girl's cheek with her fingertip before reluctantly handing her over to the housekeeper. "I mean her no harm, but I think it would be best if you did not mention my visit to Lord Louth for the time being."

The housekeeper glanced at her suspiciously. "Why is that? Why shouldn't he know?"

She sighed. "It should have remained his secret to tell me when he was ready, if he ever wanted to."

When she met Esme's gaze, her friend shrugged. "I wanted to protect you."

She smiled sadly. Esme didn't want her to be fooled but it was too late to spare her now. "I love you for it but this isn't the way."

Mrs. Hughes glanced between them and nodded slowly. "I will conceal your visit for the time being."

"I appreciate that." Iris watched the child go with a heavy heart. She'd never suspected Louth of having a child. She had actually begun to wonder if he disliked them. Either way the child would suffer. Children always did.

She turned for the door blindly as tears filled her eyes. "I'd like to leave if you don't mind. I have to think."

Chapter Eighteen

---•◆•---

After only five minutes waiting inside the Marshalsea Prison, Martin's skin crawled. This was no place for any man, woman or child to be for any length of time. He was appalled that Iris had come here every day to see her father. He was also furious that Alexander Hedley had allowed it.

Despite the likelihood of social ruin, he hadn't been able to walk away from the woman he loved. They hadn't spoken since the dinner at Ettington's and the robbery had apparently gone off without a hitch. When he'd paid a call on her the next afternoon in the hope of discussing her part in the illegal activities, he'd been informed she was indisposed for callers and requested to return in a few days' time. The time apart had made him impatient and equally worried about how she fared.

A whispery trail of fog and wood smoke clung to the eaves of the brick barracks before him where the indebted of London waited out their penance for making the mistake of having no funds to pay their way. A mean place, not one measure of elegance or beauty within the cobblestone yard he paced. He was sure that he'd made the correct decision to come here. It frustrated him to think he'd not heard of this travesty sooner.

He ignored the glances of the curious inmates while he waited for the turnkey to fetch Alexander Hedley from the room he shared high up the barracks block. It had taken him considerably more time than he'd first anticipated to settle Mr.

Hedley's debts in full to everyone's satisfaction. Each debtor had to be found, negotiated with and appeased, and then forced to sign letters that extinguished Mr. Hedley's debt to them.

The last one had proved almost unwilling to meet with him to discuss the matter of settlement, and for no good reason Martin could see. Only explaining his intention to marry Iris had secured Mr. Talbot's untidy scrawl. The man had seemed very pleased to hear she would become a countess.

At his side, a groom fidgeted, clearly uneasy with his presence in the Marshalsea. "Shall I have the carriage take another turn, my lord?"

"No." He wanted to make sure that when Hedley finally came to him, he could whisk the poor fellow out of here as soon as possible.

Voices grew louder as rushed footsteps echoed off the building around him and he sharpened his gaze on the far staircase. Martin had not attempted to meet with Mr. Hedley himself until this very moment. He hadn't wanted to make the man anxious about his release in case the resolution of the debts proved protracted.

Mr. Fitzhugh, the turnkey of the prison, was followed by a small man Martin barely recognized as Alexander. Grayed, overlong hair, sideburns untrimmed, ill-fitting clothes that marked the man had lost weight since coming to live here. Martin had imagined incarceration would have changed Hedley, but not make him appear so much older. Despite his concern, he smiled broadly, stepped forward and extended his hand. "Mr. Hedley. So good to see you again."

The little man looked up as he shook it. "It *is* you? I thought the turnkey was having a lark."

"Not at all." He glanced about for luggage. The turnkey's assistant carried a single wooden trunk. Not even a hat on Hedley's head and no gloves to be seen about him. Was that all Hedley possessed? Fearing it was so, he gestured the groom forward to collect the trunk and the man easily balanced it on his shoulder as if it weighed nothing. The groom marched smartly for the gate and the waiting carriage.

"We can be on our way now."

Hedley looked to the turnkey for permission leave. "You'll

give my best to the committee when you see them next?"

The turnkey, a man who had seemed genuinely puzzled to be rid of Hedley when Martin had first arrived, nodded slowly. "Farewell, Mr. Hedley. Conversation will grow dull in your absence but that's for the best now I'm sure. Say goodbye to your pretty daughter for me. Tell her to take good care of herself."

The assistant rushed for the gate and let the groom out.

When the door swung wide, Martin strode for freedom too. He had the overwhelming urge to return home to bathe. His skin prickled with an itch he didn't like.

Hedley seemed slower to follow and by the time Martin was at the closed carriage doorway, the man was only just sticking his head out the portal. His eyes were a little wild as he glanced around the busy roadway. Perhaps the surprise hadn't been such a grand idea after all.

Martin smiled again. "Come, Hedley. Your daughter is waiting."

At the mention of Iris, the little man hurried forward. "Yes, my daughter. Is she well? I have not seen her for so long."

"I believe so, but she will be happier once she knows you are far from here." Hedley climbed in and Martin followed. "I never mentioned my errand. I thought surprise was best all around."

Hedley licked his lips and glanced around the carriage interior. He carefully caressed the blue-velvet cushioned bench he sat on. "Why have you done this? What do you want?"

"I want nothing. It was the right thing to do." Martin tapped on the roof and had the driver move off. He placed his hat on his knee. "I had no idea you were incarcerated until the Duke of Exeter explained your situation."

The old man rubbed his thigh. "I told my daughter not to mention me."

"I wish she had. I thought something was wrong when she would not speak of you. I would have ensured your release much sooner had I known the truth."

Hedley glanced down. He seemed to shrink in size even further, and it wasn't until his shoulders shook that Martin realized his emotions were overset. The man was crying and trying to hide it. Martin glanced out the window and did his best not to notice while Hedley collected himself.

A few sniffs later, Martin dug into his pocket, retrieved a handkerchief and passed it to the other man as it appeared he had none about him. Next to Hedley's yellowed linen shirt and dark hands, the handkerchief seemed shockingly clean and bright.

Martin glanced away. Hedley needed the help of a valet, and soon. A faint musty odor permeated the carriage. The scent of stale sweat and fear. "We should discuss your situation."

"Yes, of course. I shall repay you, my lord. I promise. As soon as possible."

"Think nothing of that for now." Martin shrugged. "What I need most is your daughter, sir."

The older man peeked at him through red-rimmed eyes. "Iris is a good girl."

"And it is my intention to marry her." He took in Hedley's gaunt face and watery eyes. He would offer the man refuge for the foreseeable future. Hedley was too weak to be alone and unprotected until the robbery business was concluded. Iris would fret if her father lived anywhere else but close to her, and with good reason. He needed a month of tender care and more than a few solid meals under his belt before he would look healthy again. "I should like you to be my guest for what remains of your life, sir."

Hedley's mouth fell open. "A guest?"

Martin nodded. "There is plenty of room at Holly House that it shall be no trouble. Undoubtedly your daughter will want to see you every day, now that you have your freedom returned. Her happiness means the world to me. Staying as my guest will barely cause a ripple, I assure you."

Hedley smoothed his hand down a muddy-brown waistcoat that had seen better days and did not immediately jump to accept. "I should discuss the matter with my daughter first. It will be strange to us for me to be your guest while she lives at home."

He frowned. "Iris will make her home with me when we marry."

"Yes, of course. You were going to marry her. That's right." Hedley nodded slowly but he looked confused. "She is young of course but that is beside the point."

"You'll have to stay in my home tonight without her, of course. It's far too late to disturb a vicar to perform the marriage ceremony but I do have a license. I thought we could discuss her settlement in the morning after you've rested." He peered through the window to check their location. "Not too long now. I sent a servant ahead to Holly House to have a bedchamber prepared for your arrival. Your daughter will be completely surprised at seeing you tomorrow."

Hedley swallowed. "You go to too much trouble."

"Nonsense. I am merely repaying my debt to you. Where would I be, if not for your wisdom?"

At that, the older man winced and glanced down. "Not so wise if I ended up where I did and my daughter forced to live without me."

"Lady Heathcote was a suitable chaperone, I assure you." Holly House loomed. Martin saw no point in addressing the issue of the robberies with Hedley. He would not broach the subject until Iris was his wife, and then only if she agreed and was present to defend herself. "As for your daughter, she has handled her reduced circumstances with a grace many ladies do not manage under less trying conditions."

Hedley smiled but it seemed a touch wary to Martin. As the carriage stopped, he was grateful to step outside and escape to fresher air.

The front door opened and Martin chivvied Mr. Hedley inside past Gibbs before he was seen in his current state on the street. A bath was essential, and soon. A tailor would need to be summoned as well so he was better dressed for the wedding.

Gibbs took Martin's hat and addressed their guest. "Welcome to Holly House, Mr. Hedley. I am Gibbs, Lord Louth's London butler. A room has been prepared for your arrival and if you've no objections, I shall act as your valet for the duration of your stay."

Trust Gibbs to assume a role that required a delicate touch. Hedley likely hadn't had a servant in years and given the small dimensions of his trunk, would require many things replaced. Gibbs, of similar age to Hedley, could also be counted on to make the man at home without being obvious about it.

"Thank you." Hedley glanced around nervously. "Where is

my daughter?"

Martin smiled. "I will send a note to Lady Heathcote this evening and ensure Iris comes here in the morning rather than to the Marshalsea, as has been her habit."

"Thank you."

Gibbs beamed. "This way, sir."

Martin trailed behind the pair as they headed upstairs. As much as he wanted to see Iris' face when she understood her father had been released from debtor's prison, he was wary. Something about Alexander Hedley's behavior seemed out of place to him, and it was not just the shock of surprise freedom.

When Hedley passed into the bedchamber prepared for his use, he made no comment about his surroundings, and when water was delivered for washing, stood quietly as Gibbs attended him. He'd never seen a man so lacking animation. He was also indeed painfully thin once his coat was removed, but appeared unconcerned about his condition. He didn't even protest when his hair was cut and he was dressed in a borrowed nightshirt then settled before the fireplace with a cup of tea and biscuits.

"Iris will be expecting me soon," he told Gibbs suddenly.

"Your daughter will be here tomorrow, sir," Martin reminded the older man, strolling into the room. "A hot meal, a good night's sleep and you'll be fresh as a daisy to receive her."

Hedley nodded. "That's true. Mama always says a proper rest can take your worries away."

He raised his teacup to his lips with a gentle smile, and sipped. His hands shook the tiniest amount as he sat it back down and snatched up a biscuit. He smiled then stared off into space as if being outside of the prison was of no consequence. He hadn't even looked out the window.

Martin caught Gibbs' eye and moved toward the door. They stopped just outside the doorway to talk in private. "Does he seem all right to you?"

"Forgive me, but no. I don't think he's been well." Gibbs bit his lip. "It's a horrible thing for a gentleman to live in the Marshalsea, I'm told. I'll take good care of him tonight and I'm sure he'll be more himself in the morning."

"Thank you, Gibbs." He glanced along the hall, puzzled by the silence. "Is my cousin at home?"

"Yes, my lord. She and Lady Ettington retired to her studio some time ago."

Martin groaned, remembering Ettington's hint that his wife would lead his cousin astray. He was sure it would be the other way around. "I'd hoped to speak to her alone but I'd better share the news of our guest. She gets so shrill when surprised. The marchioness will hear what I've done anyway, so there's no point keeping him a secret."

He headed up the hall and tapped on the door of the room Whitney had taken over for her art. There was a flurry of activity inside before Whitney answered. "Yes?"

"It's Martin. I understand the marchioness is with you." He set his hand to the knob, anticipating an entreaty to enter. When he didn't get one he asked, "Might I come in?"

"No," both women squeaked. "Can you come back later?" Whitney pleaded.

"Later?" Whitney had never once sent him away from her studio so he was surprised by her refusal.

"Yes, quite a bit later, actually." There was silence beyond the door a long moment. "A few hours at the very least."

"But I have news." He listened hard. "We have a guest."

"Has Miss Hedley come to call?"

"No. Her father has come to stay as our guest."

Soft footfalls raced across the room before Whitney unlatched the door and opened it a crack. There was a smear of paint on her cheek and a bright flush to her cheeks. She had undoubtedly been painting again. "That is unexpected."

Whitney did not normally hide her projects, so he pushed lightly at the door. It didn't budge and he suspected her foot was behind the door and preventing his access. "Yes. He will be staying with us indefinitely. He'll rest tonight then tomorrow I'll send for his daughter."

"Splendid." Whitney pushed the door shut in his face and the lock turned. "I will come and see you later to discuss the matter further," Whitney promised through the door."

Martin set his hands to the doorframe as a lady giggled. "Pixie, has my cousin kidnapped you to sit for one of her ridiculous portraits? Do I need to rescue you or should I send for Ettington so he can break down another door?"

"Don't!" the marchioness screeched. "It's supposed to be a surprise for his birthday and you will spoil everything if you even mention I was here."

He stood back, satisfied the marchioness was there of her own free will. He did not want to know what kind of portrait Whitney was painting but if Pixie had arranged the private sitting he would not interfere. "Very well."

"Thank you, my lord." Pixie giggled. "And congratulations on your imminent marriage, too. Miss Hedley is lovely."

Was nothing he ever did a secret? "Thank you."

Chapter Nineteen

———◆———

Iris took a deep breath as she approached the Earl of Louth's front door. She could not believe the message in the note sent to Lady Heathcote last night and was here to see for herself if it was true.

At her side, Esme was still trying to wake up. "Slower, my dear, Alexander will still be in his bed if you do not take a moment more to behave like a lady. What would he say if he saw you rushing about like this?"

"He would give me that look he favors if he were in his right mind." Iris rapped on the wood, aware that her early morning call might not be welcomed.

Lord Louth opened the door himself. "You're early, good. He's just finishing his second breakfast."

She stared at him, her chest heaving from her anxiety. "My father really is here?"

The earl smiled and nodded. "Oh yes. Collected him myself yesterday afternoon and have been wildly entertained with stories of his childhood since he woke the house at sunrise."

Panic filled her. The past had become her father's favorite place. More so than the here and now. "Might I see him?"

"He's in the breakfast room, which you might recall is behind the stairs."

Even though it was terribly rude, Iris ran the length of the hall and burst into the breakfast room.

Her father speared a beefsteak and plopped it onto his plate. "The food is indeed excellent."

Whitney's eyes sparkled with laughter. "It is, truly. Only the best for Lord Louth's guests."

She stood and joined Iris at the door. "Your father insists we're in a posting house and won't take no for an answer. He's very good at a jest, isn't he? I swear he believes every word he utters."

Iris pressed a cold hand to her face and then she skirted the table. She took the chair next to her father and captured his hand. "Father, what are you doing here?"

"Eating." He pressed his head to hers then stabbed his steak. "I've been told to make myself quite at home and I shall."

He gobbled up a forkful and, cheeks bursting, smiled brightly as he chewed.

Esme joined them and had the butler serve her tea and toast.

"You could do with a steak too, missy."

Esme grinned at him. "And spoil my figure? I will not, sir."

"Sir, indeed." Her father rocked as he laughed, as if Esme had told the finest joke he'd ever heard, and then tossed a sausage on her plate.

Esme accepted the meat without comment but her smile was sincere. "I'll stay with him. You should speak to your intended."

She would have to explain about her father. About his illness and that his obsession with old news was no laughing matter. "Thank you."

She stood and stepped back into the hall. Lord Louth waited, propping up the wall. "He's in fine spirits this morning. He wasn't half as lively last night."

"I'm sorry if he's been any trouble."

"Not a bit." He straightened. "We should talk in private, I think."

Iris nodded but her heart was pounding as she followed him into another room.

She wrung her hands, glancing about the masculine study as anxiety filled her. Louth really must be upset if he didn't at least smile.

The door clicked shut then the key turned in the lock. "You place me in an uncomfortable position."

"I am sorry."

An exasperated expression passed over his face. "When I was a young man, I was given the most valuable piece of advice of my life. Be able to pay your debts immediately or don't commit the funds. While many of my contemporaries were wasting their fortunes at cards, and running up bills all over Town, I kept my eye on the future and funds in my pocket."

"A wise decision."

"But do you know why I took that piece of advice to heart?" He stared at her and she trembled. "I'll tell you why. Your father said it. Because of him, I have a fortune to support myself and my family, and plenty to spare."

Iris winced at the mention of her father's advice. Many men might attribute their success to wise advice but it was the first time her father had ever been specifically singled out. Lord Louth was undoubtedly not the sort to spread false praise. "I am glad of that."

"Your father is one of the few men I admire so well that I would dare to quote them." He circled her. His eyes narrowed. "My cousin has a way of saying things that might sound completely honest, but are in fact lacking certain particulars of complete honesty. You never spoke of your father so you didn't have to lie to me."

Iris closed her eyes. He likely knew it all but would he make her say the words?

"Your father's location would not have had any bearing on my decision to marry you," Louth proclaimed, his voice dropping to a soothing whisper. "I would have preferred you were honest with me about your situation from the beginning. Having the duke point out my naivety is not a pleasant experience."

She kept her gaze lowered rather than reveal her misery. "I am so sorry."

"I'm sure you thought you had good reasons." He sighed. "The moment your father lost his fortune, society turned its back on you both. Your mistake was imagining I could be just as cruel."

Iris squirmed and glanced up guiltily.

The earl shook his head. "Please don't look at me like that. I am not judging you. Everyone makes mistakes."

"So many in society have."

"You lost everything."

"Everything that was important." She gripped her hands till her knuckles turned white. Her friends, her life, her future.

He held out one hand for her to take. "You must have missed him terribly?"

Although she trembled, she placed her palm over his. Iris glanced down at their joined hands and made a sound that might have signaled her agreement.

He caught her chin and raised her eyes to his. "Why did you not tell me from the beginning where he was?"

"He is my father," she said. "I didn't want to see the pity in your eyes."

"Good God, woman, have I not proven you can trust me these past weeks?" the earl snapped. "You put your reputation at risk daily by just going to visit him alone."

She lifted her chin defiantly and found Lord Louth scowling at her. She paled. She'd had no choice but to lie about her life over the past year, particularly the past few months. She was ashamed that her father had accumulated so much debt. She was ashamed of herself.

"Alexander Hedley has no further debts at the present moment and I prefer that it remain as such," Louth continued, moving so close she could feel his breath on her face.

She stared at him. "How could that be?"

"I repaid every single mark against him. He is a free man now."

Heat burned her cheeks. "I'm sure he will agree to curb his spending."

"Damn right he will. He'll remain as my guest for the rest of his life so I have my way."

"You would keep him prisoner?"

"I would keep him, if it made his daughter happy. I have had a long discussion with your father this morning and the agreements are prepared." Louth dropped to one knee. "Miss Iris Jane Hedley, would you do me the honor of becoming my wife?"

She gaped at him. "How could you marry me? You don't

know what I've done."

"But I do. You're the spy among the *ton*, setting up all the robberies."

The room spun and she collapsed onto the floor beside him. "I was so afraid to tell you."

"Exeter thought to warn me at dinner the other night. He wasn't a happy man about the danger his nephew placed himself in with the trap that was being set. He was also the one kind enough to clarify why I was having so much trouble locating your father."

Iris bent her head. "He wouldn't look at me that night."

"Exeter will overcome it eventually. I hear Meriwether is very determined that nothing get in his way. He will find whoever is pulling the strings."

"Talbot." She squared her shoulders. "Charles Talbot is behind it all and threatened to hurt my father if I did not do what he wanted."

"You don't say? That filthy prig. He acted so concerned for you, too." The earl pulled her into his lap and settled them comfortably on the floor. "Miss Hedley, I am still waiting on an answer. I can protect my wife and her father."

But who would protect him. "I'm sure you would try."

"Then give me your answer. Will we marry today or not?"

She drew back and searched his face for reassurance she'd heard him correctly. "Today?"

"Better than too late," he said quietly. "You father will never want for another meal and you will have every luxury I can offer."

"And there are always my lessons to continue?"

He leaned forward, and kissed her cheek. "Damn the lessons. Tonight you graduate."

She tried very hard to hold back a smile but since she'd been dreaming of him for so long, she couldn't quell her anticipation. "I would be honored, my lord."

Iris climbed to her feet unaided but her knees were weak with shame and hope. The earl drew her into his arms and wrapped her tightly against him. His sure and certain grip dispelled any lingering unease that he was truly cross with her. He cupped the back of her head and held her close. "Haven't I done my best to make you comfortable, Iris?"

She turned her face into his chest. "Yes, my lord."

"Have we not become good friends these past weeks? You can tell me anything."

But would he tell her tell her of the child he'd fathered? A child she yearned to care for herself?

She placed her arms around his waist, unsure if she could deny this man anything. What had started as a desperate need for an independent future had shifted to a private wish to belong with him.

He kissed her cheek. "I won't let anything happen to you."

"My father promised much the same." She caught the earl's eye. He met her gaze with steadfast conviction. He believed every word he said. He sincerely wanted to protect her. But what about her father's growing odd manner? Did Louth know her father well enough to sense the change in him?

She rose on her toes and sought his mouth for a kiss to avoid that discussion. The earl bent himself to seal their lips together and the next moment she was swept up in his arms.

They did not kiss for long, but Iris was trembling by the time it ended.

Louth nibbled at the skin of her neck and her pulse raced. "You should return to your father. I need to go out for a little while but the vicar will be arriving at two o'clock to perform the marriage ceremony."

She hoped he wouldn't regret his generous offer to make her his wife. She wasn't exactly a good choice. "Thank you."

He swooped to kiss her firmly then took her hand and pulled her toward the door. They could hear her father's laughter in the drawing room but when they reached the doorway, she gaped in shock. Louth's mouth fell open too at the scene.

Her father crouched on top of a lovely brocade chair, waving a riding crop about as if he were racing.

"Alexander Hedley," Iris shouted.

He leaped from the chair. "Sorry, Mother."

She hurried to him, concerned by that slip. "But I'm Iris. Your daughter, remember."

He squinted at her. "Of course you are. Have you no greeting for your old father?"

She stepped into his embrace, squeezing back tears. "Papa, what were you thinking? Grown men do not stand on other people's furniture."

The man gestured to Lord Louth. "Lord Louth said to make myself at home and I have done so."

"But you still should not stand on his furniture." Her future husband merely smiled at the situation. She kissed her father's cheek, belatedly noting that his hair had been cut, nails manicured and he was wearing a new suit of clothes. "You're looking very fine today."

"Such a kind girl." He embraced her tightly. "My daughter is getting married today so I'm told I have to look my best."

Tears pricked her eyes. "Yes she is. And she's very fortunate in her husband."

When she glanced toward the door, she discovered Lord Louth had slipped away. She couldn't blame him. Her father's antics must have been embarrassing for him.

Chapter Twenty

No matter how much he tried, Martin could not wait to get his wife alone, preferably into bed. He understood her father needed her. Hell, everyone had needed her since they'd spoken their vows before a select company of friends invited for the hastily arranged wedding that afternoon.

She drew back the bedding in her father's room and settled him under the comforter. "Are you warm enough, Father?"

The older man smiled as if he were tipsy. "Right as rain and twice as tired. It was such a long day. I didn't see Fitzhugh anywhere about."

"Of course not." Iris cast an apologetic glance in his direction. "He wasn't invited to the wedding."

"Did someone marry?" Her father grinned but Martin didn't believe the man was teasing his daughter. Over the course of the day, he'd become suspicious that Hedley didn't remember very much of what was told to him and this was only further proof.

She smoothed back his hair as if he was a child and made no response to his question. Iris had brushed aside all his hints about the matter of Hedley's forgetfulness so far, much to his disappointment. The discussion could wait until tomorrow but not for much longer than that. If his suspicions were correct, steps would have to be taken for the man's care. Hedley had almost released his water off the back terrace before their wedding guests. If not for Gibbs' quick action, Hedley would have bared his backside to the entire room.

Iris bent to pick up a book her father had knocked off the side table earlier, revealing the outline of her lush bottom. *Definitely time for bed.*

He excused himself and retreated to wait in the hall. As much as he might wish otherwise, he couldn't hold back his lustful thoughts forever. They were married. He was anxious about tonight and hoped Iris never regretted marrying him after making love to him.

Just as he was beginning to fear he'd have to drag her from her father's room, she appeared at his side. "He's asleep."

"Gibbs has been instructed to remain as his valet for the foreseeable future, Iris."

Her face lit up with a smile quite unlike any she'd bestowed on him before at the mention of her title. It was as if a thousand candles had illuminated her and swamped her in their soft glow. "I like hearing that, my lord."

"Martin will do." He scooped her up into his arms and headed for his bedchamber before any other distractions got in the way. Iris looped her arms about his neck with a sigh and clung to him as if she would never let him go. And he wouldn't either. He would do anything to keep her happy.

The room was lit with warm light from the hearth and little else.

He lowered his wife to her dainty feet and knelt to remove her shoes.

When he stood again, he was reminded just how tiny Iris was. He swallowed his apprehension about the coming night and pressed a soft kiss to her lips. As always, his body hummed with lust the moment her tongue slipped past his lips to turn a tender moment into a passionate one. She tasted so very sweet. He could get drunk from the taste of her if he wasn't careful.

When their lips parted, he drew back. "Wife."

"Husband." She grinned.

She kissed him again, tangling her fingers in his short hair and pressing close. There was nothing he wanted more than to be inside her, to complete her education in the sensual arts as she'd planned. Patience would serve her better though, so he ran his hands up and down her back, cupping her delightful bottom and torturing himself with the feel of her.

He pressed her firmly against his body, the ridge of his erection hard against her belly. Her fingers delved beneath the waistband of his trousers and she slipped the buttons free. As much as he appreciated the freedom, he feared it too. Too little thought and consideration and he'd hurt her.

Martin carried Iris to his bed and paused at the edge of it. He loosened his grip, intending to place her down. "There is no need to rush."

She shook her head, and then cupped the side of his face. "Don't deny me what I want."

He closed his eyes briefly and gently laid her on the soft mattress. Iris smiled at him and his heart tripped painfully. She was not afraid. She reached for him, intending to pull him on top of her immediately. He shook his head and removed his upper clothes first.

Her eyes widened as his bare chest came into view. She sat up and ran her tiny hands over his skin. "You're beautiful and so strong."

Since his trousers were already unbuttoned they slipped low of their own accord, and he stepped out of them quickly before turning back to Iris.

Her lazy grin, glued low to his crotch, brought tingling warmth to the base of his spine. At her urging, he covered her body with his. "Is that what you want? To be under me with no chance of escape?"

"Yes, but more too." She examined his shoulders even as her hips rose to brush across his erection. "Make love to me."

He kissed her brow. He was a heavy man and, after a bare moment flush against her, he propped himself on his elbows and removed his weight until they barely touched. "I will. But it will be slowly done. I'm too big for you."

"For now perhaps, but I will grow accustomed." Iris traced his collarbone with the tip of one finger, and then dipped to circle his nipple. "We will have to practice often I expect."

"A few times a month."

"Several times a week would be better. I'm told it will be easier over time."

He jerked back in surprise. "You spoke to Esme about me?"

"No, Esme spoke to me. She thought that given the absence of a mother, she must explain intimacy to me. I'm glad she did. I'll not allow you to sway me with your own fears."

Martin flipped Iris over so he could reach the buttons on the back of her gown. "I have reason to be afraid."

Reasons he couldn't share yet. He drew back, paused a moment, then lowered his lips to her neck.

Iris sighed deeply as he nibbled on her skin. "Yes, just like that."

Martin's head clouded with lust as Iris grew pliant in his arms. He rolled her to her back and glanced at her face to find her eyes hooded, her expression one of utter trust and expectation. He kissed her lips, astounded by how she moved him. He'd never intended this but he would make love to her. He didn't dare disappoint her when she was so adamant about becoming his wife in every sense of the word. He would look after her.

He traced her skin, from her slender neck, over her collarbone and down to her chest with the tips of his fingers. She was so tiny lying at his side. He had to be careful. The modest gown she wore hid her breasts but a quick glance confirmed her nipples were hard points beneath. He covered her breast with the palm of one hand, and then thumbed her nipple gently through the gown. Iris arched her back, until she brushed against him.

The top of her gown gaped and he slid the garment down, uncovering her shoulders and the tops of her full breasts. The barrier of a corset and chemise remained between them. He tested how tightly she was bound in the corset. The garment moved and he dug his fingers beneath on each side of her body and shoved it down as far as he could. Iris gasped softly.

The chemise had followed the corset and he admired Iris in the most improper of states.

Pale and perfect. Her breasts were white and full. The pink tips of her nipples grew even more obvious as he stared at them. He touched one reverently. Iris hissed and he smothered her breast with his hand. Martin kneaded her flesh gently and then plucked at the nipple. He met Iris' gaze and smiled. "Mine now."

He lowered his head and suckled at her breast. Iris stiffened in his arms. As expected, she soon grew used to the sensations he evoked and even cupped his head to hold him against her.

Martin hitched her skirts up to her thighs and gently pushed her legs wider apart so he could settle his weight between them.

When he reseated his hips at the apex of her thighs and pressed against her there, a low moan spilled from her lips. Martin could not suck her breast and tease her quim at the same time so he switched between suckling her breast and rubbing against her sex. Iris clawed at his head and shoulders. Incoherent words tumbling from her lips.

The sound of her encouragement made him ache with need to be inside her. However, Iris could not be ready for him. He had enough experience with women to know she needed to find her own release first before he could even think of joining with her.

He slipped one hand beneath her skirts, teased up her slender thigh to touch her curls. Iris bucked again and a full-throated moan filled his ears. He parted her lower lips and skimmed her sex with one finger, discovering scorching wet heat and excitement beyond his dreams.

This time *he* moaned. He touched her clitoris with steady pressure and then swirled around the hard nubbin until Iris jerked and came apart.

He slid his finger downward and pressed inside her body. Her sex pulsed around his digit and he fingered her, mimicking making love. When her spasms eased off, he added another finger and discovered Iris wasn't quite as tight as he feared she would be.

He added a third finger to her sheath and kept them there as he eased away to see her face. A soft smiled played around her lips, her eyes drowsy with sated lust. He quickly stripped her gown and petticoat away, the corset proved more complicated but he mastered the lacing and laid her bare across his bed. He hovered over her and teased her with his fingers again. "You will need to lift your legs so you twine around me when I come into you."

Iris threw one leg around him and the action opened her body. He slipped easily in and out of her sheath. She was ready.

But still doubts filled him. She was so small. Martin withdrew and positioned himself at her entrance.

He met her gaze and his breath caught at the sight of Iris so utterly abandoned by desire. Her breasts bobbed with each breath, her cool legs lifted higher to his waist and tightened around him. Iris regarded him with obvious lust and beckoned him close.

The heat of her damp skin against his cock threatened his patience. "You are so beautiful."

He kissed her cheek and she twisted to capture his lips in a deeper kiss. She ran her tongue over his bottom lip and then caught it gently between her teeth, her eyes flashing with mischief.

Never had he wanted a woman more.

Iris cupped his face with both hands. "What are you waiting for? I'm ready."

The whispered hot words against his lips crushed his resistance. He pressed forward.

———◆———

Iris wiggled. God lord, he was big. If it were any other man, she'd be terrified to be in this situation, helpless and impaled on the largest manhood she'd ever imagined. If not for his gentleness and hesitation, she'd never have enjoyed his slow possession so much. He'd entered her so carefully she'd feared he'd stop each time he withdrew, but now he was still inside her and his chest heaved at the effort of holding back.

She swept her hands up the torso hovering immobile above her and marveled at Martin's restraint and determination not to hurt her more than necessary. His skin was slick and hot and his body tense. If he didn't continue now, she'd scream.

After a long moment, he met her gaze. "Are you all right?"

She nodded swiftly and rocked her hips experimentally in an attempt to make him move. He'd made her wait so long for this moment she was anxious that he was pleased. "Yes. Are you?"

He smothered a laugh against her hair and drew back his hips in a long slide that made her moan. "Very satisfied."

Iris didn't possess the knowledge to tell him what she wanted in words, so she covered his chest in kisses, ran her hands all over his hot skin and wriggled beneath him. Desiring him had been easy; making love to him was all she wanted for the rest of her life.

When he held back from her a little too long, she feared he would stop entirely. Iris pressed the heels of her feet against his bottom and forced him to slide back inside her again. When he reached her limit, he eased back immediately then repeated the short thrust. He kept up a steady assault on her body and she loved each and every sensation swamping her.

Iris wrapped her arms about his shoulders and held on, loving the feel of him inside her. Tomorrow she might be sore but for now she was restless with need. She tangled her fingers in his short hair and brought his lips to hers again.

The thrust of his tongue was met by her own and she chuckled softly against his mouth. Was there anything he could do to displease her?

The glide of his manhood quickened and the slap of his thighs against hers brought an ache where they joined. Would she experience another release so soon? She hoped so. Making love to him was heavenly.

Martin rose above her, fists pressed into the mattress as he possessed her with steady thrusts. There was a question in his gaze and she answered it with a smile. He could continue. He could make her body his all night long and she'd never complain. His hips rotated on the next thrust and her breath caught as undeniable lust shot through her body.

Restless and unable to hold Martin when he kept such a distance, Iris let her hands slide down his muscular arms and let one fall to her own chest. He pressed deeper and rolled his hips, but his attention followed her hand. Iris cupped her own breast as he had done and toyed with the nipple. She'd never imagined her breasts could be so sensitive but with Martin hard inside her and watching, she moaned softly.

He caught her behind her neck, rocked back onto his knees mid-stroke and brought her over his lap. The new position sank her deeper onto him and she shuddered. Her release was near. "Help me," she whispered.

Martin bucked beneath her, taking over her ability to think with his wild thrusts. He touched between her legs and she flew apart violently. She shrieked and shook in his arms, clenching him in the heat of passion.

"Fuck." His curse blistered her ears and the big man clutched her against him, chest heaving, body slick and blisteringly hot as his seed exploded inside her. Iris hung there, impaled and panting against her husband's warm skin, so overcome that she could barely move. She didn't *want* to ever move from his arms.

At last, he set her aside on the mattress. She winced as he withdrew from her body and she hugged her legs together to blunt the discomfort as Esme had suggested might help afterward.

"Iris?"

She smiled up at her handsome husband, touched his face. "I made the right decision."

His expression grew dark. "You made a foolish one."

Iris frowned. "How so?"

"Now that you've shared my bed, and so thoroughly too, I will want you again."

Oh, to make love like that again, so totally the focus of his attention and of her own. She sighed. "I do hope so."

"I have no excuse."

Iris scrambled to sit up, ignoring the discomfort of her body in the face of his shocking suggestion. "I don't want there to be any doubts between us. I wanted to make love to you so much and will not be made to feel ashamed by that."

He seemed taken aback by her suggestion. "I couldn't bear to lose you."

Iris wrapped herself around him. "You won't."

He shifted to the edge of the bed and Iris was hard pressed not to stare at his manhood, which had not softened to any considerable degree. There was so very much of him, and all of it deliciously naked.

His head fell to her shoulder. "A gentleman should have control and you shredded mine."

Iris grinned. What proper lady enjoyed being thoroughly debauched by her husband that she'd offer herself again and again? She was wicked and sinful and utterly unrepentant.

She lifted his chin and met her husband's gaze. She saw the fear in his eyes. Couldn't he understand that no matter the outcome, she wanted to be his wife in every way possible? That meant having his child. His heir. Loving them all. Even the one he wouldn't admit to yet. "And you took mine the day we kissed. I've no interest in being held on a pedestal and only allowed close on special occasions."

He frowned at her.

"No, don't say another word. It's been a long day and you promised to spend the night with me." She scrambled to her knees. "Get back into bed or you'll ruin everything."

He considered her a long moment and then slid under the comforter. His gaze slid over her nakedness. He touched her thigh then held up his hand to show her the blood. "I hurt you."

She set her hands to her hips, furious with him for stating the obvious. "At least you have proof I was an innocent."

Iris swung her legs over the side of the bed and slipped into her adjoining room to tend to her needs. When she returned, Martin appeared pensive. "I never doubted your innocence."

"Shh," she whispered as she crawled under the comforter next to him. "I know you didn't, but I am fine and the next time will be even better."

Iris cuddled up against his warmth, resting her head on his arm and letting her topmost hand slide down his side then drop to cover his erection. She played with him a moment, earning a groan for her teasing, and marveled that he was still so obviously in need. One night would never be enough to appease her hunger, and certainly not his. He'd held back.

Given enough time, enough insistence, she would win him over but for now she closed her eyes. She was too tired to argue about the depths of pleasure he'd given her and what the future could bring.

Chapter Twenty-One

Iris stood aside as footmen carried away the large, empty copper tub from her father's bedchamber. She waited at the door as he took in his surroundings again, wide-eyed with surprise, as if a child transported to a place he'd never imagined. Like Iris, he was having trouble believing he was outside the Marshalsea this morning and once more living in a fine home where he could have anything he wanted. "Is there anything you need?"

He pressed his lips together and shook his head. When he rubbed the arms of the deep-blue brocade banyan that clothed him now, a hastily purchased garment, like all of his new possessions were, her heart ached.

Iris grasped the door handle and pushed it shut to keep the servants from returning. When she approached him and captured his hand, she discovered he was shaking. "It's all right."

He nodded, staring at her in consternation. "I never expected this when I woke up."

She squeezed his fingers and swallowed the lump forming in her throat. Every day since his arrival had been the same for him. Surprise and confusion filled him. "Father, you have been a guest here for several days. You might not remember but we must be very grateful to Lord Louth for paying off your debts."

"My debts? Yes, I see, but…" He bit his lip and then released her to wander around the room. "We had such a slight acquaintance for him to do so much."

"He paid your debts as a wedding present to me, I think." She had her father out of that terrible place and far away from the danger Talbot presented. There were no words to describe her relief. He would never need to venture into proper society again either, if he didn't want to, or wasn't capable of managing the chore on his own. He could put the past behind him and concentrate on getting better. And she would put the past behind her too she hoped, but only if Talbot was caught red-handed.

"Are you sweethearts?" Her father grinned, his eyes widening in amusement at the idea. He spoke in a teasing voice and wagged a finger at her. "Mama won't like that."

Iris froze. "Lord Louth, Martin, is my husband. I married him here in this house. You were there to see me marry. You said you were proud of me becoming a countess. I am a lady now."

"Oh, I see. Lady Louth, is it?" He made a strange noise, a tease that hinted she was giving herself airs she didn't deserve. He walked away to peek out the window. "Well, only a wealthy and a well-connected young man will do for you, I suppose?"

She did not like the way her father reverted to childlike behavior these past few days. He'd never teased her before. It wasn't right and was sure to be noticed. Iris wrung her hands then joined him at the window to see what interested him so much. "He also makes me very happy and I care for him."

There was nothing outside but the press of people going about their lives.

"Love?" Her father scowled and studied his nails.

"I think so," Iris confessed.

"A wealthy husband you shall have, if I have my way, as such emotions do not last."

Her father had loved her mother and she had thought he had cared for his second wife too. Iris had never been particularly close to the woman and especially not after she'd left her father because he couldn't pay her dressmakers bill. She had not realized the extent of his bitterness. "Why do you say that?"

"Experience. Love is for fools."

Before Iris could respond, a tap sounded on the door. Her father bid entry as if he were himself again and had not just teased her like a mean little boy. Two footmen waited in the doorway, one holding a heaped tea tray. "Mr. Gibbs sent us, Mr. Hedley."

"By all means, come in. Come in." He peered at the tray. "What have we here?"

The footman laid out food and teacups on the drop-sided table set against the window in silence. Duties done, they exited the room, leaving her father grinning. Gibbs, bless him, had sent up enough cake to last her father several days, judging by the quantity provided. Iris moved to serve. She poured the tea in the fine china cups, and then chose a thick slice of strawberry cake for her father and placed it on the pretty matching plate. "Come and eat."

He stared at the plates then stretched for a covered bowl. "Sugar." The word was whispered reverently and he snatched up the sugar bowl and held it to his chest. "This of everything I have missed the most."

Iris laughed softly and took the sugar bowl from him. "Well, there is no shortage of sweets to please your palate today."

She handed him a silver spoon and as he heaped six teaspoons of sugar into his cup, she started to laugh. She couldn't help it. He'd not missed his gleaming black carriage, the dozen footmen he'd employed to fetch and carry, nor his second wife or their home. He'd missed sugar.

His teaspoon grated against the china cup as he stirred, a huge and satisfied smile gracing his lips. When he eventually stopped, he picked up his cup and slurped his tea loudly. "Ah, that is what I needed most of all. Apologies for my bad manners."

"Quite all right." She leaned close to him, amazed by how different he could sound in so short a time. "It can be our secret."

He grabbed his slice of strawberry cake next and took a generous bite. His smile while he ate was one of wonder and with a start she discovered her father likely hadn't eaten so richly in several years. When he was close to done, she handed over the plate of lemon tarts. "Another?"

He was quick to help himself to two and as he munched and sipped his oversweet tea, his animation waned. "When is the innkeeper bringing our luggage from the carriage?"

Iris pinched the bridge of her nose. "Father, please. We are at home in Holly House with Lord Louth. He is your son by marriage, not an innkeeper. Can you not remember to refer to him by his title as you used to do? Lord Louth. That's his name."

Her father shrugged and his mouth turned down at the corners. "What sort of man is he that keeps a man waiting so long?"

"He's already spoken to you today. And you do like him, Father. He is a good man. Kind to his cousin, Miss Whitney Crewe. He has a fine sense of humor."

That would be sorely tried if he spent even ten minutes with her father in his present state of confusion.

"He did boast he was well off." Her father helped himself to another tea and slice of cake and stared at nothing as he filled his mouth. He glanced at her, and then hurried to finish. He stood, dropping an avalanche of crumbs to the floor. "I'm ready to go."

"But you've only just arrived."

"Did I? Oh, well. I cannot remember." He patted his stomach while yawning. "Eating makes a man weary. I think I might take a short nap before dinner. It's been an exciting day."

"Of course," she whispered, her heart breaking.

It was only ten in the morning but she'd reached her limit for trying to convince him of anything more. Iris hurried for the bed and turned back the covers so her father could rest comfortably lying down. "I'll wake you so you have ample time to prepare for dinner."

"That is a fine idea." He lay down with a groan and curled up on his side with his hands resting under his cheek. "These places do become uncomfortably overcrowded around meal times."

Iris slipped from the room and, once alone in the hall, covered her face. His insistence he was staying at a coaching inn was growing harder to bear. She could not seem to talk him out of his delusion he was on a long journey and the strain of correcting him was already getting on her nerves.

"Is there anything I can do, my lady?"

The butler's polite question made her cry out because she'd

not heard his approach. She faced him and noticed a footman lingering a few steps behind. "No, nothing. My father wished to go back to his bed. He's very tired today."

"Very good, madam." Gibbs peeked into the room, and then crept inside to retrieve the tea tray. The familiar strains of her father's heavy snore added a comfort that she'd missed this morning. Gibbs closed the door carefully and smiled. "He never noticed me. If there is nothing else?"

Iris quickly shook her head.

When the footman hurried off with the tray, Iris assumed Gibbs would follow him. However, he opened the door to an adjacent room and stepped inside. Curious about what he was doing in a bedchamber at this time of day, she glanced around. A round table had been stacked with tarnished silver. When Gibbs picked up a cleaning cloth, and turned out a chair to sit upon, she frowned at him. "Should that not be done below stairs?"

Gibbs nodded. "Ordinarily it would be done elsewhere, however, his lordship has asked me to keep an eye on your father during the day, should he require any assistance. I abhor the idea of sitting idly about doing nothing. Brown has been promoted to answer the door, as per Lord Louth's instructions. Mrs. Clayton is waiting on your ring to discuss the menus at your earliest convenience."

"Oh, I see. Yes, of course." She turned to go but then changed her mind and doubled back. "Will you bring my father to me when he grows tired of his room?"

Gibbs nodded. "I would be very happy to, my lady."

She should also visit with her husband's cousin. Whitney had made herself scarce after their vows had been spoken and that would never do. She did not want their marriage to alienate the girl. "And Miss Crewe?"

"She is in her studio, as usual for this time of day." Gibbs gestured behind her. "The room is at the end of the hall, to the left."

She nodded, adding the location and Whitney's habits to her memory. "And my husband. Do you know where I might find him?"

The butler's gaze grew wary. "He went out, my lady."

"Out?" He'd failed to mention any errand he'd needed to run this morning. "Where? Or do you know when he will be coming back?"

The butler straightened. "He never said, and it's not my place to ask."

Iris nodded. "Of course. I merely wanted to thank him for the care he is giving my father." At least with him out, she had time to work up her courage to broach the subject of her father's scattered memory. She shouldn't put it off much longer. He seemed worse today.

Gibbs nodded. "I will pass along your desire to see him on his return."

"That would be appreciated. Thank you."

Iris headed toward Whitney's studio, a room she'd never ventured into before her marriage, and tapped on the door. Upon hearing no response, she let herself in and glanced around. Whitney stood with her back to the door, paintbrush poised in her hand as she stared at the incomplete portrait before her.

"Miss Crewe?"

Her brush lifted high and then she made a small, delicate brushstroke. "I can never get the eyes the way I want on the first attempt," she murmured and set aside her brush. "Good morning, dear cousin. You're looking very well this morning."

"Thank you." Iris glanced around the walls of the room to hide her blush.

Aside from her growing concern for her father's failing mind, she felt wonderful—full of hope and optimism about her marriage. The ease at which they'd come together filled her with relief. The earl had doubts about her size in comparison to his. That he had regretted withdrawing to prevent a pregnancy and wouldn't say why filled her with unease, though. Would he ever tell her about his child? If she closed her eyes for even a moment, she could still remember the feel of the little girl in her arms. She needed a mother and her father to love and protect her too, didn't she?

There were few pieces of art hanging but many canvases were stacked against the walls. "So this is where you prefer to spend your time. Your cousin spoke often of your interest in art but I never had a chance to see any before we wed."

"And that is how it should have been." Whitney dropped her paintbrush into a glass jar filled with liquid and stood back. "You only had eyes for him, and that is very satisfying to me."

She hid a grin. "Was my interest really so obvious?"

"To one who cared to wonder, oh my yes, indeed it was." Whitney snatched up a black satin cloth and carefully cleaned the brush on it. "You did appear smitten. I was so relieved my cousin had found the right woman to marry. I hope to claim my cooperation played a small part in your success with him."

Iris faced the woman, surprised she'd try to take credit for her marriage. Most women were not that bold. "I never quite believed my husband before when he spoke of your character, but you truly are not afraid to voice your opinions, are you?"

Whitney shrugged. "I know what I like and what I don't. Most women will never tell you how they really feel or think."

That was unfortunately all too true. "What will you do today?"

Whitney carefully set her brushes out to dry then smiled. "I am at your disposal."

"Good. If you don't mind, I would like your company for another tour of the house, and perhaps you might remind me of the servants' names and duties as we go along, too."

Whitney leafed through some papers in a side table drawer and handed them over. "This should help. I started making notes for you when we returned from the park the other day."

Iris scanned the list. Whitney had noted every servant by name, detailed their duties, and added little side notes about their character, too. Everything the new lady of the house might require at short notice.

The second to last sheet contained the names of members of society, including their London addresses. People she assumed her husband was best acquainted with. There was also a sketch of the London townhouse and of Holly Park, their country estate in Lincolnshire, and a short list of other properties the earl owned, including the Pollen Street residence where his daughter lived.

Iris folded the papers carefully without commenting on the nearby property. "Thank you for your help. These lists will be invaluable."

"Anything I can do to help the transition." Whitney smiled. "Where's that cousin of mine hiding today? I've not seen him all morning. Did you leave him in bed?"

"No. He went out alone earlier."

"Bare days after he gets married? I do hope he brings home something precious as a wedding gift."

Iris' pulse quickened. She didn't need anything more than he'd given her above marriage but she hadn't truly considered what he did when they were not together. Had he gone to Pollen Street to see the babe or did he ignore the little girl altogether? How long would Mrs. Hughes conceal her secret visits to the baby? "I've no idea of what he might be doing but I'm sure I'll hear about it later."

Chapter Twenty-Two

———◆———

"**I** can't begin to thank you enough," Mr. Hedley began as soon as his daughter exited the room, on her way to confer with the housekeeper about the chances of setting out their dinner earlier than planned. Hedley could barely keep his eyes open and Martin was growing concerned.

"You've already been profuse enough with your thanks." Martin smiled gently, admiring the color of his whiskey. "I'm just glad I had the opportunity and funds to help."

At the mention of money, Hedley swallowed hard and shifted in his chair. "I can never repay you, you know."

"I knew that from the beginning, sir." Poor Hedley, the man was extremely uncomfortable but the deed was done, money spent, and Martin's conscience was clear. Hedley was at large and Iris was happy.

In all but one respect, Mr. Hedley had no further worries. "I've been meaning to ask you about your wife. Iris hasn't mentioned her stepmother, but I understand Mrs. Hedley returned to her family soon after your losses became known. Do you wish to send for her? There is more than enough room."

At the mention of his wife, Hedley's face grew dark with anger. "She married me only for my money; came as quite a shock after fifteen years of believing myself a happy husband. But when there was nothing left but me, Jane fled to her family without a backward glance."

Martin had never met Iris' mother. He did remember the second Mrs. Hedley as elegant but a trifle brisk. She would not have fared well visiting debtor's prison. "Why did Iris not go with her to stay with family?"

"My wife accused me of spoiling her life, as if I'd ruined us just to spite her. The love of my daughter is the only thing that has kept me going. Iris would not leave no matter how hard I tried to convince her to go." Hedley swallowed his whiskey in one gulp.

Martin had had no idea the marriage had broken down so completely, but he should have suspected as much, given how neither Hedley nor Iris had mentioned the absent wife. "Would you like to write to her and give her your address?"

"And have her send her bills?" Hedley shook his head violently. "No. I'll not do that to you, or to my daughter. Jane would only meddle and cause trouble."

Martin studied Alexander Hedley and let the matter drop. "Very well."

Hedley pursed his lips a moment then sat forward. "Take one last piece of advice from me if you will before I go: When you're thinking of proposing marriage, think about it a bit longer before you speak up. A fair-weather wife isn't for any man."

Martin winced. Could the man not keep it straight in his head that Iris was now married to him and this was now their home? The only conclusion he could make was that the man was losing his mind, or had lost it some time ago. There were times he understood, but more often than not he was confused. "I am married to your daughter, sir. Do you not remember the ceremony that took place in the drawing room?"

As much as he wanted Alexander Hedley in his home, the situation was not ideal when he questioned his marital status all the time.

"A man your age," Hedley continued, unaware Martin's mind had strayed to worry for the future, "should have a wealthy wife with good connections. My Iris, to my shame, has neither advantage."

"She has enough appeal for me." He stood quickly and replenished their glasses. He was well satisfied with his decision to marry Iris and discussions like this with Hedley were beginning to irritate.

So far, there had been no upheaval in the running of his home as his wife had assumed the role. She had taken charge smoothly and by all accounts had won over the staff on her first day as countess. The matter of the robberies, Iris' part in them particularly, had not resurfaced in discussion but plans were afoot to bring an end to Talbot's thieving very soon.

He peered out the window onto the street as he stoppered the decanter, dreaming of a pleasant future ahead. He could have Iris in his bed, tease her until she woke from slumber as he had that morning. And then later he'd slip away to visit his daughter without anyone noticing. It wasn't ideal but he couldn't see how to bring his wife and daughter together in the immediate future.

After a moment, he registered a man standing opposite his home on Golden Square. The fellow was dressed poorly compared to those passing him and stood out for his lack of fashion. Those strolling the square gave him a wide berth but his attention was on Holly House.

He took a closer look and at last recognized the man as the turnkey from the Marshalsea.

Martin was moving for the front door before he fully realized what he was doing. That man had no business loitering outside his home.

He burst outside, crossed the roadway with little thought to the traffic, and pinned the turnkey with a cold, hard stare. To his credit, Fitzhugh stood his ground until Martin drew near. The man bobbed his head deferentially. "My lord."

Fitzhugh was half a head shorter, slightly rounded in the middle and clearly wearing his best clothing. "You've no reason to come here."

"I was wanting a word with Mr. Hedley but the knocker's gone from the door."

"Yes, it is." He wanted no callers at all today.

"I'm Mr. Fitzhugh, if you don't remember. From the Marshalsea Prison." He smiled widely as if such a place was a credit to him rather than a disadvantage, revealing unshapely, stained teeth.

Martin gritted his. This man had allowed Talbot access to the prison and to blackmail his wife. "I know who you are."

"I trust Mr. Hedley, and his daughter, are in good health?"

Martin narrowed his eyes and used his bulk to intimidate. "My wife's health is none of your concern, sir. Be off with you."

"You really did marry her?" Fitzhugh appeared stunned. He thrust his hand into his pocket then held out a grubby, folded square of paper. "You should have this then."

Martin stared at the note in disgust. "What does that concern?"

"It's a private matter, my lord. Best not discussed on the street."

The envelope could only contain one of two things—a note of blackmail or a threat against her life.

Martin snatched the note away before anyone noticed and shoved it in his pocket. "If you come here again, I'll set my dogs on you." He didn't keep dogs in London, too much fuss and noise, but he'd get some for the townhouse if the bastard dared to come back into this neighborhood. A dog with nice sharp teeth that could ensure the man walked with a permanent limp for life.

The man shrugged. "Dogs are only loyal to the one that hands them their next meal. Men are like that, too. Good day, my lord."

He turned away before Martin could respond, getting in the last word and leaving Martin seething with anger. He headed home immediately. Once inside, he peeked into the library to check on Mr. Hedley but found him napping. The man had an uncanny knack of falling asleep whenever a lull in conversation occurred for longer than a few minutes. Today he was grateful of it, and backed away from the man before he disturbed him.

Gibbs joined him in the hall, his gaze darting to the library doorway. "Is everything all right, my lord?"

He urged Gibbs into the drawing room. "Did you by chance notice the man I was speaking with in the square?"

Gibbs nodded slowly. "Yes, my lord. I didn't recognize him though."

"You shouldn't have, but remember his face, will you?" Martin sighed. He needed Gibbs' help so Iris would remain safe.

"Keep an eye out for him and let me know if the fellow returns. He is not to be admitted to Holly House, he is not welcome, and make sure that my wife remains unaware of his visit should he ever dare darken our door."

Gibbs nodded but then he frowned in confusion. "Is he an acquaintance of hers?"

"That is no friend to any decent woman."

"Oh." Gibbs moved to a window and peeked out. "He's gone now."

"Good." Martin touched the note in his pocket but didn't reveal it. "I don't wish to be disturbed until dinner."

"Of course. I will make sure Mr. Hedley has everything he needs."

Martin paused a moment. "Is he an easy guest?"

"Yes, my lord. The most trouble he gives anyone so far is asking for second helpings of everything we set before him."

Martin glanced toward the library. "He does need to eat."

"And rest too," Gibbs murmured in full agreement. "He's nothing but skin and bones."

"He'll recover," Martin insisted, wondering silently if that were true or not. How did one mend a mind that refused to remember?

"He will, my lord, with you watching over him." Gibbs nodded in approval and headed toward the butler's pantry.

Martin retreated to his study and examined the paper he'd shoved in his pocket from Fitzhugh. He wasn't about to pass it over without knowing what it contained first.

He scanned the sheet, expecting to read the worst sorts of demands for money. However, the poorly scrawled note contained a warning from Fitzhugh. Talbot was in a rage over Hedley's removal from the Marshalsea and had promised to make Iris pay dearly for what he considered a betrayal of their agreement.

He shoved the note in his pocket as Iris tapped on his open door. "Mrs. Clayton agreed to move dinner to an earlier hour."

"Good. Thank you."

She moved closer. "Did you have a pleasant day?"

"Somewhat. Helena Ward is still causing all sorts of problems for my man of business."

The smile slipped from Iris' face. "You saw her?"

"No, I saw Mr. Barker at his offices and that was enough. He describes her as a frivolous spendthrift with no self-control whatsoever." Martin laughed at the memory. "Poor man might be in over his head, but I'm sure he'll sort her out eventually."

"I see." She bit her lip and turned away. "Did you go anywhere else?"

"No." He'd gone to see his daughter but he would not mention that fact yet. Not until the business of catching Talbot red-handed was over and the danger he presented was past. The situation had to be handled very delicately.

He stood and crossed to a portrait of his grandparents that was made shortly after their marriage. "There is something I would like you to have."

He removed the painting and fumbled with the lock of the safe hidden behind, then removed a heavy jewelry box. He smiled at the contents. "These jewels belonged to my grandmother and I think they may be sufficient for the upcoming ball." He turned and held out the open box that, on first glance, appeared to contain a fortune in rubies and diamond.

Unfortunately his wife had covered her face and couldn't see them.

"Iris?"

She kept her face covered. "I can't wear them."

Concerned by the breathless quality of her voice, he set the box aside on his desk and pulled Iris into his arms. She buried her face against his chest and trembled. "Talbot will want them. He wants everything he sees."

He smoothed a hand down her back, understanding her concern all too well. "I haven't had a chance to tell you about my grandmother yet, have I? Clever old duck. Hated to wear fine gems for the envy they caused in others, so she had the real family jewels copied. These are paste, an exact replica of the set worn in that painting I took down. She wore them everywhere, and it was not until she'd passed away that we discovered the real set hidden inside an old hat box on the top of her cupboard. My grandfather was never sure when she commissioned the copies."

Iris drew back. "You are wise not trust me with the real gems."

"I do trust you." He kissed the top of her head. "But I don't trust Talbot and I didn't want to add to your worry, should he attempt to take your gems from you by force."

"He will try." She shuddered. "His rage is terrifying."

"Shh, love." He hugged her close. "You're safe now. I won't let him hurt you again. All you have to do is drop a note tomorrow on your way back from your outing with Lady Heathcote and the rest will happen without you as it always has."

He released her to pick up the gems, and placed the heavy pieces around her neck and wrists. She held her hand up to the light to better see the stones. "They're very good. I'd never have believed them copies if you hadn't told me."

"The trap will be sprung at Acton House."

Iris covered her wrist as if afraid to lose the gems adorning her arm. "I thought Acton's invitation was to be a smaller event?"

"That was true at first but since he has just announced his engagement to Miss Quartermane, the event will be considerably grander in celebration of the match."

"Miss Quartermane and Lord Acton?" She frowned. "I had no idea they were involved."

"Neither did I. It's a very odd pairing indeed, but it's exactly what we need to catch Talbot red-handed. The guest list is said to be staggering and his invitation assured."

"Yes, of course." She bit her lip. "Let us hope Talbot is convinced there is nothing untoward going on."

"He will be." For the moment, Martin cared not for anything but making his wife happy, so he claimed her lips in a searing kiss and tugged her into the nearest armchair so he could distract her from their troubles the only way he knew how.

<h1 style="text-align:center">Chapter Twenty-Three</h1>

Iris tapped on the faded blue door on Pollen Street with a determined heart, Esme at her side. The girl living here would be her daughter if she had her way, and she wanted to assure herself that everything required for her comfort had been taken care of properly.

An older gentleman greeted her, the same man she'd seen that first meeting with Louth's daughter in the park. "Good afternoon, sir. Might we come in?"

He recognized Iris then eased back to allow her entry. The house was hushed and he directed her to a sitting room and then excused himself. A moment later, Mrs. Hughes poked her head around the doorway with a nervous smile. "I didn't expect to see you again, miss."

"I'm sure it seemed that way but I had to come." She held out her hand. "I should introduce myself properly. I am Lady Louth now and this is my close friend, Lady Heathcote. I married your employer several days ago."

"Yes, the master mentioned he'd wed and we had wondered if it were you he'd taken for a wife." Mrs. Hughes scraped her palms down her dress. "He still doesn't know you visited this house, does he?"

"No. I thought to allow my husband the opportunity to do so on his own but he has not mentioned the girl so far in conversation."

"He should have by now," Esme grumbled quietly.

"Shh," Iris warned. Esme was only here because she'd insisted on accompanying her again. "You promised."

"I see." The housekeeper frowned. "Then how can I help you? Why have you come back?"

"I would very much like to hear about the lady who gave birth to Lord Louth's daughter. You said she died in childbirth." A gentleman's footsteps could be heard leading away from the doorway. She did not like the idea that he'd been listening to their conversation but she could understand his concern over her visit.

"It is not done to speak of the dead. My lady was beautiful and Lord Louth is a fine man. Kind, so gentle and understanding." Mrs. Hughes' gaze dropped to her hands and she winced. "But my mistress never did appreciate his generosity. She hid the pregnancy from him quite deliberately, insisting the child belonged to her new protector."

Iris blinked at the idea her husband had been kept in the dark about the pregnancy. She swallowed nervously. "I see. When did my husband learn of the child?"

"Not until after my lady's death." Mrs. Hughes sighed. "The other gentleman took care of my mistress' burial and then suddenly abandoned the child to my care. I didn't know what to do. I had no choice but to contact the earl."

"So no matter what he might have done if he'd but known of the impending birth, Mrs. Rose denied the child the chance to her father's name." Anger filled her at such obvious selfishness. "I see. Mrs. Hughes, I find myself in a difficult position and need your help. Lord Louth will not agree to us having children. I fear he blames himself, and his greater proportions, for your mistress' death."

"She did die straight after the birth, my lady. One moment there, the next gone."

Iris swallowed her anxiety. "A sudden death can be the hardest to understand. Had she been in good health before the birth?"

Mrs. Hughes frowned. "My mistress always claimed her health was delicate as a means of ensuring she was taken care of by her protectors, but now that you mention it, she had been listless in the preceding weeks. I thought it only impatience and suggested bed rest."

"A sensible precaution," Esme agreed, nodding in approval. "Did she take your advice?"

"No. My mistress was always somewhat contrary. She took picnics with Lord Fallon because he insisted she needed a change of scenery, and returned late, often well after dark on most occasions. The morning following such an outing, she had pains and her daughter was delivered later that night."

"Was a physician in attendance, or a midwife of skill and experience, perhaps?" Iris asked.

"A midwife was sent for in the late afternoon, and my mistress was very tired by then."

"Not surprising." It did not sound entirely sensible to Iris that the woman was traipsing about London so late in her pregnancy and keeping irregular hours. "So it is possible that the size of the child wasn't the cause of her death entirely. There might have been other influences at play. Exhaustion, perhaps. An illness."

"I suppose so, but I couldn't say for sure. My mistress did not care much for physician's and such."

Iris nodded. Her husband's last mistress had been a fool to put her health and that of her unborn child at risk by running about Town. She shared a long glance with her friend. Esme's answering smile was reassuring. "That is enough for me. If I am careful, take sensible precautions to remain in good health, there might be no reason I cannot give my husband an heir. Now where is my daughter?"

"*Your* daughter?" Mrs. Hughes gaped.

"Well, I certainly intend to be a mother to the child." Iris stood, disliking the mourning colors surrounding her. "What is she named, by the way?"

"She has no name still." Mrs. Hughes sighed and gestured across the hall. "The earl will not decide."

"I see. Well, that must be addressed as soon as possible."

Esme remained seated. "I will wait here until you are ready to return home."

She paused at the doorway upon seeing a woman with frizzy

blonde hair seated with her back to the door. The woman was rocking to and fro, singing a lullaby. She turned to Mrs. Hughes. "And this is?"

"The wet-nurse, my lady."

"She's not done yet," the unknown woman complained without bothering to turn. The coarse accent and possessive tone set Iris aback but she swiftly recovered her poise and stepped forward to be acknowledged.

Mrs. Hughes made the introductions. "Martha Blake, this is Lady Louth. A countess. She's come to claim the child as her own."

Iris smiled at the woman clutching the babe to her breast. "I married the earl a few days ago. I wanted to see for myself how the girl does."

"She's perfect," Martha claimed.

"I thought so too when I first met her. Might I sit?" She skirted Mrs. Hughes when Martha nodded and took a chair opposite. "I did want to meet you too."

The woman squinted at her, suspicion clear on her face. "Why?"

"Well, you are the most important woman in my daughter's life right now. I can learn a great deal about her from you."

That brought a smile to Mrs. Blake's face. "She's an appetite, this one. And a temper. Always hungry when I come."

Iris frowned. "I thought you would have lived in."

"I could if it were offered." Martha glanced up at Mrs. Hughes with a scowl and received one from the housekeeper in return.

Iris noted the friction between the women and wondered at the cause. "Perhaps tea for us both, Mrs. Hughes, and for Lady Heathcote while I become better acquainted with my daughter. And biscuits if you have some, thank you."

Although Mrs. Hughes appeared hesitant to go, she did as asked and retreated toward the kitchens. Left alone with Mrs. Blake, Iris made herself comfortable and glanced about. The mourning colors were absent from this room. "Lovely."

"It's too gloomy elsewhere." Martha patted her frizzy locks self-consciously and threw a pained look in her direction. "Mrs. Hughes' beau doesn't like me for saying so."

Iris laughed softly in response. "At least the child is too young to notice colors but it seems she likes you very much."

The babe had released the woman's nipple on her own and was staring up at Mrs. Blake with a sweet smile.

Martha cuddled her against her chest. "And I like her, too. She's such a good girl."

Although she ached to ask for the babe, Iris held back. "Do you leave because you have children at home to look after?"

"I did. They're gone now. My husband sent them away to his family."

Iris' heart ached. "That's horrible, and where is it that you live?"

"Southwark. It's good money coming here."

She travelled as far as Iris had to the Marshalsea, and back each day. "That must be a very long and tiring walk to make."

"Sometimes I wander round the fine homes during the day and peek inside the windows instead when Mrs. Hughes doesn't want me around." Martha stroked the child's head with a gentleness that surprised her. Martha must have come to care for the child as if she were her own. Iris smiled in approval. For an illegitimate child, this girl already had so much love.

The child's immediate needs were important so she decided to ensure the girl's happiness and health were assured. "Would you be willing to stay here at night, too?"

"Mrs. Hughes won't have me underfoot. She doesn't think I'm good enough."

Mrs. Hughes returned, arms laden with tea and biscuits. "It's your husband I don't care for, Martha. I won't have him coming around again."

Iris winced. "Mrs. Hughes, I'm sure you will agree that the child requires a stable environment. I should like Martha to stay close to the child and take over as many aspects of her care as possible."

Mrs. Hughes stiffened and almost dropped the tray to the tabletop. "Are you unhappy with how I run this house, my lady?"

"Of course not. But the child does need a nursemaid too. That is not a job for a housekeeper. Your time and experience is better used on other matters, where firm decisions are required for the running of the household."

"And she's supposed to be getting married soon," Martha said quickly. She glanced down at the bundle in her arms, and awkwardly buttoned her bodice one-handed. "Would you like to hold her, my lady?"

"Thank you. I would love to hold her." Iris took the babe and settled the child in her arms. Gently she caressed the child's face and smiled down into her sleepy eyes. "Such a precious girl. I will have to scold your papa. He should have chosen a name long before this."

A pair of dark eyes fixed onto her face a moment then moved on to follow the light dancing into the room from a fluttering curtain. "Violet. If he will not choose, then your name will be Violet I think."

Mrs. Hughes sank to a chair. "Her mother's name was Vivian Rose."

"Violet Rose. It has a nice ring to it. Like a sweet wine or a perfect day." She hitched the child in her arms and leaned back in the chair. "I could stare into this sweet face all day."

"I fear we all have that thought," Mrs. Hughes murmured with a shake of her head.

Iris glanced at her. "Is the gentleman who answered the door your intended, Mrs. Hughes? I remember him from the park that first day we met. He seems very nice."

The housekeeper nodded. "He agreed to wait on account of the little girl."

"Ah, that is so good of him. When will you wed?"

"I don't know. He's been none too pleased with this situation but I could not leave the little one with things so uncertain. Lord Louth has not approved any candidates for my replacement so far."

Mrs. Hughes set a cup of tea within reach and then served Martha.

First he cannot name the child, and then not find a replacement housekeeper. She'd not imagined him indecisive before but perhaps this situation was one he'd never considered he'd ever face. Iris, however, knew exactly what needed to be done. "I think you might feel comfortable making your plans to marry now if you wish, Mrs. Hughes. I hope to take Violet home soon, so a replacement housekeeper will be unnecessary."

Mrs. Blake fidgeted. "Am I to go with her?"

"I had not meant to startle you with the change but if you would be willing to come, I would be grateful. I cannot, of course, feed the girl myself. She will need you."

The wet-nurse grinned, her eyes lighting up at the news. "I'm not fool enough to say no to a better situation."

While she sipped her tea, Iris studied the wet-nurse's manner. A little coarse, but she did make an effort to mimic Mrs. Hughes after a quick glance in that woman's direction several times. She could make a perfect nursemaid with the proper guidance. A bit of polish to smooth any rough edges and Iris could be content to leave her future children in the woman's care too without any hesitation.

The child grumbled and Iris lifted her to her shoulder. She patted Violet's bottom rhythmically. The child pulled her knees upward and cried as the sensation of breaking wind reverberated against Iris' palm. She glanced at Martha and Mrs. Hughes and pressed her lips together. The other pair laughed softly and she joined in too. "Now I feel myself her mother."

"She needs to be changed soon," Mrs. Hughes suggested.

Martha sat forward, hands outstretched. "That's my job now, isn't it?"

Iris smiled softly. "Perhaps for today you would allow me the honor. I cannot always be here and I'll not have another chance for many days to come."

Having gained her staff's agreement, under their watchful eye, she moved to the baby's room and changed her daughter's garments for the first time with a wide smile plastered to her face.

Unfortunately, as much as she might wish it otherwise, she could not stay all day. She had responsibilities at home. Her father's declining health needed to be discussed with Martin. He'd wanted to talk to her, but Iris had been at a loss over how to explain his contrary nature.

She took a long goodbye, kissing little Violet's cheek gently, and then set off for home with Esme.

Talbot's boy, a child of no more than a dozen years that she'd noticed too often this week lurking around her new home, was waiting at the corner. He trailed her discreetly as she pulled a note from inside her glove and let it flutter from her fingers. She didn't look back until the front door was closing behind them. The note, and the boy, was long gone by then.

Chapter Twenty-Four

———◆———

Martin tossed his boot aside carelessly, switching his attention from the closed door to his wife's bedchamber, and back to the mantelpiece clock. He could hear her in there, talking with her maid while she changed out of the clothes she'd worn to dinner and readied for bed. He'd never expected to be so eager to meet his wife each night but then again, he'd never seriously considered himself a married man. He'd discovered that being apart from Iris made him anxious.

As soon as the door between their bedchambers swung open, he was on his feet and across the room. Gods, she was beautiful. Her dark hair spilling across one shoulder, her feet bare under her robe. "You were very quiet tonight at dinner."

She closed the door behind her firmly, her expression tense and uncertain. "I can't help but worry for the future. I have a lot more to lose now than I ever had before."

"Don't worry about Talbot. I have Meriwether's assurance that you will be protected from prosecution no matter what he might say. Do you remember the quip you made to Lady Heathcote about being invisible? Well, that is nonsense of course, but the comment inspired her and Meriwether to concoct a rather believable excuse for your involvement, if it's discovered. As far as anyone knows, Meriwether recruited Lady Heathcote, a woman renowned for her intelligence and ability to uncover any scandal within the *ton*. She has been collecting any information relevant to the robberies for him and that is how your involvement began, as her confidant and second set of eyes."

Iris rubbed her brow. "So I'm still a spy."

"For the right reasons this time." He set his hands to her tiny shoulders and rubbed through the thin robe she wore. He bent and pressed his lips to her soft cheek. When she sighed with pleasure, he continued to stroke the column of her throat and then kissed her collarbone. He'd not been intimate with her since the wedding, allowing her time to adjust to being his wife and everything else. However, he did want to try again tonight. The release might just do her the world of good and settle her nerves ahead of tomorrow night's confrontation with Talbot.

They both wanted it over and for Iris to be safe again. Meriwether had assured him the plan to catch Talbot red-handed would work but he would not breathe easy yet.

"Waiting is very hard. I feel like everyone is watching me." Iris pushed his waistcoat aside, her hands eager as they swept around his chest to embrace him. She brushed her body against his groin and although the action was probably innocent, it utterly inflamed him.

"The only eyes on you tonight are mine," he promised. He tugged on the tie to her robe and undid the simple knot. His breath caught as the silk gaped, revealing his wife had come to him utterly bare beneath. It seemed he wasn't the only one with pleasure on their mind.

He shrugged out of his waistcoat and dragged his shirt over his head. Iris swirled the tips of her fingers around his navel and then kissed his chest. When she licked his nipple, Martin groaned then swept her up into his arms and carried her the few steps to his bed.

She curled her arms about his shoulders and wriggled until her legs wrapped about his hips. "Make love to me."

"I'd intended to." He cupped her bottom and squeezed. "If you're agreeable."

Iris nodded and kissed his neck. When he felt the nip of teeth, he laughed and reached to snuff the candle on the side table. He climbed onto the bed, resting his back against the headboard, and brought Iris onto his lap so she straddled him. There was enough moonlight that he could see her face clearly and she appeared excited by the position. She eased down his body, her lips tracing fire over his skin. He unbuttoned the fall of his trousers to give his growing arousal room but didn't expose himself.

Iris glanced up, a teasing grin on her face as she traced his outline through the garment. "I need you inside me."

She moved up his body and claimed his lips in a fiery kiss that obliterated any possible denial. He would still be cautious. Telling her so didn't seem possible, given her ardor, so he stroked her bottom lip with his tongue, gently biting the pink flesh as he held her against him.

She rose to her knees and brushed her nipple across his lips. He took the bud into his mouth and sucked hard, earning a desperate moan as repayment. He pushed her soft silk robe off her shoulders slowly and swept the barrier away.

She shuddered and pushed her breast harder against his face. He widened his fingers on her lower back, urged her quim against him and increased suction of his lips. She gasped softly when he switched breasts, scraping her nails over him. He teased her until she was moaning in a near constant stream.

He loosened his grip and while he continued to worship her breasts, he slid a finger along her opening, finding her damp and hot already. He slowly prepared her to be claimed once more. It did not take long for his insistent touch to provoke her to bear down on his fingers. When she groaned and tipped her head backward, Martin replaced his fingers with the head of his cock and pushed up.

Iris met his gaze, a wild look in her eyes. She rocked against him, pressing down a little at a time so he began to enter her. He cupped her breast and squeezed the tip, even as he held his cock steady. Her fingers dug into his shoulders and she gasped as he slipped almost all the way inside. He was a bit surprised by the ease.

"Slowly, love," he warned, holding back the urge to surge upward.

Heedless of his warning, Iris lifted and lowered much quicker than she should. Her lips parted and gasping. He gripped her hips firmly and slowed her down. Iris brushed his hands aside and set hers to his shoulders, undeterred by his wishes for a careful pace. Her eyes fluttered shut as she rode him, taking him deeper with every descent, her face a picture of concentration and pure joy. She paused only when he was fully seated inside her tight, blistering heat.

She met his gaze as she rotated her hips slowly. A moan ripped from his chest at the realization that his wife delighted in provoking him. She raised her arms over her head, twisted her hair into a coil and did it again. Her flushed face and easy smile hinted she was pleased with herself and knew her brazen display of her body aroused the hell out of him.

He flipped her onto her back and pinned her hands above her head. He surged into her and out again. Her legs tightened around his back as he lost himself in her body. Over and over, he thrust to her moans of unchecked pleasure, eventually releasing her hands so she could hold tight to him. She caressed his face as she peaked, crying out her pleasure loudly. She clutched him close, nails sinking into his back as she trembled. She held him so hard he could not move an inch.

What little control he had was lost in the wonder of her prolonged climax. He shook as the wave of intense satisfaction swept through him and he spilled his seed deep inside her body, despite his intentions not to do so again. Not every coupling created a child, but he shouldn't risk it again.

When she eventually quieted, he rolled to his side, gasping for air. His bare cock poked from the opening of his trousers, large and hard and glistening with the moisture of their passions, but he was too content to move at first.

When he eventually noticed the direction of her gaze had moved to his groin, he stripped off his trousers entirely and flopped onto his back. "That wasn't slow."

She met his gaze with a teasing smile. "No? Should we start over and try again?"

He chuckled at her attitude and swept her long dark hair back from her face. "You'd like that wouldn't you?"

"Actually, yes." She grinned. "I do love how you watch me, and I'm very pleased to discover your concerns that you were too large are unfounded."

His size was only a small part of his concern. A small woman giving birth to a large man's child put herself at risk. He shifted to bring Iris into his arms as the idea of losing her pained him. She made no attempt to cover herself and he liked that very much. He traced around her nipple. "You are so beautiful. I love seeing you like this, so very exposed, so very ready for me."

"I've been waiting for you to touch me all day." She glanced up into his face, frowning. "Didn't you tell me men think of sex at all hours of the day and night?"

"I did think of you many times today." He flicked her nipple gently until it grew hard. "I thought of you at breakfast when you passed me the newssheet. I had a fine view down your bodice and my mouth watered to suckle your breast."

He cupped her breasts with both hands and kneaded them. Her feet moved restlessly on the bed and he smiled at her reaction.

She touched his cock and lightly teased him. "Is that the only time?"

"No." He pinched both her nipples firmly and rolled them between his fingers, earning a gasp. "We could spend all night discussing my lustful thoughts about you. I'm utterly depraved."

She rolled onto his chest, settling her body over his own nakedness with a groan. "I would have enjoyed being your mistress you know, but I think as your wife I'll have far more opportunities to touch you than a scandalous woman like that ever would."

She wriggled upward and his cock slipped between her thighs. She rose and set her knees on either side of his hips.

The tip of his cock brushed across her bare bottom and he sighed. "Is that so?"

She nodded and with another adjustment, he was at her entrance again. She pressed his cock into her body with a groan. Despite the earlier rush to fuck, she kept the movement gentle and sweet. She rode him at a much slower pace, while he teased her lips with kisses, caressing her body everywhere. He withdrew a little to suck on the tips of her breasts before returning fully to her and groaning against her hair.

Pleasure built much more slowly this time. Iris curled her arms about his neck and held his head to hers. Her breath a soft gasp against his ear. "Thank you for being my tutor," she whispered. "I could never have felt so free or beautiful with anyone else."

And no matter then what position he moved her to, she moaned and writhed with pleasure. He was astonished and grateful to feel so wanted. He was behind her when her fingers twined in the comforter and she cried out his name as she climaxed again, shuddering violently.

She collapsed, panting for breath, bottom raised provocatively in the air. He stoked her cheek, marveling at her, and as soon as she calmed he moved again. She twisted to meet his gaze over her shoulder as he climaxed again with a wild shout, opening a dam inside himself that he'd always hidden his desire behind. He couldn't stop himself from continuing to pump into her long after he'd come. He needed her too damn much to ever be the same controlled man again.

He fucked her despite his softening cock and then withdrew, kissed down her back. He teased the base of her spine with his tongue and then rolled her over. Iris whispered his name as she tried to hold him but he slipped lower to her quim, determined to bring her pleasure. As many times as he could, that night and forever.

Chapter Twenty-Five

---◆---

Iris gripped her fan tightly as yet another member of the *ton* expressed surprise that an earl would marry so suddenly. Only the problem wasn't that Martin had married at all, but that he'd married a nobody. Iris did her best to fume silently. So far his closest friends had most easily accepted the match, and she was very grateful for their support tonight.

She scanned the faces in the crowd, looking for one face in particular. "I don't see him."

"I do. To my left." Martin smiled down at her. "Standing near the potted palms with Miss Alice Quartermane. Where the devil has Whitney gotten to?"

Iris turned slowly in that direction, and her gaze locked on Talbot. "She's dancing with Lord Acton at the moment."

"Dear God, why?"

"I dared her to accept," Iris confessed but her attention remained on Talbot. "And told her you'd buy her a dozen new canvases if she'd end her hostilities tonight."

"Clever." He beamed at her. "I'll have to kiss your feet in thanks for that."

Talbot bowed over Miss Quartermane's hand, admiring the enormous gem gracing her wriggling fingers. Acton had been very generous with the gift to her on their engagement. The size of the ring was all anyone could talk about tonight. "Run, Alice," she whispered. "Run."

"Be calm." Martin's hand slid over hers and squeezed. "Lady Heathcote is coming this way."

Iris turned as Esme stopped at her side on a stranger's arm. The older woman kissed her cheek. "You look radiant, my dear. Marriage agrees with you."

"Thank you, as do you." Iris took in Esme's bold gown— dark-blue silk edged in black lace and smoky quartz gems—and sighed with envy. "Madam du Clair has outdone herself once again."

"I know. She's anxious to see you soon." Esme gestured to the gentleman at her side. "Might I introduce you to a very old friend of mine. Mr. Miles Hammond. He's recently come up to Town."

Iris held out her hand to the man. "A pleasure to meet you. Esme has told me absolutely nothing about you."

"There's not much to tell." The gentleman kissed the air over her glove and turned his attention to her husband.

Iris met Esme's gaze. "I think new gowns should wait."

Martin touched her elbow. "I'd never come between a lady and her modiste. I'm looking forward to the bill, actually, and the view."

He squeezed her fingers and then began a conversation with Hammond.

Esme smiled widely and then leaned close to her ear to whisper, "Wicked, generous and kind. But has he mentioned *her* yet?"

Iris shook her head. Not once, and she'd tried so hard to find a way to bring up the topic herself but to no avail. She glanced beyond Esme and discovered Lord Windermere staring in her direction. She nodded to him and although he offered a smile, it was clear his attention was on Esme alone. "Have you spoken to Windermere lately?"

"No. But I have heard he and Lady Bartlett had a falling out a few days ago. Why do you ask?"

"Because he can't take his eyes off you. Do you think he might want to apologize for his outburst?"

"I'm sure I don't need to hear it." Esme curled her arm through Mr. Hammond's and smiled. "I'm parched, sir."

A decidedly warm smile crossed Hammond's face. "That's the girl I know and love. Shall we search for a quiet corner too, my dear?"

"Darling, you're always getting ahead of the game." Esme laughed wickedly and then kissed Iris' cheek. "I will see you later. Be careful."

The pair strolled away, headed for the card room where they were certain to find a beverage to their taste.

"We should congratulate Miss Quartermane on her engagement," Martin remarked as he took her arm. He steered her in that direction, moving at a slow pace and pausing often to speak to guests. Talbot had moved on long before they reached Miss Quartermane and now she could not find him anywhere. Iris thought she caught a glimpse of his pale head as he passed out the door and into the card room but she couldn't be sure.

Miss Quartermane smiled warmly. "Here you are. I was just telling Mr. Talbot how much I admired the speed of your marriage. Congratulations. A surprise wedding is exactly the way to get married these days. I would never have said that you pair would make a match. Not a hint of scandal about you both. We're all desperate to know when and how you caught him?"

The girl wagged her fingers and the diamonds gracing them caught her attention. Talbot must have almost been drooling over the priceless stones.

"I, um," Iris stammered, and then dragged her attention back to the girl's smiling face. "I've always liked him."

Martin set his arm around her back. "My proposal caught her by surprise but I simply could not wait another day."

Miss Quartermane held her gaze. "And your father has returned in time to celebrate with you, too. How wonderful. Is he here tonight?"

"No," she said calmly enough but since no one else had mentioned her father that night, and he'd not left Holly House since his release from debtor's prison, she was uncertain how to answer the question. So far, society at large seemed unaware of his return to London. "His travels have exhausted him."

Miss Quartermane smiled and squeezed her hand. "I do understand the need for misdirection in such cases but it is unnecessary with me."

Iris fought the urge to flee. "I don't know what you mean."

The girl shrugged. "I had an uncle who *traveled* several times in his life. Most uncomfortable for the family to keep quiet, and I would never hold such circumstances against his devoted daughter."

Martin stiffened at her side. "Who told you?"

Miss Quartermane's brows drew together and she leaned close. "Mr. Talbot suggested some recent difficulties had kept your father from society, and given what I knew of his history…"

"I see." Iris bit her lip a moment. A calculated guess perhaps but how many other people would Talbot drop hints to about her father tonight. "What else did he say?"

"Nothing very interesting. We talked of Acton. He complimented me on my good fortune to snare an earl. He laughed heartily when I mentioned Everett, I mean Lord Acton, let me choose my own gift after he proposed marriage. That is how I knew he was the man for me. He left his safe open the whole time I dithered over which gem I liked best."

Iris exchanged a concerned glance with her husband. Idle gossip was the single best way to spy on society. "Did you mention where Acton proposed to you?"

"Yes, I'm sure I must have." Miss Quartermane's eyes widened slightly. "I told him it is inside the fourth stair in the hall staircase. The strangest place to keep a safe, don't you think? I should never have said that," she whispered in a shocked voice.

Heart sinking, she squeezed Miss Quartermane's hand. "No. You probably should not have done so, but I'm sure it will be all right."

But how could the night get any worse? It was not the location she'd given Talbot earlier in the week. Acton must have more than one safe. She glanced toward the entrance hall. Talbot might not be caught tonight because everyone would be looking in the wrong direction. He'd slip away without detection and the situation would go on and on forever. She searched for Meriwether or Esme to share the warning.

"Never fear." Martin signaled Acton to follow and then slipped his hand around hers. "Would you excuse us? Lady Taverham has just arrived and I must speak to her urgently about my cousin's upcoming visit."

"Yes, please excuse us," Iris said quickly too. Hand in hand, they wove through the crowded room, pausing only when they reached the winding marble staircase.

Iris glanced left and right. "Are we in time?"

"Yes, I think so." Martin hurried beneath the staircase and Iris followed. He reached the paneling and flipped back a false cover—hiding an open safe. "No. We are not. Damn. He's taken everything."

Acton skidded to a halt beside the safe. "Damn it all!"

"We must find him before he can slip them to his men." Iris caught one side of her skirts and hurried toward the card room. The chamber was full of noise and unfamiliar faces and stank of spirits, but she quickly slowed down so she wouldn't draw attention.

She rounded the central table and saw Talbot across the room as he lifted a glass to his lips and took a long sip. He set the glass aside calmly and dipped his hand into his coat pocket. A pocket that bulged in a way no decent tailor would intend.

The superior, smug smile gracing his face infuriated her. He had the gems on him and was drinking to congratulate himself at the very scene of his crime. How many times must he have done this to others and never been noticed?

"There's been a robbery," Acton shouted loudly at her back. "The watch has been sent for. No one can leave until the culprit has been uncovered."

Iris stilled as ordered but kept her eyes on Talbot even as the gentlemen in the card room came to their feet against Acton's wishes.

"Don't move," Iris screamed as Talbot was partially hidden from her view.

The gentlemen closest to her stared at her blankly and began to complain of her rudeness to each other. Talbot glared at her and edged to the side. It was only then she realized a window nearest him was open.

She rushed forward. "Talbot!"

Acton restrained her even as Talbot dove out the window. Iris struggled free of him. "He's getting away! Talbot just jumped out your window. What innocent man does that?"

She was released and Acton and then Windermere brushed past her to stare out into the night-dark gardens. Windermere jumped through the window, as did the Marquess of Ettington a minute later.

Martin hugged her. "I should have known he was on to us."

"Why?" she asked, staring up into her husband's furious face.

"The turnkey delivered a note the day after we married. It was not signed but threatened to take away what you loved most."

Iris clutched his waistcoat with both hand. "My father is safe but... Dear God, no. He couldn't know about her."

Martin met her gaze blankly. "What is it?"

"I have to go. Violet isn't safe." Iris hitched up her skirts and ran for the front entrance of Lord Acton's house, ignoring the shocked faces and her husband's demand she slow down. She had to reach her daughter in time and Talbot already had a head start.

Lord Acton's home was not far from Pollen Street and she sprinted down the front stairs, past carriages, and along the dark streets as fast as her legs could carry her. Behind her, Martin followed, matching her speed and demanding answers. She couldn't explain. But she knew where Talbot would have gone to hurt her the most.

She slammed into the front door of her daughter's home, intending to knock until someone answered, but fell through onto the floor instead as it opened. Horrified the door had been left unlocked tonight of all nights, she caught her breath and then hurried inside. "Mrs. Hughes. Mrs. Blake. Where are you?"

A muffled scream replied and she hurried in the direction of her daughter's room.

A candle was lit in that room and Iris pressed her hand to her chest as she took in the scene before her.

Talbot was on his belly, bound hand and foot, a white cloth stuffed into his mouth to muffle his screams for help.

Mrs. Blake stood between him and the baby, a trickle of blood sliding down her cheek as she glared at the man, while Mrs. Hughes brought up the rear, brandishing a candlestick holder and apparently whole and unharmed.

"Thank heavens you stopped him." She checked Mrs. Blake's

wound immediately but did not think it serious.

"No one's touching our girl," Mrs. Blake declared as she leaned forward and tugged the cloth from Talbot's mouth. A dirty infant cloth, if Iris was not mistaken. "That should teach you not to upset the little one."

"Do you know these mad women?" Talbot spat and spat. "Release me!"

"Oh, I think not." Iris crouched low, noticing the spill of gems flowing from his coat pocket and onto the carpet rug. "How dare you attempt to harm an innocent child?"

He snarled, fighting his bonds. "Ungrateful bitch."

"Ungrateful?" Iris regained her feet. "What did you ever do for anyone but terrify and steal from them?"

Meriwether stumbled through the door, gasping. He spared a glance for the man on the floor and grinned. "My God, you were fleet-footed, my lady. Almost lost sight of you."

"Well, I had something of value to protect." She glanced at Martin and noted his unnatural pallor. His chest heaved and he gave her the strangest look. Iris took a peek at the wicker perambulator behind Mrs. Hughes. Violet was wide awake and appeared on the verge of tears. She picked up the child and cuddled her against her shoulder to calm her. "It's all right, my darling. The bad man won't hurt you."

She patted Violet's bottom softly and hummed to her. Everything would be all right now. She gestured to the man on the floor. "You should find Lord Acton's gems in Talbot's coat pocket, Mr. Meriwether."

Talbot protested, but Meriwether searched him thoroughly and then jammed the dirty cloth back into his mouth when he wouldn't shut up. He spread the gems across the nearest uncluttered surface. "When did you realize he'd tricked us?"

"Almost too late. As many newly engaged women are prone to do, Miss Quartermane described Lord Acton's proposal down to the smallest detail to everyone she met. When Acton cried out he'd been robbed, I thought Talbot's behavior extremely unconcerned. Everyone else was shouting but he was playing with something in his coat pocket. I suspected him immediately, and even more so when he jumped from the window and ran away."

Meriwether smiled and glanced about. "I am very glad I confided in you, Lady Louth. You've proven invaluable in apprehending a dangerous man. How did you know he'd come here?"

Iris kissed her daughter. "We received a note threatening harm to those I love, but my husband did not mention the incident to me until tonight. I had to be sure Violet was safe but to my considerable relief, our staff had already apprehended Talbot. They were very brave indeed to attempt it."

Meriwether threw a questioning glance at her husband, who'd said nothing so far but lurked in the background. To be honest, Martin looked to be in shock.

Acton arrived, out of breath and anxious.

Iris passed Violet to Mrs. Blake. Then turned to Meriwether, "If you wouldn't mind removing that filth from the room, we'd much appreciate it. The child needs to rest."

"Yes, my lady." Meriwether untied Talbot's feet and hauled him upright. "I know just where to take him too."

The gems on the table winked in the candlelight and Acton quickly went to collect them, checking carefully that none had been damaged. One, a small cut emerald, had fallen loose from its setting and been thrown wide in the apparent struggle with Mrs. Blake. Iris bent to pick it up and returned it to its rightful owner. "One last treasure for your collection."

"Thank heavens." Acton held it up to the light and assessed the stone. "The one I was looking for most of all. Thank you."

"It's very pretty." Iris didn't think the gem very valuable but the earl placed it in his waistcoat pocket securely and tied the rest into a white handkerchief.

He bowed and made his way to the door.

When they were gone, Iris turned to face the staff. Mrs. Blake appeared triumphant but Mrs. Hughes was pale with shock. She slowly crumpled to the floor, shaking her head. "I'm too old for any more shocks. What a terrible man. What a dreadful night."

"He truly is." Iris knelt at her side and caught the housekeeper's cold hands in hers. "Perhaps it's time you married your nice gentleman."

A tear slipped down her cheek. "I'd like that."

"Good. Shall I have Mr. Cooper sent for immediately? It might be wise to have him stay here with you tonight too."

"Thank you, my lady. I don't know what I'd have done without Martha. He would have murdered us to get to the little one."

"We are indeed lucky to have our Mrs. Blake." Iris helped Mrs. Hughes to her feet and sent her toward the kitchens for the comfort of a strong cup of tea laced with brandy.

Iris faced her husband at last.

He searched her face. "I'm so sorry."

"Never mind that now." She grasped the handle of the perambulator and maneuvered it toward him. "We'd like to go home, if you don't mind. Holly House is a safer situation for the girl. For Mrs. Blake now too."

Chapter Twenty-Six

"**I** like the name you chose for my daughter," Martin murmured as he allowed Iris to precede him down the front steps of his daughter's Pollen Street home and then set the baby and rolling contraption at her feet. "It seemed so important but I couldn't decide."

"I'm glad you approve," she murmured, hovering over the sleepy child.

Violet had settled down for sleep soon after Talbot had been taken away for further questioning, and he was anxious to take her and his wife where they'd be safe.

Iris started pushing the perambulator while the wet-nurse hurried ahead with some of the child's possessions tucked under her arms. "It will dawn soon."

"Yes, the sun is just rising," she agreed, glancing about her calmly as if their whole marriage hadn't been turned on its head in one night.

Martin was anything but calm and he was impressed with Iris' confidence with his daughter. She knew what she was doing with a child and had made him feel decidedly clumsy without meaning too. She even showed up Mrs. Hughes, too, although he wouldn't dare mention that out loud. Not after the help she'd already given him.

She was obviously waiting for him to speak on the matter of

him having a child but he didn't know how to start.

"Mrs. Hughes was out of her depth and this scare will be too much for her to continue as housekeeper," Iris murmured as the distance grew between them and Pollen Street.

He sighed. "I know, but she was all I had since I learned about the child's existence and Vivian Rose's death."

Iris glanced up at him. "You must have been very shocked."

"On so many levels."

"When did you learn of Violet?"

"The morning you started asking questions about intimacy." He guided Iris across the quiet street. "I hadn't spoken with Vivian in many months. We fell out of sorts with each other and hadn't spoken since. I swear I didn't know about the pregnancy. I didn't know Vivian had died until Mrs. Hughes sent for me and presented me with my daughter."

"That's a terrible way to find out." Iris shook her head. "She's very like you."

"Do you think so?" He smiled proudly, glancing into the basket where his daughter lay sleeping without a care or concern to trouble her. "I hoped I wasn't imagining the resemblance."

Iris stopped. "You took the housekeeper at her word that the child was yours without any proof?"

"What else should I have done? Abandoned the babe to an orphanage and washed my hands of the matter? The timing was right. She was my mistress and I was not always careful enough in her bed. Vivian had one protector after me but the child doesn't resemble him in the slightest. Looking after her was the only choice I had. Vivian had no family and no responsible friends to turn the child over to."

He glanced around but they were entirely alone. "I'm so sorry I didn't tell you myself. I've been trying to find the courage to mention her existence. I'm sure it changes how you think of me but if things had been different, if I had known before the birth, I likely would have married Vivian so our child would not be burdened with the stigma of illegitimacy. That is why I was so adamant you not become a mistress. How did you find out about her?"

Iris was silent at that and Martin feared he'd shared too much of his personal life for her comfort. Unfortunately, he'd gotten into the habit of confiding in her and found it hard to hold back anymore. She moved on and he noting how calm she appeared pushing his daughter home. He'd expected an argument. Anger. Even tears.

"I've known about the babe since before our marriage. Esme took me to see her."

"What had Lady Heathcote intended by taking you to see my daughter? Can I expect to read of the scandal of my daughter's existence in the newssheets?"

"No." She touched his arm. "Esme would never do that to anyone she liked. She just… She wanted me to have all the facts about you."

"And how do you feel about that? Are you upset that I didn't tell you before we married?"

"No. I made the decision to marry you knowing all about her existence. I've no regrets in having you as a husband. We fit, my lord."

"Good." He stopped. "Iris, I have a question to ask you and I hope you will not mind my urgency. Under the circumstances, it cannot wait."

She smiled up at him. "I promise I won't tell a soul about your daughter if you insist. I'm sure Acton and Meriwether will keep it quiet and understand that a man in your position has a lot to lose, and there is Whitney to consider. She might not want to marry at the moment but the stings and barbs of association will taint the way she is treated. I know all about how unfair society can be firsthand."

"I don't want to pretend she doesn't exist." He sighed. "Do you want to be her mother? I can see you care for her already and I know I can never make it up to her for the way she'll be treated. You've made some good decisions regarding her care and I would like to ask for more. I want her to live with us but I'd rather not have your name dragged through the scandal rags because of her."

Her eyes widened then she grinned. "Talbot is in custody and cannot harm anyone. Why do you think I suggested she would be safer at Holly House? I already consider her my daughter, husband, so your question is quite unnecessary."

"You do?" He grinned sheepishly. "I won't understate the

potential difficulties that lie ahead for the family."

"I've already had ample time to consider the future and I would be proud to tell the world she is my daughter." She bit her lip and then started walking again. "Will you suggest next that my own history might make me a poor choice for her mother?"

He hurried to catch up. "Nonsense. I never gave a damn about your lack of dowry."

"I meant the other thing."

He stared at her. "I will admit to being angry about your involvement with Talbot, but believe me, it's the scoundrel's neck I want to wring, not yours."

"Well then. After we have settled Violet at home, we had better invite your closest friends to meet her so they are not surprised by any gossip."

"Whitney has agreed to visit with Miranda for a while, too."

Iris nodded at the news, but since they were at Holly House she focused on taking the baby into the house.

It astounded him that everything would work out. Iris was safe. Violet would be accepted and have a mother. All he needed now was for Whitney to make a match with a suitable gentleman, if that were even possible.

Once they were inside, he caught Iris' hand in his and held it. "There is something I've been meaning to tell you. I—"

He froze at the sounds of struggle from the nearby drawing room. "Wait here."

He snatched up a candlestick and hurried toward the disturbance. In the drawing room, furniture had been overturned and a pair of heels drummed on the floor behind a high-backed chair.

When he rounded it to see what was going on, he found Alexander Hedley sitting on top of Mr. Gibbs' chest. Both men were dressed in their nightshirts.

He dropped the candlestick. "What the devil are you doing?"

Hedley turned and his stare shocked Martin to stillness.

"You," Hedley hissed. "You stole my daughter."

The older man flew at him but being larger and stronger, Martin was able to contain his assault quite easily and pinned him against his chest. Hedley continued to twist frantically in his grip and shout out his daughter's name. Servants came running from all directions in various states of dishabille but Iris pushed to the front, holding Violet protectively in her arms. Her shocked expression made his heart ache. "It's all right. Everyone go back to bed."

Whitney appeared too, dressed in her nightgown and robe, and rushed toward the butler. "What's happened, Gibbs?"

He climbed to his feet unsteadily with Whitney's aid and leaned heavily against a chair, gasping for breath. "He's been agitated for half an hour or more. Got it in his head we'd made him our prisoner and that his daughter was in danger from you. Nothing I could say would convince him you would return soon from the ball."

Iris approached them slowly, her eyes trained on her father. "Oh, Papa. I'm here now and all is well."

"My baby," Hedley sobbed. His gaze fixed to the bundle in Iris' arms. "You've been gone so long and I couldn't find you anywhere."

Hedley sagged but Martin didn't dare release him yet.

"He's calmer now, Martin. Please sit him down beside me."

He guided his father-in-law to the settee she chose and hovered. He wouldn't allow anyone to hurt his family, not even Alexander.

Iris set the baby on her lap and then caught her father's hand. "We were only gone to a ball, Papa, and I'm in no danger here. We are at home now and soon for our beds. It's been a very long night."

Martin remained close to Iris, heart in his throat, afraid Hedley could became violent again if he looked away. God alone knew what had provoked this outburst but it could not happen again. Hedley wasn't in his right mind and not to be trusted.

The man leaned forward and tickled the baby's cheek with one finger. "He stole you from me," Hedley whispered to Violet. "You'll never have to see him again."

Iris winced. "Lord Louth has never harmed us. He is my husband. He takes care of us. Didn't you say you like living here better than anywhere?"

Martin nodded to remind the older man.

Hedley's hands clenched into fists. "But I saw him pawing you on the stairs. I'd have dealt with him then but the turnkey stopped me. He said I'd imagined it. He brought me extra food to keep me quiet, too, but I won't stand for it any longer."

Hedley glared at Gibbs.

Iris gulped and met his gaze. In his agitated state, he was confusing Gibbs and Fitzhugh into the same man.

"Mr. Gibbs is a servant, Papa. He is our butler." She passed the baby to Whitney, who'd drawn close, then rubbed her father's hands briskly. "You must apologize to him for the misunderstanding. You've hurt him and I know you did not mean to."

Hedley faced Gibbs and all of a sudden he blinked, glancing around him at the room in surprise. Martin drew closer in concern but Hedley's attitude had changed. He looked older and very confused. "Iris?" he whispered.

"I'm here, Papa. Everything will be all right." Iris put her arm around her father and held him against her side as she met the butler's gaze. "I am so sorry if you were hurt, Mr. Gibbs. It won't happen again."

"Never worry about it, my lady. He caught me by surprise. And I do understand. My mother was the same way in the last years of her life. Accidents happen. I'll have the room cleaned up before the first callers of the day arrive." He bowed to her but stopped at Martin's side. "I'd recommend laudanum," he whispered softly enough that Hedley wouldn't hear.

"A calming draft might just be the thing to ease his mind." Martin nodded. "Thank you, Gibbs, and be as quick about it as you can."

Whitney drew close, rocking the child in her arms. "I was to go to visit Lady Taverham later today but I can stay at home if you'd rather I not."

Martin shook his head and took Violet from her. "No. Go back to bed and later enjoy your visit. Say nothing to Miranda about this as yet. I'll send a note to her at midday and ask her to call on us tonight, when this is taken care of."

Whitney rose up on her toes to peer at Violet's face and then at his. Her brow rose. "If you're sure?"

"I will explain everything later, I promise."

"This should be very interesting." She smiled softly and hurried out.

When the butler and Whitney had gone, Martin drew close to Hedley. Iris might not like it but he was about to make another decision for her father. The man couldn't stay in London or the gossips would shred his reputation and see him assigned to Bedlam. He needed watching over, and that could be better done in the country than in London, where there was less disruption and late nights. And Martin had the perfect place in his possession for such an extended stay. Hedley needed the serenity of the dower house at Holly Park, and a set of footmen permanently on hand to keep him calm.

He set his hand to Hedley's shoulder. "Shall we adjourn to the library for a nightcap, sir?"

"Oh, yes. That would be very welcome. I was just feeling a bit parched, now that you mention it." Hedley eased away from Iris as Martin passed Violet to her. He escorted Hedley toward the library so the staff could begin straightening the drawing room. When he glanced over his shoulder, Iris remained behind hugging the babe tight to her chest. Her frightened expression spoke volumes for her concern. He tipped his head to urge her to follow.

Gibbs returned quickly enough that Martin could slip a large dose of the opiate into Hedley's first drink. He settled into the chair opposite Hedley, as he had done on other cozy afternoons, and spoke to the man of inconsequential matters. Iris perched in a nearby chair, rocking their daughter while she slept. She must be so afraid of the changes in her father's demeanor. He wasn't the commanding Alexander of old, nor had the sweet father she expected emerged from the Marshalsea.

Hedley grew drowsy very soon after and when he was soundly asleep in his chair and snoring, his head nestled against the headrest comfortably, Martin motioned Iris to the far side of the room. She set Violet down on a heavily padded armchair and he drew her into his arms immediately. He held her tightly against his chest. "It is over now."

She curled against his chest. "No, it's not."

"I'm sorry." He sighed against her hair to whisper, "You are correct. There is no end to this situation. Gibbs mentioned his mother went the same way and grew unmanageable, and I recall a little of what happened. I'd intended for your father to live with us forever, but can we manage him? You cannot stay at his side every moment of the day and night and neither can I. It's not the life he'd want for you, either."

She pressed her head to his chest. "He's never done this before. I'd hoped he would get better after his release from the Marshalsea. It was never very pleasant for him there but I never dreamed he could become violent."

"I thought as much." He kissed the top of her head. "Perhaps instead of staying in London, your father should retire to Holly Park? There is a little house on the property, a dower house not in use and not too far from the manor. He could be very comfortable there and have a regular routine that might soothe him. There's a bookroom decorated much like this one and I can supply company from time to time and plenty of his favorite foods. With the proper staff, and a new situation in a peaceful setting, he might not be reminded of the past year's difficulties."

"I apologize for the accusations he made against you." Her breath left her in a ragged rush. "They were cruel and uncalled for."

"Shh," he whispered. He tightened his grip around her. "He is your father and it's not surprising he's concerned for you."

She looked up at him. "I love you."

"And I was going to say earlier that I love you, too, with all my heart." He kissed her gently. "My darling brave wife. You amaze me with your strength and your acceptance of my daughter. To see your eyes light up from within because you are exactly where you want to be has made me so happy."

He trailed his fingers down her neck softly. "Iris, there will be little chance of hiding the fact he's losing his mind."

"I know. I have suspected for some time that's why he lost our fortune. He might not have been in his right mind for many years before that too and I shrugged off my suspicions. Small things at first, like forgetting names and confusing the time of day.

"He speaks like a child at times and mentions grudges against people from his past as if he's just met with them. I fear one day he will live so far into the past that he will have no memory of me. I've already had to remind him I was his daughter. That is so hard to do."

Hedley's decline was greater than he'd seen so far. "We must prepare for the worst."

"What am I going to do?"

"Lean on me. Together, you and I can accomplish anything we desire." He glanced down. "That reminds me, I've yet to kiss your feet for nudging Whitney to smooth things over with Lord Acton."

He made to kneel but she caught him about the waist, stopping his decent. "Don't you dare."

He grinned. "Tonight then? After the family are put to bed. I will suck each dainty toe until you beg me to stop."

Her eyes fluttered shut. "How do you do that? Make me ache for your touch with just your words and forget everything else."

"It's a talent." He kissed her, holding her tightly against his body.

A throat cleared and they drew apart. Gibbs had paused three steps into the room and had lowered his gaze to give them privacy.

Martin sighed. "Yes, Gibbs?"

"I've taken the liberty of arranging for two footmen to keep an eye on Mr. Hedley day and night. I'd rather not take any chances of another outburst like this."

"Thank you, Gibbs," Iris whispered softly. "I am so very sorry to be such trouble to everyone. You don't deserve this."

Martin set his arm around her shoulders to offer his support.

"It's no bother at all, my lady." Gibbs moved into the room, refilled Hedley's brandy and added a few more drops of laudanum to the liquid. "We will keep him quiet for the rest of the night and see how he is at luncheon. If there is nothing else, I'll leave you to it."

"Thank you, Gibbs." He caught Iris' hands in his as soon as Gibbs was gone again and raised it to his lips. He brushed light kisses over her cold knuckles and then blew over the damp skin. He grinned as her eyes fluttered again. "Now that your father is taken care of, I want you to take our daughter upstairs and see her settled with Mrs. Blake, then take off your shoes and gown, and lie down for at least an hour. Whitney will go to visit with Miranda and won't be returning for hours. I'll write to everyone while you rest and wake you in time for their arrival."

She squeezed his hands and then stretched to kiss him on the lips. The kiss was fleeting but solid and Martin couldn't help but feel optimistic when she smiled. "Will you wake me with kisses again?"

He brushed his knuckles across her cheek. "Always."

Epilogue

---◆---

"I cannot imagine I've forgotten anything," Whitney mused as she circled the pile of luggage stacked to the side of her bed, ready for her departure to Lord and Lady Taverham's country estate.

Iris folded her arms over her chest and surveyed the room. Whitney had stripped it bare. "If there is anything left, I'm sure you don't need it."

Whitney caught her arm and squeezed. "Always so practical. Do you ever do anything reckless, my friend?"

She glanced at Violet where she rested in the middle of Whitney's bed, supervising the packing with only the occasional gurgle or cry. "I've been reckless enough to last a lifetime."

"I am so proud of you." Whitney folded her into an embrace and rocked her from side to side. Since her marriage to Martin, Whitney had dropped all pretense of formality, and had once even climbed into bed with Iris to talk when she'd discovered her alone. "I would stay if you want my support. I don't care what anyone says about the child. She is family. The prettiest little girl there is." Whitney crept onto the bed and pressed a kiss to Violet's soft cheek. "Looks nothing like her father."

"Of course she does. The resemblance is very strong."

"You are so lucky, all the fun and none of the hard work." Whitney grinned widely. "Unless there's something you'd like to share with me."

"Far too soon to tell. But I promise to write to you as soon as I'm sure."

Whitney grinned. "I don't imagine Miranda will be as easy to laugh with as you are. I'd have to get her attention first, but I am looking forward to a month away from London. They say the views from the highest points of the estate are spectacular. I am so looking forward to painting them."

"And I will look forward to viewing them when you return to Holly Park."

Whitney frowned. "But I thought you were going to stay in London a little longer? I certainly would want to see for myself that Talbot is punished."

"My father needs me. I don't imagine the journey will be a comfortable one."

"You mean you need your father?" Whitney set her hands to her hips and glared. "Iris, have you never had a selfish thought in your whole life? You have to take what you want and forget about the consequences. If you spend all your time worrying about what people will think, you will never have any peace. I learned that a long time ago. I must be honest with myself."

What did she want? She looked about her. A home. A family. Someone to love. Food on the table. A new dress now and then.

And Martin's daughter.

She smiled. "Whitney, I have everything I need to be happy. I have a family again."

Whitney squeezed her hand. "I will miss you, sweet cousin."

"And I will miss you," she agreed. Whitney, despite her unconventional attitude and indifference to many things society expected her to care about, had proven herself over the past days. She had not judged her for her past mistakes. "Promise to write and let me know how you get on as often as possible."

"I will." Whitney glanced around the room.

Martin tapped on the door and stared at the luggage in horror. "Is that all you're taking?"

"That is everything." Whitney smiled and picked up Violet. She stared into the child's eyes. "I'd take her with me in a heartbeat, though, if I could."

"Never." Iris took Violet back and set her into the crook of her arm. "I'll not go without my daughter for even a single day."

Whitney reached into a side drawer and withdrew a sheet of paper. "Not even for this?"

The girl had drawn a portrait in charcoal—Iris holding Violet with Martin watching on. Her father was seated in the background and smiling. It was so well done, her eyes filled with tears. "Thank you."

"There will be more when I return, I promise."

With one last look, Whitney swept from the room, carrying her reticule and her brush case as hand luggage. They followed her to the front hall and watched her join Lord and Lady Taverham in their carriage. Her luggage would follow later.

"I hope we don't live to regret her going." Martin sighed as the door closed after they'd gone on their way. "Or cause trouble between the Taverhams and Acton."

"Acton is remaining in London so there can be no trouble."

"He's returning to the country too. Wants to prepare his home in advance for Miss Quartermane's arrival. I do hope Whitney behaves herself."

Iris bit her lip and moved to the front window. Lord Acton's property abutted Lord Taverham's Twilit Hill estate and he was said to be a frequent visitor. It was inevitable that upon his return, Lord Acton might find himself in Whitney's company. "It is too late to warn Whitney that her pleasant holiday might have an unwanted presence."

"Well, at least she has made an effort to be civil with Acton in London so I'm optimistic she could behave for a few weeks."

Iris sighed and rocked Violet in her arms, resigned to be the recipient of the most interesting correspondence soon. "I think a few weeks in the country might be just what they need to sort out their differences once and for all. She might even meet and eventually marry the man of her dreams if we are lucky."

Martin pulled her into his arms, careful not to squash little Violet, and smiled down at her, a question in his gaze.

"I don't have to dream anymore, husband." She kissed their daughter's brow and then caressed his dear face. "I have everything I need to be happy right within reach."

Falling in love was
never an option . . .
until they kissed !
HEATHER
BOYD
BESTSELLING AUTHOR
REASON TO
WED
Distinguished Rogues

Chapter One

Every woman can appreciate the challenge of making a man do what she wants. Unfortunately for Lady Heathcote, Esme to her closest friends, her chances of success tonight seemed to have fled along with her lover. "Now where has he gone?"

She scanned the room in search of Mr. Albert Meriwether. However, it was becoming increasingly clear that inviting him to Lord Windermere's house party in Gloucestershire had been a colossal mistake on her part. She had his attention here even less than she had in London, and no one had even been stolen from or murdered. She should have broken with him when she'd sensed his repeated reluctance to take time away from his important work in the city.

"He's across the room, making good on his intention to win every lord in attendance over to his cause," Lady Ames warned.

Again.

"I must say, if you had not mentioned your connection earlier today, I'd have had no idea you were such good friends," Lady Small whispered dramatically. "He's paid you less attention than our host and we all know you've been at odds with Windermere for an age."

Harriet met her gaze, her expression tinged with concern. "I've known of social climbers before of course, but never one so pointedly obvious as Meriwether."

"That wasn't why we came, Harriet," she complained softly to her friend and confidant.

Harriet squeezed her arm, full of sympathy. Esme had dragged Meriwether from London to reignite the spark of their affair before his obsession with his work snuffed it entirely. But he was determined to curry favor with the most influential lords in attendance. And if he couldn't gain their ears for long enough, he'd started being friendly toward their wives too.

She'd had more of his nonsense than she could tolerate, and

turned away.

Esme left Harriet to her own devices and wandered the public rooms of Windermere Park on her own. The loveliest property she'd ever visited was home of the most arrogant man she'd ever met. She'd been surprised by the invitation to come this year, but never considered refusing after reading Windermere's most sincere apology for losing his temper with her. With his last lover, Lady Bartlett, being so proficient at amateur theatricals, it hadn't been surprising the woman had pulled the wool over his eyes, professing to a pregnancy that was just a myth. And it had been Esme's unfortunate sense of fair play that had prompted her to warn him that Lady Bartlett wasn't the least bit pregnant. His vitriol had fallen on her head- first, of course, but at least he'd listened and not married the devious woman.

In the hall, she encountered Windermere's ancient butler, a kindly soul who'd served the family forever. Oswin was a sweet old man who never failed to treat her well, so she stopped to speak to him when so many others wouldn't bother. "Good evening, Oswin."

He nodded. "Might I be of service, Lady Heathcote?"

She took in the lean to his posture and his tired expression and smiled. "Yes, you can go and sit down and let young Pip run around in your stead for the rest of tonight."

Pip was the newest footman employed here, but Esme was confident the young man wouldn't mind the extra work or the experience.

"It's my pleasure to serve the family," Oswin replied with his usual dignified loyalty.

"As you wish." She'd let the matter slide but privately thought a man his age should be already training his replacement. If she were mistress of this house, she'd have begun long ago. A long house party like this could send him to his bed from sheer exhaustion, and then where would the family be?

She glanced back inside the drawing room once more.

Lingering by the hearth, Meriwether laughed with Windermere's guests, most part of her extended circle of friends too. She considered each man in turn...their intelligence, their reputations. Their chances of being won over to Meriwether's cause to formalize protection for the wealthiest homeowners with a private, trained guard. Her host, Lord Windermere, and his younger brother Lord Avery Hill were among them, and both were extremely shrewd gentlemen. They would have the greatest influence on the others if Meriwether won their support this week.

As far as causes went, Meriwether was entitled to his opinion that such a service was needed. But the truly needy of London were most at risk from robbers and couldn't afford to pay for their own private guard. Truth to tell, she was finding it hard to support Meriwether's ambitions as completely as she once did. She'd also come to suspect their affair had become a way to gain entry into the upper ten thousand by association, a means to an end for him.

However disappointed she might feel about that and his motives, Esme would never allow herself to depend on a man for her entire happiness. If she wasn't involved with Meriwether, there was always someone handsome to fantasize about and encourage into her bed down the road. Over the years of her widowhood, she'd never lacked for male companionship.

She nodded to Lord Avery Hill and Miles Hammond as they strolled past. The glow of appreciation in both men's eyes practically shouted their interest and soothed away her hesitation to break with Meriwether. She'd easily find someone who wanted to be with *her*.

Lord Avery Hill moved toward Harriet and she smiled with understanding. The pair had been lovers on and off for years, and it seemed this year would be no different.

Mr. Miles Hammond, however, was another matter entirely. A friend of hers since the final days of her largely unhappy marriage, his inclusion in the house party guest list confounded her. He was not a particular favorite of their host, or even of his brother, yet all had seemed to be in quite a genial mood with each other since the party began. She'd have to find out why Hammond had been included.

She glanced about those gathered for tonight's ball. Champagne was being passed around freely and everyone seemed happy and infinitely agreeable to enjoy the party atmosphere to the fullest extent. Parties such as these were opportunities to mingle and conduct discreet liaisons without expectation of deeper, longer-term connections in many cases. It was all very civilized. As the quartet hired to play tonight tuned their instruments, she smiled. She might find her host a trifle wearying, but she could ignore the little irritations in Windermere's company, given her expectation of every other pleasure.

She moved away from the hall as new guests were welcomed by Oswin and turned her gaze on Windermere. Couldn't he see his nearest neighbors had arrived and needed to be introduced to the first-time guests?

But no, he remained watching Meriwether talk, a slight frown on his face.

After a long moment, Lord Windermere cast a questioning glance her way, catching her watching him. Unwilling to be ruffled by his scrutiny, Esme stared back. Good God, those cornflower-blue eyes of his would render a lesser woman immobile if she was unprepared. Esme knew Windermere well though, well enough not to be affected by his handsome face. He knew he was attractive, too; he thought far too well of his appeal for her taste, and she sometimes stared at him overlong just to make him a tiny bit uncomfortable.

His grin faded slowly as she held his gaze and then his glance cut to those gathered about him and back to her, a question now in his eyes. Esme hid a smile, tipped her head in the direction of the hall, waiting for Windermere to catch on to why she stared at him so pointedly. It certainly wasn't for his looks alone.

He shook his head, as if clearing his mind of a thought, and hurried off to do his duty as host, leaving her laughing at his befuddlement.

The man needed a wife sooner rather than later to manage himself and his home affairs better. Someone to point him in the right direction from time to time, or even daily.

She turned back to her quarry only to be disappointed yet again. Meriwether was headed in the opposite direction. He snagged two glasses of champagne, glancing over his shoulder once or twice, as he navigated the crowd and slipped into the hall.

How sweet. Perhaps she'd misunderstood his preoccupation

and he was arranging a private rendezvous for them both beyond the ballroom. Esme didn't require the fuss of a perfect seduction, but his hands on her body would be very fine tonight.

She moved toward him but again lost sight. Esme drew in a deep breath in frustration. It wasn't the first time the man had vanished so completely since they'd arrived two days ago.

The hallway beyond the drawing room was filled to bursting with chattering guests and she moved smoothly through them, nodding and speaking occasionally to some. While she admired the elegance and comforts to be found in Lord Windermere's home, she kept her eye out for Meriwether. She turned into the library, but the room was startlingly empty.

"Looking for me?" Windermere asked as he came to stand near. His gaze raked her from head to toe in the most gauche way.

Arrogant and presumptuous. "Hardly. You should pay more attention to your guests and the health of your servants."

Instead of taking the hint that she wasn't in the mood to talk, he caught her hand and raised it to his lips. His blue eyes danced with amusement. "I do love when you're friendly. How have you been, Esme?"

She scowled at him and withdrew her hand to her side. "I've not given you leave to use my first name and I am not of a mood to spar with you. Go back to your other guests for amusement and send your butler to his bed. Anyone can see he's on the verge of collapse tonight."

"I already banished Oswin to rest." He laughed suddenly. "Young Pip has assumed his duties until Collins comes up."

"Just as well," she replied, thankful for such sensible decisions at last.

"Only you would ever dare tell me what to do in my own home. I wanted to thank you for coming," Windermere murmured. "But to convince everyone we're not at odds, you will have to talk to me occasionally with a little less acid in your tone."

"We've spoken as much as needed to quell any gossip." She smiled at him. "Or was it your wish to have me chivvy you out of your mopes too."

"I will say again you were right." Windermere sighed and

raked a hand through his dark, wavy hair. "You're enjoying rubbing my nose in that business with Lady Bartlett, aren't you?"

"Perhaps." She smothered a laugh. He hadn't wanted to believe he was being used until it was almost too late to extract himself from the connection. "You were so indignant that day, and after venting your pique at me, you charged down the street—on foot of all things, my man and your horse trailing after. I laughed for at least a whole day afterward. But I am sorry you were let down."

He inhaled sharply, his jaw clenching before he relaxed and shook his head. "No, you're not. You're positively gloating that you were proved right about her."

She allowed herself the briefest smirk. "You should learn to listen to good advice when you hear it, even if it comes from a direction you don't care for. I did try at first every subtle method I could imagine to make you really look at her figure and behavior. She wanted to trap you and almost did. An adventuress of her poor standard is not suitable to be your countess."

"I believe you wholeheartedly." He leaned closer, bracing one hand on the doorframe beside her head so she was partially trapped by his body. "In fact, I'm considering leaving the matter of who should be in that position in your capable hands."

She stared at him in shock. "You'd let me choose your wife for you?"

"Well, perhaps not a wife." He grinned and his attention dropped to her bust. "But I'm open to hearing your suggestion for my next lover. I seem to have the worst luck in that area and you seem to have developed an interest in those I take to my bed."

Esme laughed at his absurd suggestion and ignored the overwhelming urge to unbutton her gown for him. She did not lead a man on while involved with another, even if that *other* was leading her on a merry chase tonight. "You hardly need advice on that. Any pair of breasts will do. But next time, if the lady claims she's carrying your child, at least find out for sure she's speaking truthfully *before* you request a special license."

"Breasts come attached to the lady." He sighed again and drew back. "Given my near miss, I'm no longer confident I've the patience for marriage."

Last year, Esme had formed a suspicion about Lord Windermere, what set him to sigh so often when someone married or was heard to have fathered a son or daughter. He implied he lacked patience, but that probably wasn't true. There were countless other gentlemen of their acquaintance with both legitimate and illegitimate children attached to their names. Lord Windermere had not lived the life of a saint, but he had no children of his own that Esme had ever learned of.

She could sympathize with his situation, though she'd never let on or embarrass him by speaking of it. At his age, nearing three and forty years, he must have begun to worry for the succession, since his brother appeared even less ready to settle down than he was. After that, the estate and title fell to a cousin who hadn't the bearing of an earl, in her opinion, although he did possess a sweet wife and two sons already.

She didn't know what to say to make him feel better anyway because nothing really could. She'd long since accepted her own barren state as a certainty. "Things might be different with the right woman," she suggested gently. At least that is what well-meaning family had always advised her.

He shook his head then assumed the warm expression so common for him that lit up his eyes so brightly she wanted to draw closer. "So, are you going to tell me what you were looking for?"

She glanced away, glad he'd changed the subject and that the uncomfortable personal conversation between them was over. She wouldn't confide in him about her exasperation with her lover, but Windermere had invited Meriwether knowing they were intimately involved. It should have been clear to him whom she'd be looking for. "I'll let you get back to tending your guests and charming your next dance partner."

He sighed dramatically. "You're a cruel woman but you are correct. I have obligations. Until we meet again."

Esme turned on her heel and left the library and Lord Windermere behind. If not for the lingering feeling of shared sadness, she didn't plan to think of him again tonight.

About Heather Boyd

Determined to escape the Aussie sun on a scorching camping holiday, Heather picked up a pen and notebook from a corner store and started writing her very first novel—Chills. Years later, she is the author of over thirty sexy regency historical romances. Addicted to all things tech (never again will Heather write a novel longhand) and fascinated by English society of the early 1800's, Heather spends her days getting her characters in and out of trouble and into bed together (if they make it that far). She lives on the edge of beautiful Lake Macquarie, Australia with her trio of mischievous rogues (husband and two sons) along with one rescued cat whose only interest in her career is that it provides him with food on demand and a new puppy that is proving a big distraction.

You can find details of her work and writing at
www.Heather-Boyd.com